IR

"I can't think of something I want to do more than take you out to dinner."

"Oh." She bit her lip and blinked back emotion. "I'd like it a lot."

More than that. To be included, be a part of it. She'd love to.

"Good. After work, I'll give you a two-hour head start over to Revolution to get freshened up and then Souze and I'll come pick you up for an early dinner. Sound good?"

She smiled. "Absolutely."

He kissed her then, and his hands roamed over her.

Laughing, she came up for air. "We do have work today."

He growled against her throat. "And it'll still be there for us."

"I refuse to be late!" She squirmed and gasped as he slid a finger inside her.

"We'll be quick."

She clutched at his shoulders and answered breathless. "Okay. Quick. Quick is good."

D0035437

www.westminster.lib.org

DISCARD

Westminster Public Library
3705 W. 112th Ave.
Westminster, CO 80031
www.westminsterlibrary.org

ULTIMATE COURAGE

ALSO BY PIPER J. DRAKE

Extreme Honor

ULTIMATE COURAGE

PIPER J. DRAKE

FOREVER

NEW YORK   BOSTON

This book is a work of fiction. Names, characters, places, and incidents are the product of the author's imagination or are used fictitiously. Any resemblance to actual events, locales, or persons, living or dead, is coincidental.

Copyright © 2016 by Piper J. Drake
Excerpt from *Absolute Trust* copyright © 2016 by Piper J. Drake
Cover design by Elizabeth Turner
Cover copyright © 2016 by Hachette Book Group, Inc.

Hachette Book Group supports the right to free expression and the value of copyright. The purpose of copyright is to encourage writers and artists to produce the creative works that enrich our culture.

The scanning, uploading, and distribution of this book without permission is a theft of the author's intellectual property. If you would like permission to use material from the book (other than for review purposes), please contact permissions@hbgusa.com. Thank you for your support of the author's rights.

Forever
Hachette Book Group
1290 Avenue of the Americas
New York, NY 10104
forever-romance.com
twitter.com/foreverromance

Printed in the United States of America

First Edition: July 2016
10 9 8 7 6 5 4 3 2 1

OPM

Forever is an imprint of Grand Central Publishing.
The Forever name and logo are trademarks of Hachette Book Group, Inc.

The Hachette Speakers Bureau provides a wide range of authors for speaking events. To find out more, go to www.hachettespeakersbureau.com or call (866) 376-6591.

The publisher is not responsible for websites (or their content) that are not owned by the publisher.

ATTENTION CORPORATIONS AND ORGANIZATIONS:

Most Hachette Book Group books are available at quantity discounts with bulk purchase for educational, business, or sales promotional use. For information, please call or write:

Special Markets Department, Hachette Book Group
1290 Avenue of the Americas, New York, NY 10104
Telephone: 1-800-222-6747 Fax: 1-800-477-5925

To Uncles G&G, with love. Every time I've shown up on your doorstep, you've always welcomed me into your home with warm hearts and open minds. I can think of no other place in all my travels that offers as much peace as stopping in to visit with you.

ULTIMATE
COURAGE

CHAPTER ONE

Y ou've got to be insane."

Elisa Hall took a prudent step—or two—back as she observed the standoff brewing in front of her. A tall man stood between her and the emergency room reception desk, glaring at the woman in scrubs behind it. He stood at an angle to Elisa, so he could see the reception desk to his right and the entirety of the waiting area in front of him.

He clenched his fists.

Elisa retreated farther back toward the entrance, releasing her throbbing wrist and letting her hands fall to her sides. Harmless. Nothing to see here.

"I'm sorry, sir, but ambulances take precedence over walk-ins," the nurse repeated. She was braver than Elisa would've been in the face of rage on a level with the man's at the counter.

He was dressed in loose fitness shorts and a close-fitting black tee. His hands were wrapped in some cross between tape and fabric.

"Fighter" might as well have been printed across his very broad, muscular shoulders.

Actually, now that she was looking, his tee said Revolution Mixed Martial Arts Academy.

Well, then. Maybe she should just take more ibuprofen and forget about seeing a doctor for her swollen wrist after all. Getting her injury examined wasn't worth staying anywhere near this guy.

The nurse glanced quickly at Elisa then returned her attention to the man, her expression softening with sympathy. "As soon as an examination room opens up, we'll get you in to see the doctor. Please, wait right here and fill out these forms while I help this young lady."

Wait, what? The man's face, and his focus, turned toward her. *Oh, great.*

Usually she envied nurses their ability to sympathize with so many patients and make such a difference in their lives. Now was not one of those times.

Elisa squashed the urge to bolt. Never ended well when she tried it. Better to hold very still, wait until the anger in front of her burned itself out, and pull herself together afterward.

Instead, she fastened her gaze on the floor and tried to keep her body from tensing visibly. Silently, she sang herself an inane nursery rhyme to take her mind off the weight of the man's intense glare. *Please, please, let him walk away.* They were in public, and even though the emergency room waiting area wasn't packed, it still had a dozen people scattered around the seats.

But the expected explosion, shouting, other things… never happened. Instead, the man had quieted. All of the frustrated aggression seemed to have been stuffed away, somewhere.

She swallowed hard. Relief eased her constricted throat, and she breathed slowly for the time being. Leaving remained the best idea she had at the moment.

But he stepped away from the counter and farther to her right, motioning with a wrapped hand for her to step forward. As she forced her feet to take herself closer to the reception desk—and past him—he gave her room.

Belatedly, she realized his movement also happened to block her escape route toward the doors. He couldn't have done it on purpose, could he? But Elisa took a step up to the reception counter and away from him anyway.

"Yes, dear?" The nurse's gentle prompt made Elisa jump.

Damn it. Elisa's heart beat loud in her ears.

The nurse gave her an encouraging smile. "Don't mind him. He's been here before. I've already asked another nurse to bring ice packs as fast as possible. I don't mind if he blows off some hot air in my direction in the meantime. I would be upset, too, considering today's situation."

Elisa bit her lip. She could still feel the man standing behind her, his presence looming at her back. He couldn't possibly appreciate the nurse sharing some of his private information. And he didn't seem to need ice packs or any other medical attention. He appeared very able-bodied. "It's none of my business."

The nurse placed a clipboard on the counter and wrinkled her nose. "Oh, trust me, the entire waiting room knows what his concern is. Tell me what brought you here."

This might be the most personable emergency room reception area Elisa had been to in years, not counting the extremely angry man standing behind her. They were either not very busy—not likely if all the examination rooms were full up—or extremely efficient.

Efficiency meant she could get in and out and decide what her next steps would be.

"My wrist." Elisa held out her left arm, her wrist obviously swollen. "I thought it was just a bad sprain, but it's been more than a few days and has only gotten worse. I can barely move it now."

And if she could have avoided it, she definitely wouldn't have stopped in to get it treated. An emergency room visit, even with the help of her soon-to-be nonexistent insurance, was still an expense she didn't need. It'd been six months or so since her last significant paycheck, and she could not afford to extend her insurance much longer. Plus, it might be better not to. One less way to track her.

"Is that your dominant arm, dear?" The nurse held up a pen.

Elisa shook her head.

"Oh, good. Leave your ID and insurance card with me so I can make copies. Take a seat over there to fill out this form and bring it back to me."

Okay, then. Elisa took the items and made her way toward the seating area, thankful the nurse hadn't asked her to give her name and pertinent information verbally. It was always a risk to share those things out loud.

She'd learned over and over again. There was a chance a slip of information in the unlikeliest of places would find its way to exactly the person she didn't want to have it. No matter how careful she'd been over the last several months, it hadn't been enough yet.

But it would be. This time. She was learning, and she was free. Every day was a new chance.

Nodding to herself, Elisa looked for a seat. It might not be crowded, but just about everyone in the room had decided to sit with at least a chair or two buffer between them and the next person. The buffer seats were all that were left, and most of the other people waiting to be seen were either men, or women sitting with men.

Then she caught sight of a young girl sitting with her legs crossed in the seat next to the big planter in the corner. Slender, but long limbed, the girl had a sweet face and the gangly look of a growing kid. Elisa guessed the girl was maybe eight or nine, could even be ten. Hard to pin down age when the kid had such an innocent look to her. The seat next to her was open, and she was waiting quietly, hugging a big, blue, plush...round thing. Whatever it was.

Elisa walked quickly over, and when the girl looked up at her with big, blue eyes, Elisa gave her the friendliest smile she could dig up. "Mind if I sit next to you?"

The girl looked around, her gaze lingering on the reception area behind Elisa for a moment before saying, "Sure."

Elisa took a seat.

After a few silent moments, the little girl stirred next to her. "Are you sick?"

Well, paperwork didn't take much of her attention, and it'd been a while since Elisa had been outside of her own head in a lot of ways. Conversation would be a welcome change and a good distraction from the constant worry running in the back of her mind. "Not sick so much as hurt. I won't give you the plague."

A soft, strained laugh. "Same here."

Elisa took a harder look at the big, plush toy. It wasn't for comfort as Elisa'd first assumed. It was supporting the girl's slender left arm, which was bent at an impossible angle.

"Oh my god." *Why was she sitting here alone?*

"Don't worry." The girl gave her a quick thumbs-up with her right hand. "The doctors are really good here, and I'm in *all* the time."

Such a brave face. She had to be in an insane amount of pain. And here she was encouraging Elisa.

"Is there someone you should talk to about how often you get hurt?" Elisa struggled for the right tone. It was one she'd heard more than once when people had been concerned for her. Some places had safeguards in place for . . .

Blue eyes widened. "Oh, it's not what you're thinking. Trust me, people ask my dad. And it's not like that *at all*. I study mixed martial arts. I get bruised and bumped all the time, and usually it's nothing, but Dad always makes me come in to get checked."

It was hard not to believe in the earnest tone. But monsters were everywhere.

The girl gave her a rueful smile, still amazing considering how much pain she had to be in. "This time it wasn't just a bump."

"Which is why they're going to see you as soon as they can, Boom."

Elisa hadn't heard the man approach. He was just there. He kneeled down in front of the girl then gently tucked an ice pack around her arm while moving it as little as possible. For her part, the girl hissed in pain but otherwise held up with amazing fortitude.

Elisa would've been in tears. The forearm had to be broken. Both bones. It didn't take a doctor to figure that out. No wonder the man had been mad earlier. She'd want this girl to be seen as soon as possible, too. She dropped her gaze, unable to watch.

"Here." An ice pack appeared in her view. "Your wrist should be iced, too. Take down the swelling while you wait."

Speechless, Elisa looked up.

The man's words were gruff, awkward. His expression was blank. But his eyes—a softness around his eyes—and a ... quiet in the way he watched her made her swallow and relax a fraction. Her heartbeat stuttered in a fluttery kind of way. A completely different reaction from what she should be experiencing if she were wise. She didn't know this man and he was probably married. The girl had a mother somewhere. Where? Maybe on her way. This man was just being nice. Maybe.

Learn from your mistakes. You never know who a person really is.

"You should listen to Dad." The little girl had regained her earnest tone. "He's usually right. Even when I think he's crazy, it turns out he's right and I wish I'd listened to him. Besides, he gets hurt even more than I do. He says ice is his best friend."

"So is ibuprofen." Elisa snapped her mouth shut, not even sure why she'd let the comment pop out.

The little girl gave her a brighter smile. "Yeah. He says that, too."

The dad in question stood, his knees creaking a bit as he rose up and took a step back.

Elisa was grateful for the space even though he probably wanted to be near his daughter. His presence was intense even if his movements were all steady and smooth. No sudden or frenetic motion. Nothing to freak her out.

"Have you ever had self-defense?" the girl continued. "Dad says every person should take at least one class or seminar. It's what got me started in mixed martial arts. I liked it so much I started taking classes."

Where is your mother? Elisa wanted to ask, but kept it to herself. A thoughtlessly asked question could put a person in a worse than awkward position. Better to just stay in the conversation at hand.

"I haven't, no." Elisa wasn't sure if the man minded the line of chatter, but it did seem to keep her mind off her own wrist, so maybe it was a distraction for the girl, too. If it was, the least she could do was help a girl this sweet. "But it sounds like good advice. Will you be worried about mixed martial arts now?"

The girl gave a slight hake of her head, grimacing as she unintentionally shifted her arm. "I want to go back as soon as this is fixed. I've got a belt test at the end of the year, and I want to make black belt before I get to middle school."

"We'll let the doctor take a look and get some x-rays," the man interjected, his voice low and maybe amused.

"Then we're going to follow doctor's orders to let you heal up correctly."

"*Then* I'll go back to class." The little girl was not to be deterred.

Elisa couldn't help but smile. Dauntless. So much conviction in such a young package.

"Rojas?" A new nurse stood in the double doors leading from the waiting room back into the emergency room area.

The girl's father straightened. "Here."

The nurse nodded and motioned for a young man in scrubs pushing a wheelchair.

In moments, the girl was eased into the wheelchair, big round plushie support and all. She gave Elisa a wave as she was wheeled away to see the doctor.

Elisa waved back.

Wow. Just wow. Elisa took a deep breath. There was one heck of a personality. Someday that little girl was going to grow into a powerful, confident woman.

Someone cleared his throat near her.

She jumped.

For the second time in the space of a few minutes, the man had snuck right up on her. This time, he was holding out a cup of coffee and a card. "Revolution Mixed Martial Arts. It's local, if you're staying in the area. There's a women's self-defense workshop coming up in the next couple of weeks. Boom made me promise to come give this to you."

Words stuck in her throat as she stared at the proffered card. The hand that held it was strong, the fingertips callused, and the nails trimmed back out of practicality rather than aesthetics. Even wrapped in the tape as his hands were, she took note of those details. She imagined they were a sign of honest, hard work. The hands of a good person.

If she could believe she knew how to recognize good anymore.

This man had been very gentle with his daughter and with Elisa. And here he was, being kind again. Her chest tightened, and she savored it, this small act.

It took a long minute for her to pull her wits together enough to take it from him—and the coffee, too. His hands remained steady until she had both in her own. He didn't give any sign of impatience, didn't try to shove either cup or card at her to make her hurry despite probably wanting to get back to his daughter.

Oh no, she shouldn't keep him.

As she gingerly took the offerings, he didn't extend his fingers to touch her the way some men would.

Warm brown eyes the color of dark chocolate studied her, saw straight through her and left her feeling exposed. "The workshop takes it slow and easy. It's assumed everyone is a beginner. If you mention my name, you'll get a discount. Rojas."

She blinked. "Oh, but that's not nec—"

"You distracted Boom for a while. I appreciate the help." His tone had gone back to gruff. "And she's right. You'd benefit from the workshop."

He turned on his heel and headed back to the ER.

Okay, then. Elisa studied the card for a minute. She was too new to the area to recognize the address, but if she could get a hotel room with Wi-Fi, she could map it pretty easily.

Exhaustion rolled over her in a wave. *If* she decided

to get a hotel room tonight. Everything she owned was stuffed into her car, not that there was much. Just as easy to sleep in her car if she could find a safe place to park, tucked away and secure. She could find an out-of-the-way rest stop and catch a little sleep before trying to find a job tomorrow morning. It'd be cheaper and not as easy to find her.

The thought of stretching out in a king-sized bed—hell, a queen-sized bed, even—tempted her to be reckless. She shook her head and took a cautious sip of hot coffee. This was comfort. Splurging on a hotel room was ill-advised at best.

Even trying not to think of the worst-case scenario, her heart rate kicked up and she glanced at the entryway. No one was there. Not yet. Hopefully, no one would come in looking for her.

Once upon a time, she'd had a steady salary in a corporate environment and an expense budget for travel. A king-sized bed was a given. Now, she'd be glad to get an hourly job with some sort of benefits. Even fast food restaurants had full-time positions if it came down to it. But she'd try bookstores or maybe a nearby mall first. Anything fast to get an income going while she looked for a more stable position. Practicality first, bruised pride later. Better than other bruises that took months to heal.

She'd think more on it. Later, when her thought processes weren't skipping around between what she ought to do and what might come through the door at any minute. After she had her wrist examined. One step at a time.

As she worked through her jumbled thoughts, realization washed over her in a wave of caffeine. She'd completely misjudged the man at first. He'd done one nice thing after another, and she hadn't thanked him. Not once.

Elisa looked around the waiting room. A few people had entered, but the room seemed emptier somehow, without the girl and her dad. Boom, he'd called her. Had to be her nickname. Elisa could picture the girl kicking butt in a martial arts class. "Boom" was probably appropriate. Imagining what her father could do was something Elisa shied away from, but the thought was tantalizing more than frightening.

Elisa shifted her position in her seat, her hamstrings and backside aching from hours of driving. This time, it'd been too close. She'd driven up Interstate 95 for as long as she'd been able to manage it before stopping. This was about as far away from where she'd started as she could get and stay on the same continent.

Her foot hit something, and she looked down to see a stray glove on the floor, almost under the chair. She bent to pick it up and found a tag on the inside wrist of the glove.

Boom.
Hope's Crossing Kennels.

Elisa rose and wondered if she could ask the nurse to return the glove to Boom and her father. After all, they'd be here a while.

But as she approached the desk, the nurse took the clipboard from her without looking at her. "Thank you, dear. They'll be calling you any minute now to take you back. Have a seat."

Before Elisa could say anything about the glove, the

nurse had turned her attention to another person who'd just entered. Elisa jumped, then silently cursed herself. And there were two more people coming through the doors. The night was getting busier.

Heart pounding, Elisa returned to her seat and struggled to remain watchful without letting fear get the best of her. Hopefully, she'd either catch sight of Boom in the ER area or ask a nurse to find the girl and her father to return the glove.

She really wanted to manage to thank him if she saw him again.

CHAPTER TWO

Some mornings were just a little more challenging than others.

It was a good thing getting to work didn't involve traffic, driving, or more than a two-minute walk. Life had its simplicities that way, and Alex Rojas reminded himself that things could always be worse.

He could have to wear a tie to work, for example.

He hurried out the front door of his home, letting it slam shut behind him as he tugged the one clean polo he had left over his head. He jogged down the porch steps and across the yard to the side entrance to the main building of Hope's Crossing Kennels. Living on the property was another thing to appreciate.

The dogs in residence came to their feet to greet him as he passed by each of their enclosures.

"Sorry, boys. I'll be back for you in a minute." His pace didn't slow, and he let his momentum carry him right into the main building. He passed the common kitchen area and snagged an apple out of the basket on the counter, thankful for Sophie's thoughtfulness. Sophie might be a childhood friend of Forte's, but she'd adopted Rojas and David Cruz as big brothers without hesitation. It'd been awkward when they'd first arrived a few years ago, but Sophie hadn't been deterred by the kind of walls he and Cruz had built around themselves. She walked right through them, over them, whatever.

When Brandon Forte had established Hope's Crossing Kennels, he'd built it as a new proving ground. It was a place for men like Rojas to start over. The support people like Forte and Sophie provided just by being themselves...it was a good feeling to be surrounded by it.

"Rojas? I'm up at the front." Forte's voice echoed down the hallway, and Rojas headed for the main entryway. Forte, Cruz, and Rojas usually had breakfast together before dawn, but Rojas had missed the meal after staying up most of the night watching over Boom. His daughter was currently still tucked in and he was here, catching up with the day.

The waiting area was empty, but it'd be crawling with people and dogs within the next few minutes. Rojas surveyed the reception area and grabbed a broom from its hiding place behind the front desk. The place was clean, but this was a dog training and kennels facility. There was always random fur to be swept up. "Remind me again why you decided to offer obedience classes for troublesome twos and threes."

They already had a steady class schedule for the general public, teaching basic and advanced obedience classes. Adding these troubleshooting classes for dogs, and their owners, who'd been through obedience and still hadn't quite worked things out, took more energy out of every trainer at the kennels.

Forte pushed away from the reception desk. "Because we want the community to feel safer with us here, not afraid of our dogs or us. The more people who have classes with us, the better. It's beneficial all around."

Good point. A fair amount of PR could only be helpful. Rojas had endured his share of crap experiences when he'd been fresh back from deployment, before he and Boom had moved here. Times when he'd still been in culture shock from coming home and people made things worse by reacting out of fear. He still hated going off the property into busy places like grocery stores or malls; too much going on and too many triggers for his overreactive reflexes. But now, when he did go out, people recognized him. Some even had smiles for him, though mostly they welcomed Boom. And that was more important.

If the community was afraid of them and the dogs they trained, Boom wouldn't have those positive experiences.

"Besides," Forte continued, "anyone can go to a local pet store for basic obedience and puppy training classes. We've got the skill sets to handle the older two-year-olds, give or take a few months, and make behavioral corrections. Maybe prevent a few dogs with potential from landing in shelters."

Rojas grunted. To be honest, usually it was more about training the owner than it was about training the dog. "Retraining isn't my favorite pastime."

"Sometimes it's worth it." Forte set a pile of clipboards on the front of the reception desk. "When you're done with sweeping, can you find some pens?"

Rojas finished up, got rid of the gathered dust and fur, and stowed the broom. Then he started going through drawers on a search mission for the damned pens. "The occasional older rescue with bad habits or a tricky history is worth the effort."

Actually, he enjoyed working with those. It was time well spent, helping the owner willing to give such dogs another chance.

He liked to think they all deserved another chance from time to time.

"Yeah, you've got a soft spot for those." The clipboards fell with a clatter. Forte cursed. "There's got to be a better way to do this."

"We need an admin." It wasn't the first time Rojas had made the suggestion.

"Yeah, yeah. Cruz mentioned it."

Rojas snorted. "And Sophie and Lyn, too. Lyn's reputation is enough to bring more people in on top of what we've already got, so it's only going to get harder to manage."

Lyn Jones was a civilian dog trainer with a solid consulting business. She'd come in four or five months earlier on consult to work with Cruz and Atlas, a high-profile military working dog. Both Cruz and Atlas had had it bad for Miss Jones, and she'd developed a strong partnership with Cruz. With her less structured, more psychological approach to working with dogs, they were seeing more civilians come to them for dog training.

Good for the kennels. Maybe not so good for him.

The more he had to deal with people, especially the ones milling around in the waiting area before a class got started, the edgier he got. All the frenetic activity, the sudden moves, and random raised voices drove him crazy. Half the time he found himself ready to head for cover, sure something was trying to kill him. The rest of the time he struggled to quell the instinct to take out the potential threats first. This wasn't a danger zone and, theoretically, nothing was trying to kill him. Or at least he was trying to convince himself of that one day at a time. He'd been getting better, but the hard days still outnumbered the peaceful when it came down to it.

"Business is good." Forte finished retrieving the clipboards and gave up on keeping them in a neat pile, leaving them spread out across the counter. "I just don't like to keep all my eggs in one basket, so having some buffer from these training classes doesn't hurt."

The majority of their income came from providing well-trained working dogs to both military and law enforcement organizations around the country. They supplied dogs trained to track humans or detect explosives to some private security groups, too, though they vetted those organizations carefully.

"The business plan was your brainchild." Rojas held his hands up. "I thought it was a great concept when you invited me and Boom here three years ago. It's come a long way, so if you want to develop more, I'll follow your lead."

Forte had started the kennels when he'd returned from his last tour of duty and invited Rojas and Cruz to join him a year later. Cruz's romantic partner, Lyn, had her own established training company for civilian clients but had been sending additional references their way. All in all, business had ramped up over the last few months but their business administration was nonexistent. They needed an ops person, or department, depending on just how much Forte wanted to expand. The three of them couldn't stretch to cover it anymore and the bookkeeping was suffering for it.

"You want to keep growing, got to get the support team in." Rojas came up with three pens. He could've sworn they'd opened a fresh box only a week ago. Did the damn things get up and walk?

"I hear you. We'll get an ad up online, stat. In the meantime, we need more pens."

Rojas's back pocket buzzed. Coming to an immediate halt, he yanked his smartphone out of his pants and answered the call. "You okay?"

Boom's voice came across the line. "Yeah. Dad, can I watch an anime?"

His daughter wasn't quite back up to speed, but she was a hundred times better than she'd been the night before, and relief washed through him all over again. The pain meds were working, and her broken arm was set and immobilized in a solid cast. He'd kept her home from school to give her some time to rest.

Of course, even with enough pain medications to put down a camel, his daughter was up and bored.

"A what?" Rojas searched his brain for whatever his daughter was asking for.

"Anime. It's a Japanese cartoon." Boom had her innocent tone going. Which meant it couldn't be as simple as all that.

But it was a cartoon. How bad could that be?

He mouthed the term to Forte. Forte held up his hands in a "nope, no clue" kind of signal.

"Why don't you watch one of the movies I got you for now and I'll come up at lunch to take a look at these *Animaniac* things you want to watch."

"Anime, Dad. Not *Animaniacs*. Totally different." Boom huffed. "Okay, but if I can't watch them this morning, can you bring frozen yogurt for dessert tonight?"

Rojas narrowed his eyes as Forte motioned for him to keep looking for pens. Boom was at the stage where she was big into negotiating. If she didn't get what she wanted in the first place, she angled for bonus deals to make up for the loss. Still, she'd been a trooper last night at the hospital, and she was doing a good job managing the pain from her broken arm. She deserved a little spoiling. "You got it. Frozen yogurt."

"Thanks!" His daughter's happy chirrup made him grin as she ended the call.

Forte had a matching grin. "Glad she's holding up well."

Rojas tipped his head. "Going to need to drop everything if she needs something today, but so far she's taking it as a fun day off."

"Everyone deserves one of those once in a while."

There was a knock at the front door.

Forte cursed. "Still need to get those forms printed out. Can you get that?"

Rojas nodded, already headed for the door. "See if there's any pens hiding near the printer back there. Or in Cruz's office."

The front door had panes of glass set into the center,

and Rojas got a glimpse of brown hair and pale skin. One person, alone. No dog. It was enough of an impression to know what he was dealing with as he opened the door.

Beautiful blue-gray eyes met his briefly before the woman dropped her own gaze to focus on someplace lower on his face, like his nose or mouth. Subtle. Most people would probably not even notice the way she avoided direct eye contact.

But then again, not many people made eye contact a challenge the way he and his colleagues did. It wasn't on purpose, really; more of a common quirk in their personalities.

Funny, he hadn't expected to see her again. Okay, maybe he'd been hoping to find her at Revolution MMA for those self-defense classes he'd recommended. But here she was. A weird tingle jolted through his chest.

This woman was about as non-aggressive as possible without cowering outright. Despite her upright posture, her hands hung at her sides in a loose, non-defensive position. Her left wrist was covered in a brace and it was easy to see she held something in her right hand. She was far enough back on the landing to easily drop down a step or two without having to back up more than a few inches.

But the mannerisms didn't fit her energy, the straightness of her shoulders, or the set of her jaw. Whoever this woman was, she'd developed habits. She wasn't a mouse by nature. He wouldn't be as irritated to see these behaviors if these things came naturally to her.

Who had forced her to assume those mannerisms to survive?

"Mr. Rojas." Her voice was steady.

Another sign of her being more than what she seemed, as far as he was concerned. The timbre was almost soothing, and he realized he'd balled his hands into fists. *Well, shit*. He let his hands loosen.

She presented the object she held in her right hand. "I think your daughter left this behind at the ER last night. I hope you don't mind, but the logo for the kennels was on the inside label, so I googled the address."

Slowly—because he didn't want her to snatch her hand back—he took the glove from her. "Thanks."

"The hospital lost and found was overflowing, and I wanted to make sure Boom got her glove back," the woman continued, then bit her lip. "And I wanted to be sure to thank you." Her cheeks took on a fascinating pale pink blush.

Caught by surprise, Rojas raised his eyebrows. "Me?"

Maybe his tone had been the right encouragement, because she looked up again, her gaze meeting his, and the chemistry shocked him right down to his toes, hitting every vital organ—including his balls—along the way.

Blue-gray, cool as a calm day out on the water, her gaze held his. "You were very kind last night, and I didn't thank you then. I try to thank the kind people I meet. So thank you."

Rojas cleared his throat. "You're welcome."

He didn't know what else to say. He'd only given her some ice, a cup of coffee, and a card about the martial arts center. Boom had a good sense for people, and when she'd said the woman needed the referral for the self-defense classes, he'd been inclined to agree.

She broke their eye contact, and he felt the loss as if

someone had broken the circuit on an electrical current. "I should be going now."

"Wait." He didn't know what made him ask her to. But she paused, balanced on the balls of her feet at the edge of the landing. He was sure if he didn't catch her now she'd be gone for good. "I didn't get your name."

"Oh." She turned to face him. Another sign that she'd learned caution but she wasn't afraid by nature. She was open. A people person. Or at least more of one than he was. "Elisa Hall."

He dug up his best behavior smile from somewhere. "Nice to meet you, Elisa. You new in the area?"

She gave him a tentative smile in return, though she kept her focus in the vicinity of his nose again. "Maybe. I'm looking to see if I can find a place to settle for a while, but it depends on if I can find a job."

Wasn't that just a coincidence?

"Pens. I found pens," Forte called from the hallway. "Damn printer is taking forever. Are people showing up yet?"

Matter of fact, there were cars coming up the drive.

"I should let you..." Elisa began to step away again.

"To be honest, we're actually in need of serious help." Truth. And he wasn't in charge of hiring, but Rojas tended to go with his gut. What harm could she do in one day? "If you're interested in an administrative job, we've got an opening. Trial run today and see if it's a fit."

She paused. "Seriously?"

"As a heart attack." Because he did not want to have to spend one more day greeting all those people and getting their dogs signed in with all the associated paperwork. For him, it was death by a thousand paper cuts.

"I'm qualified for administrative work." There was a touch of irony in her tone, and her lips pressed together in a line as if she held other words back. He'd be interested to learn about the story there. "Word processing, typing, filing."

"Sounds good so far." He stepped back and motioned inside. "Bonus if you can start right away. We've got a dog training class starting and people showing up. If you can greet them and get the paperwork taken care of—"

"Then you don't have to," she finished shrewdly.

He shrugged. Not the least bit ashamed. "Exactly. We're dog trainers. It's what we do. The pleasantries and paperwork aren't our thing."

She huffed out a laugh, glanced up and met his gaze. "If I'm dressed okay..."

Even as she trailed off, he knew she wasn't inviting him to look for any reason other than surface value. But he looked anyway, because there was a whole lot of chemistry going on in holding her gaze and he needed to break eye contact or he might do something stupid. So he tore his attention from those stormy eyes and checked out her clothes as asked. And damn, he liked what he saw. Petite but athletic build. She wasn't frail or tiny by any definition, which was good because the men and the dogs of Hope's Crossing tended to knock those types over. Her clothes were clean, sensible. Her jeans hugged her legs enough to make his mouth water but weren't painted on the way some girls wore theirs. She could move in those.

He forced himself to look back down the drive before his assessment took too long and spooked her. She'd already tensed despite her own implicit invitation.

"Fine for today." And they were, but if she was going to work with them for more than a day, he should think about the business. "But maybe if we do decide together to extend this arrangement, you might want to wear a collared or button-up shirt. It's what the rest of us try to wear when there's people on site for classes."

Her smile was back, still hesitant. "I think I can manage that."

"Come inside, then." He waved his hand toward the interior since he was already holding the door open for her. "I'll introduce you to Forte, and between the two of us we'll try to brief you on what you need to do for the day. If we're all happy by the end of the day, we'll do the whole resumé, questions-and-answers thing."

She hesitated a moment longer, then stepped inside. "Let's give the day a try."

CHAPTER THREE

Hope's Crossing Kennels was in need of a serious administrative overhaul.

Elisa shook her head as she assessed the piles of forms from previous lessons. Oh, the piles were neat enough. Brandon Forte and Alex Rojas, and the currently absent David Cruz, kept the front desk clear of clutter. But the truth was hiding in the deep drawer where they kept release forms from previous classes. All the forms had been dumped in there and forgotten.

Technically, if an incident ever occurred during a class, they did have access to the emergency contacts and liability releases because they weren't scattered or trashed. It'd just take forever to find a specific form if a person had to sift through all of these. Plus, from what some of the friendlier dog owners had told her, they'd had to fill out the same form every time they came to a class. Weekly, in many cases. And who knew where forms went after they didn't fit in the drawer anymore?

"Inefficient," Elisa muttered.

Then she glanced around the empty waiting area to be sure there were no witnesses because she'd probably twitched.

They had a good laptop set up at the front with basic software for the usual business office needs. More than sufficient to set up a client database, scan the forms, and have them on file and searchable with the appropriate metadata. The correct information at a moment's notice meant loyal clients wouldn't have to keep filling out the forms every time they came.

She didn't want to snoop around on a computer when her duties so far had been limited to greeting and asking people to fill out a form. A paper form. With random pens.

Damn it, the pens didn't even match. They'd been grabbed from anywhere, apparently. Others had been chewed a bit on the ends, and she was pretty sure the chewing hadn't been done by any dog. And some of them disappeared as people absentmindedly took them with them.

Shuddering, she'd tossed the chewed pens in the garbage. No way should any clients have to use those.

The first class would last about an hour, according to Alex. He'd also said there was an hour break between classes, too. So she had a whole bunch of time to sit and wipe imaginary dust off a clean desk area.

She studied the laptop again. It didn't even have a screen saver set to turn on after a specified amount of time. No password protection. If she hadn't been sitting there, anyone who walked in could sit down at the laptop and have access to...

Nothing.

Elisa blinked. She hadn't even realized she'd started to poke around on the desktop of the computer. It had access to Wi-Fi for Internet browsing plus connection to a printer and a scanner, but that was it. She couldn't see any other computers on the network but there had to be. Both Brandon and Alex had mentioned offices farther down the hallway. At least the network security had this laptop separated from the rest of its computers.

To her, what she'd found indicated someone here was IT savvy. But if one of them was, why hadn't anyone made a client database and reduced the need for all this paper?

Gah. Forget waiting for Alex or Brandon to come back. How mad could they really get at her, anyway? The worst they could do was fire her, and this was just a trial run. If they *did* offer her a steady job and she *did* decide to take it, she'd want to get a better system in place. And if this job opportunity didn't work out, she'd be saving somebody else in the future.

Good enough reasoning for her.

Opening up one of the applications on the desktop, she set up and formatted a simple spreadsheet. It could easily be imported into a more sophisticated database later, but this would be sufficient to at least start organizing the data on their clients. Turning to the pile of papers from today's class, she dove in. Once she entered those, she'd go for the deep drawer.

It was nice to exercise her organizational skills. The few jobs she'd been able to pick up over the last six months had been under-the-table jobs at mom-and-pop shops, running a cash register or serving ice cream.

Here and there, even last night, she'd considered a retail job or something with a chance at benefits, but once she'd woke up in the morning with a clear head, she'd decided it wasn't worth the risk. Anything that required filling out a W-4 might be a bad idea, at least for the time being.

After a while, Elisa straightened in her chair and sighed. She rolled her shoulders to ease some of the tension caused by working at a laptop and stretched her arms over her head. Taking in a deep breath, she let it out slowly, then grimaced as her left wrist throbbed. She'd taken off the brace in the midst of her data entry because it hampered her typing speed. Probably should put it back on.

An ice pack landed on the desk next to her.

She jumped, reaching for her neat piles of paperwork, but the ice pack was well away from them. Then she looked up at the man on the other side of the desk.

The expression on Alex's face might've been irritation. Difficult to tell because his mouth was perpetually set in a hard line, and it was hard to read expression in a person's eyes when all you ever looked at was any place on the face but the eyes. Because direct eye contact was asking for trouble.

She shuddered.

Not with everyone. Maybe. But better safe than sorry. Better not to if she didn't plan to get to know someone in any case. She'd rather have a polite, nice impression of everyone she came into contact with, and not see the potential monster lurking behind the public face.

"Hey." Alex's gruff word brought her out of her musings.

"I'm sorry." The apology came immediately, followed by the guilt. She was always sorry, even if she didn't know what she'd done yet.

The corners of his mouth turned downward into a frown. "You haven't done anything wrong as far as I know."

She swallowed. *Oh, good.* "I wasn't sure if I could work on the laptop, but if I could show you—"

He held up a finger, and she shut up. Right away. Her chest constricted. He was going to be mad. She should have known better than to mess with their laptop. She'd overstepped her bounds. Miserable, she started to put her careful piles back in the drawer as quickly as she could.

"Hold up for a second." There was exasperation in his voice, and she froze.

She should've waited to hear the rest of what he said. Damn, she should've...

"First, put the ice pack on your wrist." His tone wasn't angry, and there was no edge of censure to his words. "Second, when was the last time you had something to eat?"

"Huh?" Surprised, she looked up into his face and was caught by his dark gaze. Now that she was giving him direct eye contact, it was hard to look away. There was a magnetism about him, and a calm that drew her in, like she was being pulled into the eye of a storm.

It was...enticing.

He held her in his stare for a long moment and she didn't want to look away, but then he seemed to shake himself free, too.

"We're ordering hot subs for lunch. I wanted to be sure to include something for you in the order. Do you like Italian?" Gruff, but kind. Maybe awkward. He kept his sentences short, imparting the information he wanted to communicate with minimum verbiage.

She reached out for the ice pack without breaking their eye contact. Suddenly, she didn't want to. Self-preservation or no. She couldn't read him very well, but she did notice that he seemed to like it better if she did meet his gaze. The cool pack was an instant relief on her wrist, and she berated herself silently for having ignored it. It needed to heal.

"Italian is fine; great even." She ventured hesitantly. "If you're ordering hot subs, I could go for an eggplant parm or meatball parm if they have one or the other."

He nodded.

"How much?" She started to go for her wallet in her back pocket.

He shook his head in a sharp negative. "Lunch is on us."

The statement brooked no argument.

She subsided. Unsure. "Thank you."

"Serena was hungry anyway." He glanced out the window toward a house beyond the main yard.

Elisa drew her brows together. "Serena?"

"Boom." He turned his attention back to her and the full impact hit her, making her breath catch in her throat. "Everyone at Revolution MMA and her school calls her Boom, but her real name is Serena. It's just me and her. Her mother passed away a few years ago before we moved here. I guess because it's mostly me and Forte and Cruz, her nickname became more of a habit than we intended. But Serena likes being called Boom. Says it makes her sound awesome."

Of course. Boom was fun, but it was obviously a nickname. Warm pleasure spread through Elisa at being included in the circle of people who knew the engaging young girl's real name. It'd been a while since she'd been included in such a way. A small thing. Probably not significant to Alex or the people at Hope's Crossing or maybe even Serena herself, but it meant something to Elisa.

"Next question." He reached over the desk and tapped the top of the laptop. "What's with the spreadsheet?"

"Oh." She swallowed. Well, best to give him her logic and see whether he liked what she'd done. So she turned the laptop screen toward him. "I thought it might be helpful to organize your client information, all the stuff you gather on the forms. There's an identification number for every client so we can scan in the filled-out forms and associate them with each record."

He grunted. "Nice. We've been meaning to do something like this. No one's had the time yet."

"Oh." She was saying that a lot. But she wasn't sure if he liked what she'd done or not. "I kept it in a spreadsheet so it could be imported into any database you'd want."

"Makes sense." He tapped the completed forms. "There's a scanner in one of the back offices. I'll show you where that is tomorrow so you can scan and set up the digital files on this laptop."

"It should be backed up to a network-shared drive." The recommendation popped out before she could hold back. She winced. She shouldn't be correcting him.

He huffed out a brief laugh. "We'll talk to Cruz about it when he gets back. We wanted this laptop separate, but if we do start keeping client information on it, it should be backed up somehow. Could be we'll get secure cloud space."

"Cloud." She repeated the term. Music to her ears. Not every office or even corporate organization was familiar with the concept of storing their data in the cloud yet. "That'd be good, too."

One corner of his mouth ticked upward in a hint of a smile. "We'll take a few minutes to show Forte your format and see if he wants to store any additional info. But so far, this looks way better than all that paper."

She smiled, relieved he approved of what she'd done. "Yes. Definitely."

He cleared his throat. "Next class should start arriving shortly. After that, lunch."

"Okay." Once he left, she sagged into the computer chair and chewed on her lip.

Alone again, she was a weird combination of relieved and disappointed he was gone. He had a knack for sneaking up on her. Not exactly the best thing for her heart rate. But once she'd realized he was there, his presence had filled the whole room with its intensity. Her entire focus had been on him. But not in a fearful way. Not really. She'd freaked out a little but she only had herself to blame. Her brain had been running in circles instead of listening to what he'd actually intended to communicate.

She needed to work through her issues. Preferably sooner rather than later.

But he hadn't seemed bothered by her odd behavior. Thankfully. He was patient in his own way. And she appreciated it. Definitely a good trait in an employer.

It didn't hurt that he was incredibly gorgeous, either. But she wasn't noticing his charms at all. Nope. Job first. Rebuild her life second. Men, later.

Much later.

*   *   *

"How many dogs do you have on property?"

Rojas did his best not to grimace. Elisa's hesitant tone wasn't necessarily an indicator of how she would be with the dogs. From long years of experience, he'd learned people could be completely different in their interactions with other humans versus with animals. But if Miss Hall was going to work for them, they all needed to know she could face the kind of dogs they worked with on her own without fear.

She didn't have to be able to control the dogs, though that would've been a bonus, but for her safety and the dogs' well-being, she needed to be able to interact with them without triggering their aggression. Some things could be learned, but it'd be best to see how she did right off the bat with minimal coaching.

"We've got one dog here permanently at this time. Another four or five could be with us a few months at a time, some as long as a year, as we work on their training before they're placed. I had two breeding dogs here, but it was time for them both to retire so we found them permanent homes with families. We're not sure if we're going to continue a breeding program on site. Forte's always experimenting with the business plan." He led her out the back of the main house and across the covered walkway that connected to the kennels. "We've never had more than a dozen staying with us long term at any given time, but we have the kennel space if we need it."

"That's a lot of dogs." Her voice was quiet, but more reserved than anything else.

Surprisingly, she wasn't fidgeting or shifting her weight back and forth from one foot to another. None of the anxious or nervous body language that came from someone about to meet big dogs for the first time. Even if a person was looking forward to it, they tended to project their nervous excitement. But Elisa Hall had learned somewhere to stuff all of her nervous tells away and project a non-threatening, almost docile presence instead.

The possible reasons for it made his blood boil. The way she dropped her eyes, jumped when someone caught her by surprise, flinched when someone—mostly him—made sudden moves. It all pointed to a very shitty history, and it made him see red just thinking about the possibilities.

"Ever been around more than one or two dogs at a time?" They didn't usually have many of their dogs out at the same time without a handler for each dog, but the civilian classes could get unruly. Dogs got loose occasionally. He needed to know if she might panic.

"Yes." Her answer was soft. There might've been a hint of darkness there. Whatever it was, it wasn't a good memory. "The place wasn't like this. The people weren't as nice."

He tipped his head to one side. "You think we are?"

She nodded. "You are."

The conviction in her tone caught him by surprise. She wasn't leaving any room for doubt, not even for herself.

"You seem sure." He kept his own tone deliberately light. "You could be wrong about us."

"I could." She pressed her lips together, watching the dogs. "I have been in the past, but I decided I wouldn't let that stop me from meeting new people and giving myself the chance to be right again."

And that was something he needed to store away to consider at another time because anger was definitely not something he wanted to broadcast to the dogs the first time he introduced her to any of them.

He took a deep breath. Time to get a better read on her and see if she could maybe have a place here.

Alex stopped at the first kennel and gestured down the line with one hand. "Why don't you take a walk down the line and choose one of the dogs to meet? Don't actually try to touch any of them yet. We'll do introductions as the next step."

"Okay. I can do that." She said it out loud, but he got the impression she was talking to herself.

She walked slowly down the line of kennels, pausing to look at each dog. Every dog had a different personality, and it showed in the way each reacted to her. One or two came right up to the chain link of the kennel trying to get a good look at her or catch a better whiff of her scent. There were a couple of reserved tail wags for her, too. Others stayed lying or sitting where they were, the only sign of their interest in the way their ears came up to listen in her direction.

"These aren't all the same breed, are they?" she asked as she continued to walk from kennel to kennel, almost at the end.

Good eye.

"Three of these are Belgian Malinois, and the rest are German Shepherd Dogs. Easiest way to tell the difference right now is by coat color." He paused. "All of our current GSDs are black and tans with black saddles across their backs. The Belgian Malinois are...mostly tan," he finished lamely.

He needed practice explaining the differences to a non-dog person, obviously.

"The German Shepherds are bigger, too, longer fur." She made the statement slowly, and he wondered if it was because she wasn't sure she was right or wasn't sure how he'd react to her making a statement rather than asking a question.

"German Shepherd Dogs," he corrected. She hunched her shoulders, and he cursed himself inwardly. It'd come out matter of fact to him, but she was pretty sensitive to correction. "We try to make sure to refer to the dogs by their correct breed name or a standard like 'GSD.' It avoids confusion when we're working with some of our clients."

Still standing about midway down the corridor, she looked back at him and nodded. "I'll try to remember."

Good recovery. None of the men of Hope's Crossing Kennels, least of all him, was great at saying the right thing at the right time. He didn't want to tiptoe around on eggshells every single moment with someone he'd be working with on a daily basis. But if she could take constructive feedback, that was a start.

"But, yeah, the GSDs tend to be bigger. It's a good observation." She straightened under the kudos, so he figured he was coming out about even with her. Maybe with the right environment, she'd develop a thicker skin and more solid confidence. "They can outweigh a Belgian Malinois by ten or more pounds, and they've got some other physical differences you start to notice once you're around them more."

She nodded. "But you work with both breeds?"

"They tend to have the traits we're looking for when we're training working dogs." He leaned against the door frame and waited. She didn't seem to be trying to delay, but she wasn't rushing to pick a dog to meet, either. "But we would work with other breeds if the dogs themselves had what it takes for the job they need to do. We do assessments when we acquire the dogs."

She looked at each of the dogs, her face a strange play of expressions. "They're all pretty intimidating."

True. He considered how to address that, though, because he wouldn't soften what any of the dogs were and it didn't have to be a bad thing. "The dogs we train go on to perform very specific duties, some in active combat situations. Aggression, prey drive, intelligence, and other traits are absolutely necessary to the survival of their human team and to them. That said, we're also careful to socialize them. We teach them the difference between friend and foe, when they're on duty and when they're not. Our dogs aren't vicious, indiscriminate killers the way some can mistake them for."

She shook her head. "None of them look...crazy or anything. They're just intimidating." She let out a shaky laugh. "Honestly, getting to know dogs like these would go a long way toward making me feel safe, if they liked me."

He'd take that. It was actually a fairly positive attitude. At least she wasn't afraid, and wary was smart. "I can't promise they'll like you, but I've found dogs are generally good judges of character."

"Huh." She drew in a breath and let it out. "Then they've got better instincts than I do."

There went her confidence again. Not too long ago, she'd been determined to give herself a chance to judge people correctly. The moment he thought he had a solid read on her, she shifted gears.

"I don't know about that." He didn't go closer, but he did lean in until he caught her attention and drew her gaze back to him. She had to look up through long lashes to do it, and if she'd lifted her chin, she'd have been within easy reach for a kiss. But he was *not* going to think about that and focused instead on how she was making eye contact more readily now. Good progress for a day. Bad manners on his part, thinking about totally inappropriate things, no matter how pretty the curve of her lips was. He tried what he thought might be an encouraging smile. "You gave this job a shot and survived the day. It could be a good fit."

She gave him a small smile in return, her sweet lips curving even more temptingly. "We'll call it a work in progress, then."

Someone or several someones had done way too much damage to this woman. Whether she decided to stay on for the job or not, he wanted to offer at least one reassurance that she'd believe.

"Well, I'm pretty sure about one thing." He tried for every drop of articulate skill he had. "What comes next is your choice and no matter what you decide, it'll be the right thing for you."

CHAPTER FOUR

Elisa stared at him as his words sank in.

He hadn't tried to convince her to trust him, or even any of the people she'd be working with. And somehow, it made her want to. Trust *him*, at least.

Alex Rojas had no way of knowing what she'd escaped from, but she wasn't delusional enough to imagine a perceptive person like him couldn't figure it out. She hadn't had enough time to work through her reactions and get them under control yet. Too little time and too many experiences fresh in not only her mind, but her muscle memory.

Perceptive, intelligent men were a threat to her. She should leave before she was too tempted to stay. This was how she'd gotten into trouble in the first place.

Practicality made her grab that reaction and get a handle on it. Well, that and a hint of courage. She was standing in the middle of the most unpredictable place she could think of. She needed a job, and this one had a lot of benefits to it. It was a veritable sanctuary if she had the protection of these employers and their dogs. And her hands itched to dive into their paperwork and put some organization into the way this place was run. She could always leave if it started to go down the familiar path.

My choice.

Steadied, she returned her attention to the dogs. One in particular stood out to her. He hadn't come right up to the kennel's door, wagging his tail, but he was watching her. His eyes had tracked every movement she made, and it might've creeped her out but he'd just been lying relaxed in his kennel. He gave her the impression of polite interest. Not too scary and not too friendly, either. Reserved.

"I'd like to meet this dog, please." She stepped toward the kennel. The way the big dog's ears came up was encouraging, a good sign in dogs like him. At least, she thought so. Eyes and ears focused in her direction. Not dangerous, just... intense. The impact of being the center focus of his attention hit her in the chest. Wow. He still hadn't risen from his relaxed spot on the cool kennel floor.

Alex joined her, standing close but not crowding her. "Okay. Can you step back so I can bring Souze out?"

Souze. It was an unusual name. She did as asked, mulling over the dog's name as she did and moving a few feet away.

Alex took a long leash off a nearby hook, and she noted that every kennel had a similar hook with a leash handy. When she'd first come in, she hadn't noticed them, but she guessed it was a lot more convenient than storing them all at one end of the row of kennels or another.

Opening the kennel's door, Alex murmured a few words. His tone was calm, firm. Not sweet or coaxing, the way she'd heard some people talk to their dogs in public parks or stores. And Souze's attention was completely on him, where other dogs in her experience were too busy looking at everything around them to pay attention to their owners.

Souze rose to his feet and crossed the few steps to Alex, then sat in response to another quiet command. The big dog even turned his head slightly so Alex could easily hook the leash to his collar. A moment later, Alex was leading him out into the hallway area.

"Why don't we all walk over to the training field?" Alex jerked his head, indicating a direction over his shoulder. "Plenty of room, no distractions, and the others won't get jealous."

So considerate. It hadn't even occurred to her that the other dogs might be jealous of seeing attention given to one of them and not all of them. But then, her mom's friends had a pair of little Dachshunds that spite-peed any time a person picked one up and not the other. It was probably wise not to inspire such behavior in bigger dogs.

Had to be a lot of pee.

She followed Alex out of the kennel hallway and across a yard. There was another fenced area, probably the training field. It was a wide open expanse of grass, clear of trees and shrubs. The fence took her by surprise, though. "I'm guessing having a fenced-in field is important when you're training dogs—maybe to let them off their leashes or something—but it's taller than me. Why build the fence so high?"

Alex walked a few yards into the training field and grinned at her as she closed the gate behind her. "Any of these dogs could jump a normal fence."

Wow. "So you're keeping them from running?"

He shrugged. "None of the dogs would run from a trainer so much as decide to go after something. They've got really strong prey drives. Spotting a squirrel or rabbit on the other side of the fence is a big temptation, especially early in their training when they're still working on discipline."

"So having a fence that tall will stop them from going after whatever caught their attention?" There was something else she was missing. Alex was grinning too wide for it to be that simple.

"You're close, but it's easier to show you than tell you. Besides, Souze could use the easy exertion after being in the kennel all morning." He bent and whispered something to the dog. One big ear swiveled to listen. Alex reached into his pocket with his free hand and pulled out a tennis ball. The dog's gaze locked onto the tennis ball, and a fine tremor passed through the dog's entire body. Suddenly, the dog was eager and ready. "Just stay where you are and watch."

Then Alex removed the leash. Souze stood still, his complete attention on the trainer. Alex drew back his arm and tossed the tennis ball over the fence then uttered a single word. *"Brrring."*

Souze exploded forward. He was a black-and-tan blur, covering the ground to the fence in seconds. When he reached the fence, he gathered his hind legs under him and launched upward, catching the chain link in his paws. Perched high up on the fence, the dog proceeded to climb the rest of the way to the top. Once he got there, he dove from the top of the fence to the ground on the other side and snatched up the tennis ball. He looked back at Alex and returned the same way he'd come.

Once Souze was back at Alex's side, Elisa let out a breath she hadn't been aware of holding.

Alex looked at her. "Climbing the fence takes them longer than jumping straight over. We've got a little more time to react if one of them gets over excited and decides to go up and over."

"Does that happen a lot?" It'd been exciting to see, actually. She wondered if all of their training was as interesting.

"Not once they've completed obedience training." Alex cocked his head to one side. "Mostly it's the puppies and their attention span. They all learn quickly, though, so as early as six months, they're solid with obedience and already have a decent foundation in some of the more advanced training."

"How old is…Souze?" Remembering the dog's name wasn't hard, but her tongue tripped over it as she tried to say it. Besides, she wasn't sure how the dog would react to her saying his name.

The dog in question remained unconcerned. His attention was on Alex, or possibly on the pocket in which Alex had stowed the tennis ball. She tried not to follow the dog's gaze since staring at her potentially new boss's groin didn't seem like the best of ideas.

"Good question." Alex motioned for her to approach. "He's about a year old, closer to thirteen months."

Elisa took a few steps closer, standing where Alex pointed. "Is he full grown, then?"

"I'll answer in a second. Hold your hand out in a loose fist first and keep talking to me," Alex instructed. "Let him make the choice to close the space between you and sniff. Don't lean in on him."

Okay, then. She gazed up into brown eyes the color of caramel and realized her mouth was hanging open. Suddenly, her brain blanked, and she had no idea what line of conversation she'd been following with her previous questions or how to continue. "Wh-what were we talking about again?"

Great. Fantastic.

Her cheeks burned as she snapped her mouth shut on her own inane question. Belatedly, she remembered *she'd* been the one asking questions.

Thankfully, Alex didn't laugh...out loud. Humor shone in the crinkles around his eyes and at the corner of his mouth. He was fighting not to grin. Of course, if he had one of those lopsided grins maybe his amusement at her expense would be worth it. She was a sucker for a hot guy with a lopsided grin.

Which was not anything she should be considering right now. The last thing she needed was to get tangled up with a man, and why, oh why was she constantly wandering back to considering bad ideas?

When a cool, slightly wet nose touched the back of her hand, she almost jumped out of her skin. As it was, she managed not to jerk her hand back, but she did gasp and look down, locking gazes with Souze. The big dog had jerked back a few inches and was looking up at her with a wary expression.

She gulped and really hoped she hadn't blown it. This was probably the first job interview where her ability to make friends was part of the job description.

"I'm sorry." She directed her apology at Souze. "I messed up, didn't I? I didn't mean to flinch. My brain wandered, and I completely forgot you'd be deciding whether to say 'Hi.'"

Souze's ears didn't relax from their alert, upright position, but he rose up out of the subtle crouch he'd been in and his nostrils flared. She left her hand out for him.

"He's not quick to make friends," Alex mentioned offhandedly.

Great. "You could've mentioned that earlier."

"You chose him, and I wanted you to be comfortable meeting any dog you chose. He's safe."

Somehow, she couldn't take her gaze away from the dog's. She should, though. Alex had told her to look at him. But the trainer hadn't reiterated the instructions. She decided to compromise. "Is he a full-grown adult? Is that why he's safe?"

Souze's nostrils flared again. This time his sniffing was audible, and he began to stretch his neck as he approached the back of her hand again.

"Not quite." Alex didn't seem to mind the current progression of things. "In terms of physical growth, he's about as tall as he'll get, but he'll fill out significantly over the next year or so."

"So he's going to be a hefty dog." Maybe it wasn't the right way to put it, but to her, Souze was already a big dog. Now that Alex mentioned filling out, she could see how Souze's legs seemed slightly long and awkward for the rest of his frame and his paws seemed disproportion-ately big.

For his part, Souze continued his approach millimeter by millimeter.

"Mmm, I wouldn't describe it as hefty." Alex paused for a moment, considering. "He'll be heavier through the shoulders and chest, but his overall lines will still be sleek, and he'll be trim through the waist and hips. The Belgian Malinois might be smaller, but they're boxier through the frame."

"I think I'd have to see a side-by-side comparison to get what you're saying there." Her patience was re-warded as Souze's cool nose touched the back of her hand again. Elated, she smiled as she looked back up at Alex.

Alex returned her smile. "A comparison can be ar-ranged. You think you can get comfortable with the dogs here?"

Souze was still sniffing her hand, but he didn't shove his head under her palm the way some dogs did when she'd met them in the past. She didn't think it'd be a good idea to try petting yet.

"Is this about as friendly as any of the dogs get?" The lack of jumping and slightly uncomfortable tongue baths could be a relief.

Alex shrugged. "Depends on the dog. Some of them are more open to petting and play. Souze here has some history, though."

Instantly, her heart cracked open. "Was he abused?"

Alex gave a slight shake of his head. "Not tech-nically, no. He and other GSDs were acquired for a specific purpose—to guard. Their owners invested a lot of money into obedience training and as much Schutzhund as the dogs could absorb. But they were intended to be outdoor security, so they were never socialized with humans on any sort of friendly level. They worked with their trainers and chased people off private property. That's it. No affection, no friendships, no human pack. When the owners got divorced and liquidated their property, they ditched all of the guard dogs into the shelter and didn't spare a thought for what would happen next."

Souze had moved forward to sit between them, his head turned away from her but his shoulders right next to her hand. She took the hint and gently ran her fingertips through the thick fur of his shoulder. The big dog acted as if he wasn't aware of her touch at all.

Alex regarded her with a raised eyebrow.

She bit her lip and tried not to smile even wider than earlier. "How did he come to you?"

"I wish I could say it's a standard practice for the shelter to call us when they have a dog with as much potential as him." Alex frowned. "But it was dumb luck. One of the volunteers working that week called us. Souze and two other dogs had been taken in and determined unadoptable. The shelter just didn't have the resources to rehabilitate dogs like them. If it hadn't been for that volunteer knowing us, and having a fairly good idea of what we could retrain, the dogs might have had no future."

Elisa ached in response to the genuine sadness in Alex's voice. The man truly cared.

"There's a lot of hard realities out there." She withdrew her hand from Souze and let it fall to her side. "As many people as there are trying to help, there are some things volunteers and shelters just can't handle."

People had tried to help her. And they had, in small ways. It'd taken a long time and a hundred tiny gestures before she'd gathered the courage and resources to leave. A dog like Souze didn't even have that option.

No wonder he was slow to open up to meeting new people.

"This place is made for second chances." Alex was looking out over the grounds. "Forte and me, we met overseas. He was an Air Force handler with a military working dog attached to my SEAL team. We stayed in touch over multiple deployments and I was out there a lot, too much probably. Relationships are hard with that kind of life. He was there through my marriage and my divorce. When I came back from deployment for the last time, I needed a place to raise Boom and get back into civilian life again. He invited us here."

She didn't know what to say, but she looked around her with new perspective. This place, these people, there were stories here. And not just what had happened, but what they were creating for themselves moving forward. It was...tempting.

"Thank you for the introduction." Whether she was talking to Souze or Alex, she wasn't even sure herself, but she left it to both of them. "But I should be going now. It's getting into evening."

Maybe this wasn't the right place for her after all. She could see herself caring too much about the people and animals here. Becoming too attached. She'd promised herself she would be self-sufficient, and more importantly, ready to move on at a moment's notice.

Too much of a good thing would make her comfortable, complacent. She didn't ever want to be there again.

Souze turned and looked up at her. Dark brown eyes, deep and sad and fierce all at the same time. It never ceased to amaze her how expressive a dog's eyes could be.

Alex shifted his weight, catching her attention. "Will you be coming back tomorrow?"

Her chest tightened. "I'm not sure."

Truth seemed the best she could commit to right now. Fortunately, it seemed to have been the right answer.

Alex nodded and gave Souze's leash a slight tug. "Let's get back to the kennels then, and I'll walk you to your car."

"You don't have to..." She started to protest then thought it through. She'd just said she wasn't sure she was taking the job. Of course he'd need to escort her around the property. Besides, it was getting into evening and the staff here probably needed to close up to head home for the night.

"It's no trouble," Alex continued, oblivious of her thought process. "Tomorrow's Saturday, and we start classes at oh-nine-hundred. If you decide to come back and give the job a try, try to be here by oh-eight-hundred to help set up. The rest of us are up earlier working with the dogs."

"Okay." She hoped he hadn't caught the relief in her voice. It might be too obvious, and she didn't want his pity. He'd already been far nicer than he needed to be.

Abruptly, her phone issued an obnoxious multi-toned alert. She jumped and fumbled to pull it out of her pocket, fumbling as she tried to silence it.

"Whoa." Alex raised both eyebrows at her this time. "If you do come back tomorrow, try tuning that down. It could freak out some of the client dogs if it goes off at the wrong moment."

"It freaks me out now," Elisa admitted wryly. "New phone. I haven't figured out all the settings yet and didn't realize the text notifications were set to *that* alert."

Alex chuckled. "I'll get Souze back into his kennel."

Embarrassment was quickly becoming her state of being here. She gave him a nod and looked down at Souze. "Good night, Souze. It was nice to meet you."

On the off chance the big dog might give her a token sniff, she held out her hand as Alex had instructed her before, relaxed in a loose fist.

Souze studied her for a moment, stretched out his neck, sniffed the back of her hand, then gave her a very small lick.

"All right, then. That's new." Alex sounded pleased.

Simple happiness bubbled up inside her at Souze's response.

Alex started to turn away, paused for a moment, then turned back. "Was there anything that I did, any of us did, that made you feel uncomfortable? Hesitate? You don't have to tell me, but if we can fix it somehow, either me or Forte would welcome the feedback."

She blinked in surprise. It could be a trap, a way to get her to voice a criticism and give him an excuse to snap at her. Her brain froze for a full second before she could kick it back into gear. Dropping her eyes so he wouldn't see her consider the possibility, her gaze fell on Souze.

Steady. Calm. Absolutely capable of dangerous things and not in any way threatening.

She drew in a breath and let it out slowly. "You've been very considerate and so was Brandon. I've just… got a lot of history myself."

There was a long pause. "Whatever else you take away with you tonight, consider this: No man here will ever intentionally harm you, and no dog anywhere will ever lie to you."

She fumbled for some sort of coherent response, but he was already walking Souze down the row of dog runs. She quit trying for a verbal response and watched him give Souze quiet praise before sending the dog back into his kennel. Truth might be a tough thing to find these days, but she thought she could still recognize it. He'd meant what he'd said at least, believed in it with incredible conviction. And it made her believe his words, too.

Glancing down at the phone in her hand, she tapped the notification to view the text.

Ping. How long do you think it will take?

Elisa froze, staring at the phone screen unable to move, speak, anything. He'd found her. Already. What could she do?

CHAPTER FIVE

Alex started to close the kennel's door and stopped. Souze always watched when Alex put him away, almost as if he was waiting for Alex to forget to secure the door. Souze might be one hundred percent obedient and have perfect recall so far, but the dog considered his chances of getting out on his own every single day. It was one of the reasons Alex was still working with him so closely and why Souze hadn't been considered ready for transfer to either the American military or a law enforcement unit. He needed to know the inside of every dog's head at Hope's Crossing Kennels to be sure they were ready for their next mission.

At the moment, Souze's mind wasn't on what Alex was doing. Instead, the big dog's head was turned toward where Elisa stood waiting. A second later, Souze stepped to the corner of the kennel in her direction, leaning forward slightly, his body language tense and alert.

Alex followed the dog's gaze to Elisa, finished locking up the kennel's door, and immediately headed toward her. Her face had gone pale, and she swayed where she stood, staring at the phone in her hand. Concern hit him in the gut hard.

He slowed once he was in arm's reach, not wanting to scare her further by sneaking up on her while she was distracted.

"Elisa." No response. Not a good sign. She was too exposed like this, her fear raw and leaving her vulnerable. He gritted his teeth and repeated her name, putting a little punch into it. *"Elisa."*

She jumped out of her skin and dropped the phone with a clatter, reaching out to grab the doorjamb at the entrance of the kennels to steady herself.

Satisfied she wasn't going to faint—at least for the moment—he bent to retrieve her phone and give her time to pull herself together. He'd gotten the impression through the course of their interactions that she put a lot of effort into facing him with composure. To be honest, he'd snuck up on her once or twice this morning just to enjoy her discomfiture a little because he was a rat bastard like that.

But now was a good time to let her have her composure if it would help her feel safer.

As he straightened, he glanced at the text. Seemed harmless enough, but experience told him the most innocuous-looking things on the surface could blow an unsuspecting person to pieces.

He'd seen it happen more times than he ever wanted to remember.

"Is this a problem?" He held the phone out to her.

Elisa stared at the proffered phone as if it was a viper.

He let his arm drop, phone still in hand. The tightness in her shoulders eased a fraction, but overall she was wound up so tight he wouldn't be surprised if she started shaking.

And what the hell was he going to do if she did? He wanted to hold her, stroke her hair, and reassure her. Kissing her was at the top of the list of things he'd like to do, too. None of those was the right thing at the moment and, damn, why was he even thinking along those lines?

Through the course of the day, he'd observed a capable woman dive into work with enthusiasm. She'd listened to instructions and also taken initiative, demonstrated a solid work ethic, and seemed to take a practical approach to things.

Elisa Hall wasn't the type to get dramatic over nothing. This text was significant and a threat to her. His anger started at a slow burn, and he set his jaw in an effort to keep it from showing. It wouldn't be good to frighten her further.

"Elisa." He tried for quiet, gentle—the same tone he used with an upset dog. Not that she was a dog or anything, but damn it, he was going to go with what worked for him. "I know you've only just met me, but can I help you?"

She continued to stare at his hand holding the phone for several long seconds before she came to herself with a start. Her eyes were wild as she looked up and met his gaze then quickly away. "No."

Too fast. She'd responded automatically, and it didn't sound like what she really wanted, but he wasn't going to make any assumptions.

"Okay. How about I walk you to your car, then. Just like I said I would." That was reasonable, wasn't it? In actuality, he wanted to pound the living hell out of whomever had terrorized her so bad a random text could blow her carefully constructed confidence to pieces.

She swallowed hard. "You would need to, wouldn't you? Since I don't officially work here. Sure. I should be going now."

The distance she'd put between herself and Hope's Crossing was a palpable thing. She made the idea of not officially working there sound like a decision and her leaving now something even more final.

He didn't like the idea of not seeing her tomorrow. "Are you okay?"

There was a pause. "Not right now. But I will be."

Despite his misgivings, he smiled. Truth and determination. He was getting to like her more and more. "I believe that."

"Do you?" There was still a tremor in her voice, and her steps weren't precisely straight as she headed up the aisle toward the door to the main building the way they'd come earlier. "To be honest, I said it more to convince myself."

He'd done the same in the past. There could be dark times when you had to talk yourself through to the other side.

"Yeah." He followed her as far to one side as he possibly could and still walk with her, so she could see him at the edge of her peripheral vision and not feel chased. Spooked wasn't the word for whatever was going on with her, but he could give her space without leaving her alone. "I think you're in the process of building what you want for yourself. That sort of thing takes time."

She huffed out a bitter laugh. "True. Work in progress. That's me."

"That's not a bad thing," he answered quietly. Because he was in progress, too. He didn't say it out loud, though. If it sounded corny inside his head, it'd be worse out loud.

Anyway, this was about her for the time being.

Through the main house and out to the small parking area, they walked to an old compact car. It'd seen better days, but it was one of those rice burners Sophie's dad loved. Old man swore the engines in those little cars would last forever. This one hopefully was taking good care of Elisa.

She'd retrieved her purse from behind the front desk and was fishing around for her keys so he took the opportunity to look for what else there was to see. The back of the car was neatly packed with items. In fact, he'd bet there was a lot more tucked into the back of that car than anyone would guess. It was like a master game of *Tetris* back there. If the trunk was similarly filled to capacity, she could live out of her own car.

And probably was.

"Do you have a place to go tonight?" He winced. He probably could've put it in a more diplomatic way, but diplomacy hadn't been his thing. Ever.

She went rigid. Clearing her throat, she responded, "Yes."

Not quite a lie. "Do you have a safe place to sleep tonight? Inside your car does not qualify as sufficiently safe."

Silence.

Deliberately, he leaned against the driver's side door. She started to protest, but he held up a finger and pulled out his own smartphone. "Hey, Boom? You going to be okay if Uncle Brandon checks in on you?"

He and Brandon had taken turns through the morning checking in on her, but despite her request to watch television shows she'd napped a lot. Now she sounded more awake.

"You're not coming up to the house?" Boom's young voice came across loud and clear, and he watched Elisa to be sure she could hear.

"I've got a couple of errands to run if you think you'll be okay."

There was a pause. "Will you bring me back frozen yogurt?"

He grinned. "I will definitely bring you back frozen yogurt."

"Awesome." Boom sounded all sorts of better than yesterday. "I've got my phone right here so I'll text Uncle Brandon if I need anything before he checks on me."

"Perfect. You're the best." And he meant it. His kid rocked.

"Nope. You are. Love you, Dad."

Ending the call, he looked at Elisa. "Let's get you someplace safe so you can get a good night's sleep then decide what you want to do in the morning."

Elisa regarded him warily. "Where?"

He shrugged. "I know this place right next to the best frozen yogurt shop in the area."

* * *

"How are you going to get home?"

It was a good question. Elisa was full of them. She was possessed of a detail-oriented mind and a no-nonsense practicality he was coming to enjoy. It was also fun to mess with her some more now that she'd had a chance to recover from earlier. "I could walk home. It's only a dozen miles, give or take."

She scowled, her hands gripping the steering wheel hard. "It'd be dark before you even got halfway home, and your daughter is waiting."

"True." He couldn't help baiting her, though. He'd bet she got spunky if her buttons were pushed in the right order. Even though she was quiet on the surface, he got the impression she was a woman of passion by nature. Her controlled façade was a learned behavior. "Turn right into this parking lot and go ahead and park in one of the first row spaces."

She did as requested. Despite whatever was going on inside her head, her driving was smooth. She wasn't heavy on the brake or jerky with the turns in response to his directions. He appreciated her slow acceleration and deceleration, too. Erratic driving set his teeth on edge, and he couldn't take most drivers' habits around here. He'd actually made the walk back to the kennels from here a time or two, rather than accept a ride from a driver who'd set off too many memories.

Turning off the engine, Elisa waited expectantly. She didn't turn her head to look at him. Her posture was tense, her shoulders hunched. He got out of the car to give her space and walked around to her side to open the door.

"This doesn't look like a hotel." Her statement was laced with a hefty dose of wariness.

She hadn't gotten to the point where she was ready to bolt yet, but she was close. He backed up as she got out of the car, reining in the temptation to put his hand on her lower back and guide her. She might take it as an invasion of her private space.

"No. Exactly the reason this place will be safe as a temporary fix until you can find a more secure solution." He walked alongside her again, gesturing to the MMA school. "Boom and I train here. The owners are good people. They renovated the space above the school into a sort of studio. It's got a private bathroom and everything you'd need for a short stay without ever having to come down to the school part of the facility."

"Oh." Beside him, Elisa blinked quickly a few times.

Alarm pinged in his chest. Could be she'd caught some dust in her eyes. More likely he'd bothered her somehow. "Did I say something to upset you?"

Elisa paused on the sidewalk in front of the school. "No. Not at all. I'm just...not used to immediate help like this. First you offered me a job, now a safe place to stay. It's a lot to take in, and I don't even know how I can begin—"

He held up his hand to stall her. "It's not about repayment. I'd want someone to help me or mine someday if we were in trouble. Just pay it forward someday."

Because he'd rather eat his shoe than have her feeling beholden to him in some way for doing what any decent person would do. Well, maybe not any person. But it was what people *should* do when someone was in need.

"Besides," he added, "we really do need a good administrative assistant, and you're the first person not to be driven crazy by us or the dogs in the first few hours."

He stepped forward and pulled open the door, motioning for her to proceed inside. There was a class full of kids in session, maybe close to two dozen seven- and eight-year-olds. A tall, lean man in a clean black polo and loose black athletic pants presided over them as they went through a series of fun warm-ups while a half-dozen parents sat on benches along the wall to the right.

At least Rojas assumed the exercises were fun based on the squeals, giggles, and generally jubilant chatter coming from the kids. This class was a couple of years younger than Boom's, and warm-ups were as much about burning off excess energy so the kids could concentrate more on the class as actually improving their agility and stamina.

Elisa paused a few feet inside and watched the controlled chaos with wide eyes.

"Hello, there." Directly to the left of the entrance was a wide counter with a sleek tablet and stand that served as their register and a paper sign-in sheet. The counter also doubled as a merchandise display with "Revolution MMA Academy" t-shirts in various colors arranged alongside a variety of MMA gear. The speaker was a broad man, no less fit for his bulk, dressed in a similar black polo. His first greeting had been directed toward Elisa, and then the man gave Alex a nod. "Rojas, good to see you. How's Boom?"

Rojas strode forward and shook hands. "Fine now. Quick thinking getting those ice packs and helping me immobilize her arm for the ride over to the ER. Doc says she'll heal up quick."

The man sighed and smacked his chest with an open

palm. "She gave me a heart attack, not going to lie. Glad she's going to be okay."

Between the kids in the class shouting and the distance to the benches along the wall, low conversation in the reception area was fairly secure. Too much random noise to listen in on a quiet conversation.

Rojas smiled, then angled his body to include Elisa in the conversation. "We met a new friend at the ER."

Eyebrows raised so high they almost disappeared into the other man's hairline. Rojas paused to consider what he'd said. "Boom made a new friend. I mostly disturbed the peace."

A sage nod. "Sounds more like you."

And that was more than enough talking about himself. Elisa seemed to cheer up at the exchange, though. Maybe it was worth a little personal embarrassment.

Rojas cleared his throat. "This is Elisa Hall. She and Boom hit it off last evening. She also had the excellent timing of showing up with the bag gloves Boom forgot at the ER right about when Forte finally gave in and admitted we needed to look for an administrative assistant. Not only did she save me a trip back to the ER but she also saved me the trouble of posting to some online job site. I owe her big time."

Long story made short and it was still so many words. He was going to be tapped out for conversation when this night was over. He hadn't realized how much he relied on monosyllabic responses to get him through most exchanges. He'd talked more in the last twenty-four hours than in as long as he could remember. And most of it had been with Elisa.

"Administrative assistant." The man grunted and

came out from behind the counter, offering his hand to Elisa. "More like you need a keeper and a bouncer to keep those drooling women with their yapping puntables at bay. I'm Gary Boulding."

There was a split second of hesitation, then Elisa took Gary's hand and gave it a firm shake. Rojas wondered if Gary would interpret it the same way he did. A moment of assessment. It was a good habit to have for any person. Elisa Hall was fairly subtle about it, but a trained eye could still catch her.

"Mr. Rojas gave me the card for your school." Elisa's gaze wandered to the children's class. "He mentioned you gave self-defense courses."

Gary gave her a closer look while her attention was elsewhere. The man saw more than most, and Rojas appreciated his way with reading people. "We do, and you're welcome to join our next workshop, but I don't think that's why Rojas brought you here tonight. We've only got the kids' classes for another hour, then some of the advanced adult classes. Beginner's adult classes are Monday and Wednesday evenings, and Saturday mornings."

"We like to look out for our new employees." Rojas tossed it out there before Elisa could reply. Her cheeks flushed a very attractive pink, but he didn't want her to wrestle awkwardly with asking a stranger for help. She had her pride and might find a way to excuse herself and leave.

He hurried to continue. "I suck at explaining things, so I just brought her over here to introduce her. A hotel isn't going to be the right fit for her, so I was wondering if you'd mind letting her stay upstairs in the studio for a night or two until she has a chance to find a place to rent somewhere in town."

No need to air her private issues until she was ready. Rojas had a good idea of what was going on, but he was sure he didn't have the full story. And Gary was good at hearing what wasn't said.

Gary nodded slowly. "Sure. The studio's reasonably clean. One of the boys slept up there the night before his fight last weekend, and Greg swapped out the sheets and towels during the week. Should be fine to take you up there now while Greg's managing the class."

"I could pay . . ."

Gary shook his head, holding up his hand to stall her. "It'd be complicated to add that income to the books. Why don't we make a trade instead?" He jerked his thumb to indicate the instructor surrounded by kids. "My husband over there hates sweeping the mats every night and every morning. If you could take on that chore and a couple of others, it'd be more than the boys do when they sleep here for the odd night or two."

Elisa blinked.

Rojas wondered what she was processing faster: the proposed trade or the mention of a husband. "Greg is always griping about the way the mats constantly collect dirt even when no shoes are allowed on them."

Tension melted out of her shoulders, and she breathed easier as she gave Gary a genuine smile. "I'd really appreciate the place to stay."

Gary grinned. "Good. Let's take you up now and introduce you to Greg between classes. Then you can have some peace and quiet to yourself for the rest of the evening."

"Peace, maybe." Rojas coughed and looked pointedly at the ceiling. "But quiet, not so much. The adult classes aren't as high-pitched as the kids', but there's a fair amount of noise until about twenty-one hundred hours."

"That's nine o'clock p.m. for those of us who remember we're not wearing a uniform." Gary rolled his eyes. "You boys are holding on tight to your old habits."

Rojas shrugged. "Some habits are good to keep fresh."

"And some are worth letting go." Gary's gaze held his for a long moment. This wasn't the time to be working on those issues, though, so Rojas remained silent until Gary huffed out a breath. "You training with us tonight?"

Rojas shook his head. "Wanted to get Miss Hall here settled in then head next door to get Boom some frozen yogurt."

"Are you seriously going to walk back?" Elisa sounded appalled.

"Sure." Rojas grinned.

Gary rolled his eyes again, uttering a groan this time. "Don't let this roughneck jerk your chain. We're friends with the owners next door. One of their kids will give him a ride back on a delivery run. Boom's frozen yogurt won't even have time to melt."

CHAPTER SIX

Elisa sat on the edge of the bed and looked around her, bemused.

Oh, it was a pleasant enough studio and much nicer than some of the motels she'd stayed in over the last several months. The room was minimally furnished with a bed and nightstand. The bathroom had the essentials: toilet, sink, and shower. Despite the somewhat bare furnishings, the room was painted in pleasant cool blue-grays with white trim. The carpet was thick and lush under her bare feet.

It was welcoming. Not just the room, but the school and its owners. Gary had brought Greg up for personal introductions just a few minutes ago, after she'd had a chance to retrieve an overnight bag from her car. Both men were warm and friendly, and didn't seem bothered in the least by her intrusion.

Gary had waved off her apology. "Any friend of the boys at Hope's Crossing is good people. All we ask is that you leave your mental baggage at the door and come inside ready to do good things."

The boys at Hope's Crossing.

None of them were boys by her definition. As far as she could tell, Alex was a couple years older than she was and Brandon was around the same age as Alex. That put them in their mid-thirties if she was guessing right. She hadn't met Cruz yet, but she'd gotten the impression they'd all served together in the military sometime in the past before they'd reassembled at the kennels.

But both Gary and Greg looked to be in their late forties, with an equal amount of laugh and worry lines around the corners of their eyes and mouths. The men of Hope's Crossing and the owners of Revolution Mixed Martial Arts Academy had seen things. All of them. She'd have to be blind and deaf not to get a sense of the life experiences each of these men had had. Each of them had gone out and *lived*.

Leave your mental baggage at the door.

She shivered at the memory of her first night in a motel. She'd driven for as long as she could manage to stay awake. Long enough to refill her gas tank at least twice. And she'd given in and gotten a room only because she might have fallen asleep at the wheel. As tired as she'd been, she'd lain awake for hours listening to every sound in the dark. Certain her ex had found her. Or that some other predator was planning to mug her or worse.

She had her own issues, for sure. And she was very much hoping those wouldn't catch up to her here.

Her ex had a knack for finding her. The knowledge

that he could do it repeatedly, consistently, but not knowing how he was doing it had been driving her progressively insane. He was a man with a temper and a whole
lot of patience. He wanted to make her regret having left
in the first place, and every time she managed to escape
him was only adding to the eventual payback. Of that
she was sure.

But she didn't plan to ever be under his control again.
Five years had been enough. Once she'd gotten a clear
understanding of the special projects he was overseeing,
investing in, she'd decided she didn't want any part of
the life he'd arranged for the two of them.

The last six months had been a constant effort to get
away and build a life of her own.

The important thing right now was to get some rest,
think clearly, and plan her next steps. Hopefully she'd be
able to come up with something unpredictable.

So far, her attention had only managed to stay focused on Alex Rojas and his incredible generosity.
Okay, and she sort of wondered if the tennis ball was
still in his pants pocket. As random thought processes
went, she was going to need to go for more constructive stuff.

Standing, she groaned. Today had included a good
mix of sitting, standing, and even some walking, but
she'd done a lot of driving in the days prior. Her hamstrings were tight and aching and no amount of stretching so far had made the soreness disappear completely.
Maybe she needed to get into better shape.

Staying above a mixed martial arts school was already influencing her mindset.

She reached for her overnight bag and pulled out a

clean tee and pair of soft sweats. They were comfortable to sleep in and perfectly reasonable to roll out of bed and drive out of town in.

As she was pulling her current shirt over her head, a knock sounded at the door.

She jerked her shirt back down to cover her breasts and belly, reining in a moment of panic. "Who is it?"

"It's Alex."

Oh. Her hands shook as she opened and closed them a couple of times to get them to quit clenching by default. Trying to ease off the rush of adrenaline, she focused on who was on the other side of the door.

It wasn't her ex. And Alex hadn't shown any signs of wanting to take her back to her ex, either.

In fact, his gruff tone had returned and she was starting to realize it came out when he was about to do something nice and felt awkward about it.

He was really sweet, in a super rough and ready kind of way.

"You okay in there?"

The man gave good voice. She wondered whether he knew it and if he was the person who usually answered the phones at the kennels. It'd explain a lot of disappointed-sounding callers with very ridiculous questions from this morning.

"Can I come in?" He sounded uncomfortable.

"Oh!" She hadn't realized how long she'd kept him waiting for a response. Crossing over to the door, she unlocked and opened it, backing away as she did.

"For you." Alex held out a small container. He had a bag dangling from his other hand, presumably with Boom's frozen yogurt.

She took the container and her mouth watered at the sight of the pristine white swirl of frozen yogurt inside. Abruptly, she realized how insanely hungry she was. One problem. "No spoon?"

He fished around in the bag and came up with a plastic-wrapped utensil. "Got one."

The man thought of everything. He might be heaven sent. She could dream about him with wings later.

"How much do I—"

He waved her off. "Come to work in the morning and work it off. We seriously do need an administrative assistant, and I don't want to conduct interviews."

Frustration churned in her belly for a minute, warring with the sharp hunger. She shouldn't accept favors from him. Favors and unspoken expectations were how misunderstandings got started. And she hadn't decided to stay yet. Part of the reason she'd been able to stay on her own this far was because she'd always taken off at the first sign that her ex had found her again.

The text was more than a sign. It was a bright red warning flag.

Alex's voice cut across her train of thought, calm and mater-of-fact. "I got you plain frozen yogurt because I wasn't sure what you'd like, but I've got a couple of containers on the side here with strawberries, kiwi, graham crackers, and random candies. Didn't want to set off any allergies. It's been a while since you've eaten and you don't want to keep thinking so hard on an empty stomach."

Hunger and appreciation for his consideration won out. "The strawberries, please. And the graham crackers."

"They've got a cheesecake flavor down there. You

might like it with these next time." He handed over the containers and she thought there might be a hint of amusement in his eyes.

He was really good at disarming her. Or she was tired. Probably a little of both. Either way, his presence was comforting and exciting at the same time. She didn't think it was a good idea but she also didn't want him to leave just yet either.

Taking the offered goodies, she headed over to the nightstand to save herself from a clumsy fumble and drop. The last thing she needed was to spill food all over Gary and Greg's wonderful carpet. Opening her frozen yogurt, she carefully shook out a portion of each topping into her container then closed everything up again and handed the sides back to Alex.

As he took them and stowed them back in his bag, she risked a glance at his hips. The tennis ball was gone. She had no idea when he'd taken it out of his pants, but she didn't have an excuse to be looking anymore, so she risked a glance up at his face.

He was watching her, a bemused sort of half smile shaping his lips.

Heat burned her cheeks and she was pretty sure embarrassment was going to strangle her to death in the next few seconds. Curiosity. It was such a bad idea to give in to curiosity.

Alex cleared his throat. "I'm going to get this back to Boom. In the meantime, take this."

He reached into his back pocket and held something out to her.

It took her a long minute to recognize what he had in his hand. A new phone.

"Oh no." She held up her hands and shook her head. "I can't take that from you."

"It's a pre-paid loaner." He shifted to a firmer tone. "If you're running, and I think you are, you need to get rid of your current phone. Now. I'm going to take it for you and ditch it someplace away from here. I'm not going to ask you why right now, or from what, but I won't let you stay here with friends while you still have something that could lead whoever you're running from to you the minute you turn it back on."

Her breath left her in a rush. He was right. She'd felt a little bad and worried some, but she hadn't considered the full impact. He had. And he was taking action.

Alex came a step closer, still holding out the phone. His jaw was set, but his eyes held a kindness, an understanding. "It's okay to accept help. We don't know your story, but we know how to take care of ourselves. Part of that is taking simple precautions like this. I could've recommended for you to do this and you probably would've on your own. Right?"

She nodded, her mouth dry. "Maybe not as fast. Maybe too late."

And she'd been lucky she hadn't been found sooner. Each time she'd left a place, she had gotten a new phone. But not until she'd safely reached her next destination. It'd seemed more prudent to have a phone with her while she was traveling, for the GPS and to call 911 in case she got caught up in an accident. The way Alex presented it, she'd be wiser to get rid of the current phone right away and grab a pre-paid along the way.

It was just that every time she'd left in the past, there'd been no time. She'd been rushed and panicked and had to get as much distance as possible between her and her pursuers.

His voice broke in on her thoughts, quiet and almost comforting. "Don't start going down those routes. Asking 'what if' too much is going to ruin your night."

He was right. So right. She reached out and took the phone from his hand. Their fingers brushed in the exchange, and she tried to ignore the zing the minor contact gave her. There were so many other things she needed to concentrate on, but suddenly all she wanted to do was look him in the eye and find the stillness in his gaze again. The eye of the storm. Instead, she pulled her phone out of her back pocket and gave it to him. She hadn't even realized he'd turned it off earlier.

"The new phone is a pre-paid number, like I said. I got it with cash, so it's not traceable to any name, and we can take the cost out of your paycheck if it'll make you feel better. I programmed a couple of numbers in, but you'll have to remember which they are. Better than having names in the phone in case someone gets a hold of it. First number is for this school. Second is Hope's Crossing Kennels. Third is my personal number. Fourth and fifth numbers are Gary and Greg. You need any of us, we're just a phone call away." He pocketed her phone. "Gary and Greg will set the security system when they leave to go home. You should be fine to move around up here, but if you go back downstairs, the motion will set off the silent alarm. You won't realize you've set it off until the police arrive. Gary and Greg won't be far behind. They live in the neighborhood behind this shopping center, literally a five-minute run. Best to stay up here in this room and avoid all of it."

She nodded, stunned. He'd given her all those numbers and she silently repeated the order over and over in her head. If he'd gone to the trouble, she wasn't going to make him tell her more than once. Revolution MMA, Hope's Crossing Kennels, Alex, Gary, Greg.

He was inviting her to call him again. He wasn't telling her to leave.

"Hey." He reached out slowly, giving her enough time to step away if she wanted. He brushed a lock of her hair away from her eyes. Then his gaze dropped lower, and he brushed another lock away from her collarbone, raising goose bumps all along her skin in a delicious way.

His eyes were a warm caramel, very kind at the moment, though they could burn with anger readily enough. She reminded herself of how scary he'd been the night before.

For a good cause, a small part of her mind pointed out.

In any case, he was generous in offering her employment and making sure she had a place to stay. She was not going to ponder other things, the kinds of things to make a new job complicated and totally inappropriate.

Because she shouldn't be thinking anything inappropriate about a well-built man with an expressive mouth and incredibly sexy stubble across his strong jaw.

She swallowed, hard.

After a moment, he said, "It looks like you've come a long way. You can rest here. It really is okay."

New people in her life, all ready to help her with no explanation but what they'd been able to put together themselves. Her throat tightened. There'd been a long time there when her own family and friends, who'd known her since childhood, hadn't believed her when she'd been looking for help. They'd been fooled the same way she had, and it was so much easier to wonder if maybe, just maybe, there was some unfortunate misunderstanding. Easier to believe she'd made a mistake than the unpleasant reality.

"This is all too much." She hated to suspect his kindness, but it was too good to be true. "I can't even begin to repay you, and you've only just met me."

Alex was still. It wasn't a question of simply not moving. Everything about him had gone motionless. She shrank in on herself, sure he was going to explode with anger.

But he didn't.

Instead, he turned away from her and faced the door. "You can leave if you feel safer. Do it before classes are over and they set the security system. I'll have a word with Gary and Greg, and no one will ask any questions or try to convince you to stay. No pressure. Do what's right for you."

If he'd even sounded upset, she could've gotten angry back. Could've built up the momentum to leave.

She was very tired of running. What she was looking for, hoping for, was a place to rest long enough to build a life again.

"I could be playing all of you," she whispered.

He balled his free hand up into a fist, then let it go. "You could be. Not likely. I've heard a lot of lies over the years. Met more liars than I care to count. I recognize lies when they're right in front of my face."

She didn't have an answer to that. Her fear, suspicion,

guilt spiraled down into her gut and left her chest feeling hollow. "I'm sorry."

He still didn't turn to look at her. "Boom liked you. Souze liked you. That's enough for me. The great thing about kids and dogs: they don't know how to lie. Not really. They don't know how to hide themselves from the world, and it gives them a simple perspective. When I suspect I'm thinking too hard, I fall back to their opinion."

Something to think on, if she could pull her thoughts into any kind of comprehensible order.

He pulled the door open and stepped out, pausing in the doorway. "They liked you. That's enough for me. Sleep well, Elisa. You're safe. And if you're not here when I swing by in the morning to pick you up, it was nice to meet you."

And he left. Just like that.

CHAPTER SEVEN

Finally home, Rojas gave his friend a wave as the car backed down the drive toward the gated entrance. He decided to skip the main house altogether and cut around the side to head directly to his house.

House. Home.

Damn, he'd have never thought he'd have one like this—or one at all. It wasn't huge or anything his ex-wife would've deigned to live in, but it was still a two-story with three bedrooms, two and a half baths. It was enough room for him to raise Serena up right.

Coming to Hope's Crossing Kennels had been the smart thing to do. Hell, he could have gone elsewhere and gotten higher-paying work, but Boom would've spent too much time home alone. Here, there were people to watch his back—and her.

He trudged up the porch steps and let himself in the front door.

Forte sat on the couch with a beer in hand. "Boom took her meds. She's asleep."

Rojas grunted. Just as well, with her yogurt half melted. He'd only meant to spend a minute talking to Elisa, but something about her had drawn him in. He couldn't help but linger. And he had no idea what in hell had possessed him to reach out and touch her. But her dark hair and those stormy blue eyes tugged at him in too many ways. And the way she bit her lower lip made him want to kiss it better.

It'd been a long time since he'd stopped in his tracks and daydreamed about a woman.

The yogurt was melting more.

He continued into their small kitchen and popped the whole bag from the shop into the freezer. Boom could have some frozen yogurt in the morning after a solid breakfast.

His stomach growled, and he snagged his own container from the bag before shutting the freezer door. Heading back to the living room, he sat heavily in the armchair opposite Forte, who sat on the couch.

His armchair and his couch. He let out a sigh. Good to be home.

Forte took a gulp of beer and scratched his belly. Rojas was reasonably sure Boom had learned how to belch from him.

The exemplary role model in question yawned. "So what's up with our new logistics person?"

"I'm pretty sure civilians would call the role an administrative assistant. And she's only our new admin if she takes the job." Rojas twiddled his spoon between his fingers. "She's still deciding."

"You seemed to be getting acquainted with her pretty well." Forte was fishing. He liked gossip almost as much as Sophie did, and nothing got past either of them. If Cruz was around, Rojas would bet him a twenty that Sophie would be over bright and early with some of her homemade baked goods the first chance she got to find out more about Elisa.

Since Cruz wasn't here tonight, Alex held his peace. Forte tended to be a touch sensitive about all things concerning his childhood friend. There was a lot of history between Forte and Sophie.

Speaking of history, Elisa definitely had some to discuss eventually.

"Don't know if we actually got to know each other or anything, but we did have a few interesting conversations." Rojas shoveled a spoonful of less-than-frozen yogurt into his mouth and swallowed, letting it go down slow. When he could speak again, he uttered a relieved groan. "I talked more today than I probably have all year."

Not sure if that was a good thing or a bad thing, but he wasn't planning on classifying it. Especially not after he'd discussed almost the same line of thought with Elisa. She'd been damned cute chewing on that bit of logic.

"Happens when you interact with people." Forte was all sorts of agreeable this evening.

"She's got some serious personal baggage, though." Rojas took another spoonful and chewed on the accompanying gummy bear. He tended to give Boom fruit with her frozen yogurt, but tonight he'd indulged in sour gummies, gummy bears, and gummy worms. Because he was an adult and could choose to dive into a sugar high before bedtime with no one to hold him accountable but himself.

Forte snorted. "We've all got personal shit tossed in the back of our closets."

Rojas waved a free hand in the vague direction of the front door. "And here, we all know enough to watch each other's backs. That's my point. If she's going to work here, we need enough of a briefing to be prepared for any issues."

Forte raised an eyebrow. "You think she's bringing actual trouble to our door?"

No doubt. It was his practice to keep his teammates informed in as timely a manner as possible, so he suffered no guilt bringing Forte up to speed on the text Elisa had received.

"Huh. All on its own, the text is harmless." Forte took a slow pull from the beer.

Rojas waited. They'd all sent similarly harmless texts, messages, and various electronic communications in the past. Worded properly, such a communication could be completely overlooked when taken out of context. And they were meant to be. It was the context they'd been trained to look for in the right circumstances.

"You think someone's looking for her." More fishing. It was Forte's way, and Rojas didn't mind at the moment. Helped him get his thoughts straight.

"She went paler than a ghost when she got it. Thought she was going to pass out right there in the kennels. Souze tuned into her reaction from three kennels down." Rojas closed his mouth as his temper started to heat his words. He took another mouthful of frozen yogurt.

His temper needed to be kept cool anywhere near Boom. Asleep or not, she could wake at any moment, and she deserved a dad with his own issues under control. He still struggled with keeping his calm in public, crowded places, but here at home he could keep his shit together. This was a controlled environment. Secure. Safe.

"Yeah? Souze?" Forte sounded surprised. "Whole reason we didn't place him along with the other two was because he didn't take well to any of the potential handlers. That dog doesn't warm up to anybody."

Rojas didn't blame him. The dog in question didn't miss much of anything, true, but he also didn't spare strangers more than the amount of attention it took to warn them away usually. For Souze to react to Elisa's fear, it had to be unusual.

"If we make some assumptions..." And Forte made them all the time, though they were more like educated guesses. But it made him excellent in the field, able to anticipate and plan for unusual circumstances that might otherwise catch a team by surprise in a very bad way. "We're figuring she's got unwanted attention to deal with and a need to stay hard to find. Could be an issue with authorities or a stalker. I'm thinking the latter more than the former, though. She didn't seem the type to participate in illegal activities."

Forte wiggled his eyebrows.

Rojas barked out a laugh and nodded. Elisa Hall did not have a good poker face. Every thought showed up on her expressive face, and it was fascinating to watch. It also made her a seriously bad liar. "She seemed relieved to hide out at Revolution once she got over a hefty fear of strangers."

And she hadn't flinched at the idea of the police showing up when he'd warned her about tripping the security alarms. If anything, she'd filed the bit of information away as if it could be used in the future, like a lifeline or an escape route.

"Gary and Greg are good with twitchy personalities," Forte said approvingly.

Forte went over to train at Revolution on occasion. Not as much as Rojas did when he was up to dealing with people. Actually, the training helped take the edge off his anxiety, so Rojas tried to get there at least once a week. Sparring with some of the better martial artists in the smaller, private sessions helped him work off tension.

But neither Forte nor Rojas was good with the shyer students normally. The ones who came for self-defense too late and already had the bruised look of someone irreparably harmed. Those people generally had learned the hard way to seek out training or had been recommended to self-defense as a form of therapy after a traumatic experience. It was a good way to build up confidence, whether it hadn't yet been gained or had been taken away. Gary and Greg worked with them, coaxed back their confidence, helped them rebuild some of what they'd lost.

It was why he'd thought to take Elisa to them in the first place. She wasn't as bad as some, but she had the look.

"Yeah. Not sure if she'll stay. She's got a serious chip on her shoulder about accepting help. She might not be around tomorrow." And normally, he'd wish a person well if they came and went so quickly. He wasn't generally one to get attached, not even to the few women he'd dated in the few years he'd been living here.

Serena was his focus. His daughter. Boom.

"But you decided to give her a reason." Forte straightened to a more upright sitting position and placed the half-finished beer bottle on the coffee table. "You've got a soft spot for the ones like her."

"Not sure I know what you mean." Only he did. He and Forte had built a lot of history over the years, first in the military and then back here in the States.

"Doesn't matter if it's a woman or a dog or a green recruit, you step up to give the rescued ones an extra chance or three." Forte wagged his finger at Rojas. "It got you into trouble when we were deployed."

And back at home, too. He'd given his ex-wife a few chances too many even after she'd presented him with divorce papers and she'd gone down a slippery slope. By the time he'd realized she'd gotten too entrenched in her painkiller addictions it was too late. She'd died while he was on the way back to home soil. He hadn't been able to do anything but comfort his daughter when he'd returned, and fight for custody of her when his ex-wife's parents tried to claim he was unfit to raise her.

Rojas finished up the last of his yogurt and gummy candy.

"Granted, she seems like a good person," Forte continued. "It pisses me off to think about what probably happened to her to make her as twitchy as she was. I wasn't sure she'd last the morning with the way she'd look up at either of the two of us coming in and out every ten or twenty minutes. It was almost like she was suspicious."

Frowning, Rojas shifted his weight in his seat, moved to defend her some. "Nothing wrong with acknowledging people as they come and go. Better than her ignoring us or pretending we're not around. She's got some steel strapped to her spine."

Figuratively speaking.

Forte chuckled. "Oh, I saw it. She sat bolt upright whenever I came through. Watchful. Alert. Determined to put up a strong front."

To call it cute would've been insulting to Elisa. Rojas was glad his friend hadn't. If either of them was prone to using their vocabulary, maybe they'd call it endearing. Worth some extra effort to foster it, give her a place to come into her own.

He got a sense from her that there was a lot more under the surface.

"For what it's worth, I hope she comes back in the morning." Forte picked up his beer and drained the rest of it.

"Cruz is back tomorrow, right?" Rojas asked, standing as Forte did.

"Yup."

Rojas held out his hand for the empty beer bottle. "I had her give me her phone, swapped it out with a clean pre-paid. I pulled the sim card and dropped her old phone off across the way at a cell phone shop in Jersey."

The detour was another reason why the frozen yogurt was mostly melted.

"Yeah?" Forte spent a few seconds considering. "Cruz could probably track down the number sending those texts to her, with her permission. Sim card should have the data."

"I figure if she comes back tomorrow and gets to know us, maybe it'll be worth it to take a closer look at who we might be expecting on our doorstep." Rojas shrugged. "With her permission, of course."

"'Course." Forte headed to the front door. "Can see why you didn't tell her tonight. It'd be creepy for her potential new employer to suggest tracing the phone numbers in her call and text history. Goes beyond the usual background check and way into what-the-fu—"

Forte glanced up the stairs toward Boom's room and finished lamely, "Fudgery."

Rojas didn't respond, embarrassed.

Elisa thought of them as dog trainers. And, yeah, they trained military working dogs. But she didn't yet have a complete understanding of the backgrounds of her employers or what they were each capable of, what they'd done in the past. If she did, he was willing to lay odds she wouldn't come back in the morning.

Granted, a lot of normal administrative assistants might prefer not to work for them for similar reasons. Rojas was hoping that having the chance to get to know them all would help.

Or it could chase her away. Either way, it'd at least be on the basis of their personalities and not their background.

Forte studied him. "Well, no harm in easing her into the full introductions slowly. It's a lot to take in all at once and we already buried her under paperwork, fussy clients, and dogs. Maybe if she does show up for work, we should let her settle into the familiar for the day and give her the rest a little at a time over the course of this week. Give her time to get settled."

Good idea. Great, actually. Absolutely sensible. Rojas nodded. "Sounds like a plan."

He didn't know why he was so concerned with whether or not Elisa came back, but if he got right down to it, he wanted to see her again.

No idea why, but there it was.

* * *

Joseph Corbin Junior sat on a worn sofa, the only decent seat in the living room. Mary Hall, Elisa's mother, clattered around in the tiny utility kitchen putting together refreshments.

"Really, Mary, there's no need. I don't have time to stay long." Truly, he preferred not to linger even a minute more than necessary.

She came out with a glass of tap water and a plate of haphazardly piled cheese and crackers. "Oh, I know you're busy, Joseph, but it's been so long since either you or Elisa has visited. Does she really have to be away for so long?"

Joseph glanced at the jumble of orange and white squares of cheese and made an effort not to wrinkle his nose. Thankfully, he'd educated Elisa to have a more discerning palate. "This is the trip of a lifetime for her. You know that. She's off checking on my European offices and exploring the sights to see along the way."

"You're such a wonderful fiancée to send her on an adventure like that. I can't believe she's called and pretended to still be in the States. Her own mother and she won't tell me where she really is." Mary sighed. "To be honest, I'm a little bit hurt she didn't think to take me with her, since you couldn't take time away from your main office to go. I'd have loved to travel around Europe. It must be nice."

Oh, of course she would. Mary Hall lived in a modest ranch house on the edge of suburbia in one of the least affluent neighborhoods in this part of California. She'd never been across the country, much less an ocean. A single woman of limited means and from no background worth noting, it'd been amazing she'd managed to raise a flower as exquisite as Elisa.

But Elisa was his now and Mary Hall was only useful as long as there was a chance to tie Elisa to him through her mother.

"Maybe she knows how disappointed you are." He smiled. "But it is entertaining to hear what different places she's pretending to be visiting. Please do keep me up to date on the latest locations. She's got such an imagination."

"It's been a while since she last checked in. Couldn't Elisa at least remember to call me—"

His phone rang, cutting her off. He retrieved it from the inner pocket of his suit jacket. "Excuse me, I'm expecting an urgent call."

Mary stepped back, a flush in her cheeks. "Of course. I'll just be in the kitchen."

Putting the phone to his ear, Joseph didn't take his gaze from the hallway mirror. The reflection showed him Mary standing in her kitchen space, busying herself with straightening postcards and pictures on her refrigerator.

How quaint.

"Yes?" He answered his phone.

A man cleared his throat on the other end of the line. "Got a hit on Elisa Hall, sir."

Finally. It'd been days since he'd last had a confirmed report on her whereabouts.

"Is the item of interest accessible?" Conscious of Mary still within earshot, he kept his choice of words ambiguous.

Locating and reacquiring Elisa was becoming critical to his business interests. He'd given her time to run, but he was done waiting for her to come back to him on her own. And she should have. She would understand that once she was back under his supervision.

"No. I mean, not currently. Sir." The man didn't have the quality of his usual employees but Joseph had hired him more for intimidation than for professional polish.

"Explain." Joseph allowed his impatience to come through in his tone.

"I tracked her to a hospital in Pennsylvania."

"Is there damage?" Joseph stood and began to pace. She shouldn't have been injured. He needed to know if it was permanent, if there'd be scarring of some sort. The nature of her injury was important.

"Don't think so." The man coughed. "I can send you the name of the hospital, but it looks like she went into the ER and left the same night. She wasn't admitted. I found her car in a nearby town parked in a shopping center."

Joseph stopped pacing. It couldn't be serious if she hadn't been admitted. Good.

"I'm watching her car now. It's only a matter of time before I have eyes on her," his employee continued.

"We'll want to have a means to track the shipping

container." Hopefully unnecessary, but his Elisa was perceptive. She might run again, and there was no time to waste searching for her further. "Then keep an eye on the item for me. If you have the opportunity, collect it and hold it for me. I'll pick it up personally."

"Understood." There was a pause. "Should I still send you the hospital details along with the location of the car?"

"Send all of the information to my phone." Joseph ended the call and turned toward the kitchen where Mary stood, peering around the doorjamb. "It seems I have to leave now."

"So soon?" Mary stepped back into the living room. "It must be hard, your work. Always so busy."

"Yes." He didn't deny it. His work was a priority, and so was retrieving what was his. "I'll have a word with Elisa the next time I speak with her and make sure she knows to give you a call."

CHAPTER EIGHT

Okay. Sleep had been good. Better than good. Elisa felt rested for the first time in a while. But no epiphanies had come to her in the middle of the night. She still wasn't sure what her next step should be.

So here she was standing in front of a donut shop a few doors down from Revolution MMA. Gary had been in the office, but on the phone when she'd come downstairs. He'd given her a wave as she pushed out the front door, and it'd felt awkward, but she'd returned it with a smile. He and Greg were genuinely nice people, and she hated just slipping out the front door without even a thank you.

She took a careful sip of hot coffee with enough sugar in it to complement her freshly baked donut and figured being unpredictable was a good thing. So she wasn't going to give herself a hard time for not having decided what to do yet. Instead, she was going to enjoy her breakfast and the morning—just as they were right now.

The air had a cold bite to it, and she wrapped the fingers of one hand more securely around her cup to ward off the chill, relying on the wrist brace to keep her palm from getting burned. She made quick work of her donut, then held the cup carefully with both hands to nurse the warmth as much as the caffeine. This was autumn on the East Coast, and already colder than it got back in California.

A few thoughts crystalized with the clarity of caffeine. Apple cider donuts were amazing. Maybe she'd try following up with hot apple cider next time, but coffee had definitely been the right choice this morning. And she definitely liked the contrast of seasons here.

That established, her next choice could only be great, right?

She sighed. Maybe. It was still early.

Then she caught sight of a random guy in a hoodie and sweatpants leaning against the wall. Just...there. No coffee or paper in hand or any reason to be where he was. The store he was next to wasn't open yet. He could be waiting for it, but somehow she doubted he was dying to get into a beauty supply shop. Nope. Everything about him was creepy, especially with the hood pulled up over his head.

She took another sip of her coffee and willed her hands not to shake. Looking out over the parking lot, she saw that only a few cars dotted the blacktop. Because it was still early. People were arriving to open up the bigger stores, but there weren't many shoppers yet. Her car was parked where she'd left it, all the way on the other

end of the shopping strip past the school because she'd
wanted to leave it under a streetlight.

She risked a glance back over at the creepy guy. He
was looking directly at her.

The martial arts school, and Gary and Greg, were
closer.

Swallowing hard, she started walking toward Revolution MMA. The cold air burned as she breathed in
through her nose and out through her mouth, trying not
to betray how utterly freaked out she was.

Turning her head slightly, she saw the man push away
from the wall and step in her direction.

Oh no.

She picked up her pace, suddenly regretting having
left the school at all.

As she passed the next store she could see only his
feet in the reflection from the storefront glass because
of the decals on the windows. But he was following and
closing the distance.

Keep walking. Keep moving. Almost there.

The next storefront had broad, clean windows. She
caught sight of him in the reflection as he took his hands
out of his pockets and lengthened his stride.

He was almost on her.

She dropped her coffee and bolted for the front of
Revolution MMA, yanking the door open and blunder-
ing straight into another man.

Elisa screamed.

"Hey!" The voice was low, urgent, and familiar. "Hey,
Elisa. It's okay. Come inside. You're safe."

The terse words cut through her blind terror. Her
heart was going to pound a hole in her chest, but strong

hands steadied her and released her. Alex gave her space and stepped over to the front door, shielding her from whomever was out there.

Gary and Greg were suddenly at her side, too, flanking her.

These people were here, ready to help, making sure she was safe. They'd dropped everything. She wrapped her arms across her chest, trying to pull herself together, literally.

Then Alex barked out an angry curse. "Cannon! What the fuck?"

Cannon? So they knew him? Elisa leaned to one side to peer around Alex, abruptly conscious again of how imposing the man was. It was a weird kind of comfort to have him standing between her and the rest of the world. The man she'd seen earlier was standing a few feet from the door with his hands held out to his sides and spread wide. A sheepish grin split his unshaven face.

"Sorry, man!" Cannon called to them. "I was just hanging out waiting for her to come out of the donut place."

Gary and Greg instantly relaxed. Gary muttered a quieter curse of his own. "I sent Cannon to keep an eye out for Elisa since I was on the phone. He came in to pick up some gear he left last night and I figured it couldn't hurt to keep a pair of eyes on her. I didn't think he'd be a thug about it."

* * *

Elisa still considered hopping in her car and driving until she ran out of gas a valid option. Even as she stepped into the reception area of Hope's Crossing Kennels at eight a.m., sharp.

She hated herself for it.

Of course, Alex had driven her here to the kennels since she'd been a complete mess after freaking them all out this morning. So she'd have to ask for a ride back in order to make her escape. Not exactly practical. And she still wasn't sure it was what she wanted to do.

She was off balance, shaken, and embarrassed.

Indecision hadn't been one of her shortcomings once upon a time. She'd always prided herself on being able to consider all the options she might have and making the best decision possible. She'd been a detailed, thorough person with enough intuition to make the mental leap to fill in gaps when there might not be sufficient information. Once she'd committed to a course of action, she'd never had regrets.

That was before she'd gotten involved with Joseph.

Elisa stopped in her tracks. *Joseph Corbin, Jr.* Even internally, she hadn't let herself say his name since she'd first left. She didn't want to give him space inside her head—not him and not the shady business he'd had planned. Instead of the anticipated dread—speaking of the devil and all—she experienced a tiny spike of elation. Triumph. She could finally think of him without having his name terrify her.

Looking around the reception area with its hardwood benches and flooring, deep blue walls, and naturally homey feel, the twisting in her gut eased. She'd agreed to let Alex drive her here because this was the last place she'd felt calm and capable. It'd given her back a measure of pride. She'd done work efficiently and set up processes, however small, to make things better than they had been when she'd arrived.

It was a far cry from the corporate offices and conference rooms she'd worked in as a project manager and so much more personable than the sterile walls of Joseph's house. There were good people here, ready to lend a hand or jump to her defense, and this morning Alex had proven it. What's more, he'd asked her right afterward what she wanted to do next.

So she made a decision. She'd stay and give this a try.

Because something about this place and these people was different. Or maybe enough time had passed. Or maybe it was because she'd gotten her first chance at an interesting job and her first good night's sleep. Could be any number of things, but they all added up to her coming back here to see what else might change. For the better.

"Welcome back." Alex entered from the hallway leading back to the kennel run.

Her heart jumped up into her throat, and she resisted the urge to beam happily at him like an idiot. "You drove me here."

He shrugged. "Still seems like a good thing to say."

He, in particular, was different in all sorts of good ways. The undemanding, accepting, not-too-many-questions kind of ways. A big part of what had convinced her to give this a try was the way he hadn't acted entitled to know everything about her in exchange for his generosity.

He'd changed out of the sweatshirt he'd worn earlier and stood in the doorway dressed in jeans and a light, short-sleeved button-up shirt. Hope's Crossing Kennels was embroidered in a circle over the breast pocket around the silhouette of a dog. After having met Souze last evening, she sort of thought it was probably a German shepherd.

German Shepherd Dog, she mentally corrected herself.

Whether she was going to stay or not, she wanted to remember to refer to the kind of dog by the proper breed name. It was important to her to have details correct.

Abruptly, she remembered he wasn't a mind reader and would have no idea what she was so happy about. No need for her to get all excited at the sound of his voice, either. Even if he spoke with a rough sort of morning growl, the kind that sent tingles through her at the sound of it.

Brandon and Alex were her employers, and she needed to consider both of them with a certain level of professionalism. He was right; this was a good place to start the day over.

"Good morning." She plastered a polite smile on her face as she met Alex's gaze.

He gave her a friendly smile as he stepped forward to offer her his hand. "Glad you've decided to give us a chance, Elisa."

He had it backward. They were the ones giving her the chance. It was more than a job, more of a new beginning. But she didn't want to come across too cheesy. Instead, she went with another truth. "Yesterday's work was interesting. I thought today might bring some good surprises."

Alex raised an eyebrow, humor twinkling in his eyes. "Well, we do have a tendency to experience the unexpected around here."

She blinked. "Is that a good thing or a bad thing?"

He shrugged. "Do all things have to be classified as good or bad?"

Now there was a question. "Generally, things do fall under one or the other."

"True, but then again, whether something is one or the other tends to depend on point of view." Alex headed over to the desk and placed a fresh pack of pens on it. "I find I experience fewer nasty surprises if I just leave off on the opinion altogether."

"Nasty?" She took a few steps toward the desk. It was ridiculous how glad she was to see an entire pack of matching pens. Then she paused again. They were purple.

Alex gave her a toothy grin, but the smile didn't reach his eyes. "I've done some traveling. What one individual or group might think is a good thing can be received as downright evil by another. It can result in some... unpleasant reactions."

"Ah." She considered him for a minute. Both he and Brandon were very fit. Yesterday, she'd accepted it as part of running kennels and training dogs. It was a fairly active profession, requiring them to be on their feet most of the day. Plus, Alex trained at Revolution Mixed Martial Arts Academy. There'd already been fighters getting in their early morning training when she'd left, and they had some impressive conditioning as far as she could tell. But it occurred to her that maybe Alex and Brandon were in excellent condition for other reasons.

Former police, maybe. Or ex-military. Maybe even reserves. They were in shape enough to still be involved in something requiring a uniform. Her mind did her the favor of conjuring up mental images of Alex in a succession of uniforms. *Yum*.

"Oh." Alex rolled his shoulders in what seemed like a self-conscious move. "What do you think of the shirt?"

Whoops. She must've been staring while her mind wandered. *Damn*. He was going to think she was weird. "It's nice. I hadn't realized there was a...uniform."

Must delete mental images.

Or at least tuck them away for some other time.

"There isn't. Yet," Alex responded with wry grin. "Sophie brought a few of these over this morning. It's one of her ideas to make us look more businesslike or something."

"Whoever Sophie is, she has a good point." Elisa bit her lip. Might have been better to keep her opinion to herself.

"You think?" Alex didn't seem irritated. The opposite, actually. "It's not as comfortable as polo shirts, but I guess I could work in it. Sophie says these are washable and stain resistant. She keeps our books for us and ambushes us with new ideas for the business."

The button-up and collar put a polish on Alex, taking him a step away from muscular and ruggedly attractive to downright handsome. The light fabric contrasted with his darker skin tone, providing an accent against the bronze of his arms. The cut of the shirt and short sleeves complemented his broad shoulders and muscular arms. Close-fitting T-shirts suited him, too, based on what she'd seen yesterday and the other night at the ER, but she liked this look in a safer, sort of easygoing way. Tees were more casual but made him look ready for action.

This look made him look ready to settle in for a day of work.

"It's more professional." She struggled to sum up what she thought without coming across as creepy. No need to let him know how much she wanted to see what he looked like in a suit now. "And uniform shirts make it easy to immediately differentiate the trainer from the rest of the class."

He jerked his head in a quick affirmative. "See, I can get behind a practical reason like that. Just wearing a uniform for a uniform's sake didn't make sense to me."

Pleased by his compliment—being considered practical was a good thing in her mind—she reached for something else to say to fill the conversational lull. "Just before we left, Greg asked me to remind you it's your turn for parents' night."

Alex scowled and dragged his hand through his hair.

"Not a good thing, I take it?" She really didn't like to be the bearer of bad news.

"No, no." Alex waved away her concern. "All of the instructors and some of the regulars take turns to supervise. I just lost track so it snuck up on me. Besides, Boom loves it when I'm in charge of parents' night at Revolution."

"You've been doing a lot of favors on my behalf," she said slowly. "Could I help, then?"

See? She could find a way to repay every one of them for the favors. Not just because they were kind but because she didn't want to owe anyone anything.

She'd learned the hard way how things could add up and trap a person when they least expected it.

Alex was studying her. "Let's get you settled in to

work for the day and we'll talk next steps this afternoon. I'll try to think of a couple of extra things we've been meaning to do around here but haven't had the chance to get to. If you could do a few of those, we could call it even."

No anger, not even the stillness she was starting to associate with him controlling his temper. He'd taken what she'd said into consideration. The novelty of it triggered a slow swell of happiness in her chest, and she breathed in deeply, then smiled. "Okay, but I still want to know more about this night at Revolution MMA."

*   *   *

The morning classes were significantly less chaotic than those of the prior day. Rojas was glad they'd moved the obedience training to the weekdays and saved Saturday mornings for more specialized classes. There tended to be a lot fewer single women with newly acquired dogs or borrowed friends' dogs and more people who genuinely wanted to work with their companions.

Standing in the center of the agility course in his spiffy new shirt, he saw Elisa peeking out the window of the front office and gave her a wave.

Sean Cannon stepped to his side, careful to give him plenty of space and time to see him. Rojas appreciated the courtesy, though the caution wasn't as needed on kennel property where he felt at ease. Cannon's pug, on the other hand, rubbed against the side of Alex's leg in greeting and sat on his shoe.

The other man crossed his arms, following his gaze toward the main building. "Some nice new scenery in your reception area there, Rojas. Sorry about this morning."

Uh-huh. Cannon needed to tread carefully. Even if he'd been referred to these classes to train his rambunctious pug—Revolution and Hope's Crossing tended to give referrals to each other when it made sense—Rojas wasn't inclined to be friendly toward the guy today, or any time soon.

"I'm going to pretend I don't know what you're talking about for now." Because Cannon had been a dick this morning and Elisa wasn't scenery ever. Rojas's temper, never too far beneath the surface, simmered. He clamped down on his reaction. Cannon wasn't a complete ass, just not the most thoughtful person out there. Guy tended to talk without a filter for polite company. Most times, he got along fine with the fighters at Revolution MMA and he was a good dog owner, too. But there was a reason the man didn't have a steady girlfriend.

"Your new employee. I should go introduce myself to her and apologize for making her drop her coffee." Cannon jerked his chin up toward the window Elisa had been in a minute earlier. "Very ho—"

"Stop. Don't finish that. Don't approach Elisa without me there when you go to apologize. And you will." Rojas didn't even bother to try sounding nice. "And if you don't adjust your thought process, maybe we need to take up this discussion next sparring session at Revolution."

Cannon turned to look at him and gave him some more space, lifting his hands in a surrender gesture. His pug grunted as his leash grew taut. "Ah, hey, no offense intended."

The other man visibly struggled with the awkward moment, the tips of his ears turning red in embarrassment. Rojas let him stew a while longer. But the situation had caught him by surprise. Women attending classes at the kennels had no problem expressing their interest in Rojas or any of the other trainers. It was a sort of easygoing thing to fend off those advances. However, having Elisa there was new, and she shouldn't have to fend off anything untoward. It'd be good to nip this in the bud now, and Cannon wasn't actually a bad guy. Plus, he'd spread the word if Rojas set the precedent.

"Same rules as Gary and Greg have at Revolution," Rojas said. "Don't say anything about anyone you wouldn't say to their face, and I don't want to hear you saying anything like that to any of our employees."

"Yeah. My bad." Cannon bent to pick up his pug and backed away. "Seriously, man. I'm sorry."

Rojas waved it off. "Time to focus on your dog and this morning's agility elements."

No need to think too deeply about why he was so short-fused when it came to Elisa. After the scare this morning, he was completely justified on her behalf. Maybe later he'd consider whether he'd do the same for anyone else employed at the kennels. Most likely he would. But he was a special flavor of irritated at the moment, and it was better to work that sort of thing off with some exercise.

Rojas put his thumb and middle finger to his mouth and whistled to bring in the rest of the class. About half a dozen men and women approached with their dogs. Mostly herding and sporting class breeds this morning, plus Cannon's hyper pug. "Everyone warm up with a jog around the outside of the course."

Cannon gave him a wry smile, knowing the warm-up was mostly to get him running instead of his mouth. It wouldn't hurt to burn off a little energy for the rest of the class, too. The dogs were all game for it, and their humans could use a few extra minutes of cardio.

After watching them all do a lap, Rojas joined them. He could do with burning off some excess energy, too.

CHAPTER NINE

An hour later he checked on Boom, then headed to the main building for a glass of water and figured he'd grab a glass for Elisa, too. They kept bottled water in a cooler out by the kennels for convenience, but using glasses was better for the environment, or so Boom told him repeatedly.

Or he could quit justifying his impulse to come by and check on Elisa.

They had an hour break between classes this morning, and there shouldn't have been anyone in the front reception area besides her, but the sound of her talking accompanied by a low male voice came down the hallway. Rojas's grip on the glasses tightened, sloshing water over the rims.

Muttering a curse, he relaxed and headed right on to the reception area. There was no good reason for him to get worked up about Elisa talking to a man. And if it was Cannon pursuing her, Rojas could always run the guy off. Especially if Cannon was making her uncomfortable.

As Rojas came around the entryway, taking the time to visually pie the corner out of habit, he noted there was no one in front of the reception desk. No. Whoever was talking to Elisa was behind the desk with her.

He entered the room and strode to the near end of the reception desk, setting the glasses down with a thunk. Elisa jumped in her chair and swung around to face him.

"Yo." Cruz sat on the counter along the wall behind the desk area. Plenty of space between him and Elisa.

"Hey." Rojas paused, sparing himself a moment to let go of the building anger he'd been gathering. "Didn't recognize your voice from down the hallway. What, you swallow a frog?"

Cruz waved a hand. "Caught a cold on the flight back this morning. Lyn took it harder. She's staying in bed until her fever goes down. But Forte said our new admin might need some additional IT set up to organize our stuff."

Elisa gave Rojas a shy smile. "I've got the client spreadsheet started, but I figured it'd be good to set up a new calendar to help schedule the private lessons. Maybe set up a newsletter, too."

Cruz nodded. "We've been using the private e-mails so long it's about time somebody set up an e-mail and calendar specifically for the kennels. Elisa here is on the ball."

Rojas agreed. He also wanted to tell Cruz to quit breathing on her, but his friend was sitting a decent distance away. "Maybe we have some vitamin supplements around here somewhere to ward off whatever plague you've got."

Cruz pulled a tiny bottle from his pocket. "Have some hand sanitizer. Feel free to chug it."

Elisa wrinkled her nose, laughter sparkling in her eyes.

Okay, at least she was being entertained. Rojas relaxed some. "Don't let me stop you all from doing the tech thing. Carry on."

Leaning over, he slid the glass of water across the desk to Elisa. She gave him a smile, and he figured it'd been worth the extra few steps into the kitchen after all. "Thank you."

Cruz looked from Elisa to Rojas and lifted an eyebrow. Rojas pointedly ignored him.

"Back to what I was saying before *someone* interrupted. It's safe to log in to any websites you need from the computers here." Cruz tapped the laptop in front of Elisa. "Go ahead and create the accounts you need for the plans you had in mind: general e-mail for the kennels, calendar, newsletter. Just make a list of the sites where you created accounts so I know about them and can add them to the trusted sites list for the firewall."

Cruz paused and gave Rojas a different, more sober look, then returned his attention to Elisa. "You can check your personal e-mail and online stuff here, too. We won't pry, and you keep your own passwords to yourself. We're set up with a proxy server, so it'd be hard for anyone to track you down by IP address. But if you're someplace else on Wi-Fi or at a public computer terminal, log in using a free proxy site."

Apparently, Cruz had talked to Forte before coming to meet Elisa. Good. The three of them kept each other in the know when it came to important information.

"I..." She hesitated, glanced at Rojas and sat up a little straighter, then pressed onward. "I use an incognito window."

Rojas liked the way she was gaining confidence. Yesterday, he thought she might have held her peace and not spoken up. He was not going to admit that her warming up to Cruz was getting under his skin, though. Nope.

Cruz bobbed his head to one side then the other. "An incognito window isn't horrible, but it's insufficient. It protects the computer you're using from any websites that leave cookies or similar information-gathering tools on your machine. It doesn't hide your tracks, your IP address."

And that was at least one way her ex had been able to find her in the past. Rojas figured there were any number of ways the asshole had tracked her, maybe laughed every time he'd found her location by tracking down her IP address. It didn't take much specialized skill, either. Once a person learned how to look, an insane amount of information was available to the regular public.

"I didn't know enough," Elisa said in a small voice, but the delicate muscles in her jaw jumped as it tightened. She was frustrated, maybe, but not defeated.

"Hey." Rojas touched her shoulder, making sure to move slow and keep the pressure as light as he could make it, but wanting to give her more than just words. Contact. Comfort. "You're a fast learner and you're smart. Don't doubt it. There's always something new to learn out there. None of us is perfect."

"I don't know." She reached up and placed her fingertips on the back of his hand to let him know his contact was welcome. The contact zinged through him, short-circuiting his original train of thought. "Boom is close to convinced that she's omniscient."

Cruz chuckled.

Rojas groaned, but he didn't withdraw yet. Her touch was featherlight on the back of his hand, and her shoulder was warm under his fingertips.

"Anyway, we've got your back now and we'll make sure you've got the knowledge you need to protect yourself." He cleared his throat and withdrew his touch.

Cruz didn't add to what Rojas had said but nodded in agreement. "Stick around and Boom might teach you a few things none of us know yet."

Rojas's phone buzzed in his back pocket. He retrieved it and gave it a swipe. "Speak of the devil."

"I'm not a devil, Dad!" Boom's laughter filled his ear, and he grinned despite himself.

"You okay? Need something?" He'd been up there only a few minutes ago and she didn't sound like she was in distress, but a gang of worry hit him in the chest anyway.

"Yeah. I forgot, though." Boom dropped her voice the way she did when she knew he wouldn't be thrilled. Which meant it probably had to do with schoolwork and maybe not the best study habits ever.

"Homework?" He figured it couldn't be all bad. It was only Saturday, after all. He wanted her to rest, but if she was going back to school on Monday, which the doctor had said she should be able to do, then she should have her homework done.

Technically, she should've had any homework from the last day of school she'd attended done *before* they'd gone to Revolution MMA for her class in the first place. House rules: homework done before martial arts class or going out to play. And her teachers hadn't sent any assignments for the day she'd missed.

"I finished most of it." The statement came out in a rush. Meaning it hadn't been done before she'd gone to class and broken her arm. "There's a project due on Monday and that's not the same as homework."

He frowned. Technically, she had a point. "What kind of project?"

"I need to make a presentation for science class. It's supposed to be of the solar system." She went on to tell him about what she had planned. "I really want to set it up to put a spotlight on Pluto. I feel bad for Pluto because at first they thought it was a planet and then they thought maybe it wasn't and now it's supposed to be a dwarf planet. And there's all these cute pictures on the Internet of Pluto and how happy it was to have the New Horizons spacecraft fly by and take pictures."

His eyes glazed over.

Not that he didn't like science. He did. But there were only so many facts he could absorb about a planet that wasn't a planet in the space of thirty seconds. Which was about how long it took for Boom to tell him all of those things.

He glanced at Elisa, who now had her hand covering her mouth as she unsuccessfully hid her giggling. Cruz had a grin on his face, too. Great. Well, it was what Rojas got for keeping the volume up on his phone.

"Okay, slow down. The bottom line is you need to go

to the craft store. Yes?" He was fine with briefings, but he always wanted the takeaway, the action items.

"Yes." Boom sighed. "Can you take me now while my arm isn't hurting and I'm still awake?"

Rojas chewed on the inside of his cheek. No way was he going to be able to make it out and back before the next class started. On the other hand, Boom had a point about her arm and being awake. There was a relatively small window in which she was alert and not in pain with the current medication schedule. He didn't want her to get overtired rushing, either. He looked at Cruz.

Cruz's eyes widened and the other man whispered, "I would, but sick. Remember? Last thing she needs is to catch a cold on top of that broken arm."

Man had a point.

Rojas wrestled with the problem. Boom needed supplies, and as much as he hated going to public places filled with strangers—especially stores where there was always someone with the kind of twitchy habits to push his buttons—he still went because his daughter needed him to. But he'd already burned his fuse short with Cannon, and it didn't bode well for his temper for the rest of the day. He knew his limits and his own warning signs. It could be bad news for him to go out and around people today. Hell, the upcoming class would be tiring for his tolerance levels, but at least he'd be on home territory and in control of his environment.

Elisa raised her hand slightly and wiggled her fingers. "Does Boom know where to go? If you have a car to lend me and she gives me directions, I could drive her."

It was a generous offer. And at the moment, the best

solution Rojas could think of outside of making Boom wait until this evening, when the stores might be closed. She'd need all the time she could get to work on her project. He was predicting she'd be working on it in bursts of energy and napping hard in between to heal. The earlier she got started, the better. Even then, it might not get done before Monday.

Shame spread across his tongue with a bitter taste. It'd been a couple of years since he'd left active duty and every day was still a balancing act like this. If he wasn't so messed up in the head, he'd be able to juggle teaching the class and taking his own daughter to the damn store. It irked him to admit the biggest hesitation was exposing himself to random people right now.

"You can borrow my car." Rojas fished for his keys and handed them over.

Elisa took them then narrowed her eyes at him. He hadn't mentioned his car when he'd ridden with her to Revolution MMA the night before. Honestly, he'd ridden with her so she'd be less likely to drive off and not stay. Then this morning, he grumped about not liking anyone driving his car but him. It'd been to give her an excuse to settle into the passenger seat and get her nerve back after the scare she'd had. Those instances hadn't exactly been lies and could arguably be considered manipulation, but with good intentions.

This was probably how Boom felt after she'd pulled a similar set of actions on him and he caught her.

The thought diffused some of his tension, and he grinned at Elisa. It shouldn't amuse him so much to make her irritated with him, but it was turning out to be a lot of fun.

After a moment, she seemed to get over it. "Should I wait until the next class comes in and then go get her?"

He nodded an affirmative then addressed his phone. "How you feeling, Boom? Think you can wait another twenty minutes and still make it out to the store and back? You okay if you go with Elisa and not me?" He paused, back to being a concerned father. "If you're too tired, just make a list and we can go get it for you."

It'd probably mean a few repeat trips. Even if Boom made a list, she was a kid. There'd be something she'd forget or described vaguely. It was going to be a relay run back and forth to the craft store.

"I can make it. I'll get dressed now and wait downstairs." There was a pause. "So she came back?"

He'd told Boom about Elisa's visit yesterday and caught hell from his daughter for not bringing Elisa to the house to see her. As far as Boom was concerned, Elisa was a new friend.

"Yeah." His face was heating up as Elisa stared at him. "She came back."

"Good! I'll be ready." There was a rustle as Boom apparently scrambled out of bed.

"Careful, take your time."

"Dad." Boom drew out the word with exasperation. "I'm ten, not two. All I've got to do is pull pants on. You helped me into a clean shirt this morning. I'm totally okay with Elisa taking me. She's not a stranger. We met her the other night and you offered her a job and everything."

His daughter was talking about Elisa as if she was a longtime family friend. He wasn't exactly sure how he felt about that.

"If you're not comfortable, it's okay," Elisa whispered. "I could hold the class or something until you got back."

He waved in the negative. "It's a plan. Take your time and go slow, Boom. It's okay to sit and rest. Got it?"

"Got it!" And his daughter very obviously was not going to go slow at the moment. Maybe he should head over to the house to help her.

"You sure you're comfortable?" Elisa asked, her eyes filled with understanding. "I am a stranger and it's completely reasonable."

Her consideration was exactly why he nodded in the affirmative. She was good people and they weren't going any place out of touch. It'd be fine.

"The craft store is right near Revolution MMA. Same shopping center." He paused to consider this morning again, and the reason Elisa had been so scared. "I'll call ahead to Gary and Greg so they know to look for you in the parking lot. If you run into any issues or if Boom needs a break, you two can duck into the school for a rest. Gary and Greg are literally within shouting distance of the store. I appreciate the help."

Elisa huffed. "I'm glad to. Besides, Boom and I could always stop for some frozen yogurt too. Maybe we'll eat it in your car on the way back."

Aw now, some things in the world just weren't a wise idea.

CHAPTER TEN

We've got poster board, spray paints in blue and purple, a glue stick, and Sharpies." Elisa ticked off their loot on the fingers of one hand as she stood with Boom surveying the trunk of Alex's car. "What do you think might be missing?"

Boom pondered for a moment, rubbing her chin in what was probably an adorable imitation of one of her father's habits. Elisa couldn't wait to see Alex do it.

"I can print out pictures of Pluto to glue onto the board." Boom sounded unsure. Standing next to Elisa, she usually came to about chest height but now she drooped into an exaggerated slump. "I thought they'd look great, but none of it seems to stand out much. All the kids are going to be doing space stuff and we don't get an A unless we really stand out from the rest of the projects."

"Hmm." Elisa wondered when elementary school had gotten so competitive. Though honestly, she liked Boom even more for going after the top grade instead of simply planning to make a science project good enough to pass. Boom was a tomboy, no doubt about it, but she had a sharp mind, too. Some things that came out of her mouth were way more mature than what Elisa would've expected from a ten-year-old. "We could get some fluorescent spray paint and rig your poster with some mini backlights we saw on sale in there. It'd make your versions of Pluto glow."

Boom turned to her with wide eyes. "Really? Will it work during the day at school?"

Good question.

Elisa wrinkled her nose. "Depends on how bright your classroom is and how many windows there are. If you turn off the classroom lights, you might be able to see it, but the teacher would have to let you pull all the blinds to block light coming in from the windows, too."

"I don't think Miss Patrick would let me take the time to do that during my presentation." Boom began to worry at her bottom lip with her fingers. Her lips were chapped, and Elisa had noticed Boom putting on lip balm before they went into the store, but the girl hadn't reapplied since. Maybe Boom only remembered when they were going into a place and not when her lips actually felt dry. "There's a lot of kids in the class, and our presentations should be short and almost speak for themselves."

Miss Patrick must give those instructions fairly consistently. Boom had fallen into a sing-song sort of cadence when she'd recalled the teacher's words. To Elisa, it meant the child was repeating something she heard all the time.

"Not a bad point." Elisa didn't want to undermine the teacher's instructions. She closed the trunk and held out her hand to Boom. "Are you feeling up to going back into the store? Maybe we'll find something inspiring if we walk inside again."

Boom gave her a big smile. "I'm okay. Totally."

Elisa returned the smile. Really, Boom made it easy. Still, the girl was starting to look a little glassy-eyed. Elisa had better come up with an epiphany quickly and get Boom back to the kennels before she ran out of energy.

Besides, Alex might get worried.

The thought of Boom's father brought on a few mental images. He'd stood out during class, even from far away. He cut a great figure against the backdrop of the grassy fields and trees lining the perimeter of the property. Even in the new button-up shirt, his built body was clearly noticeable. He filled out the fabric with a solid chest, broad shoulders, and even his biceps were noticeable inside the sleeves. When he'd started running with the rest of his class in the morning, Elisa had snuck more than a couple of looks out the window. Alex, standing, was a sight to see. Alex in motion was worth several minutes of staring and drooling. Then, the fabric of his shirt and pants moved and the musculature underneath was even more impressive. It didn't take much of a mental leap to imagine muscles rippling under deliciously bare skin.

With an effort, Elisa wrenched her brain back around to the task at hand. Science projects and standing out from the crowd.

"Do you really think the other projects will be that

much more different?" Elisa fished for some clues as to what Boom's teacher might be comparing Boom's work to. "What sorts of things do the other kids put together?"

Boom's normally bright expression dimmed somewhat, and the girl looked down at the floor, her short blond hair falling forward to conceal part of her face. Elisa wondered if Boom's hair would darken as she got older. Despite summer highlights from being out in the sun all day, Alex's hair was a darker brown and probably almost black in winter. "Well, there were lots of different things. Glitter and stickers, and one girl even had oil paints because her mom does paintings to sell in New Hope."

"Ah." Elisa cursed herself for bursting the girl's happy mood. It had to be tough for her and for Alex to go day to day without her mother. No way was Elisa going to ask about the mother, either. Definitely had to be a difficult topic. "Well, it sounds like your teacher likes to see texture and creativity in your projects."

Crafts had been some of Elisa's favorite hobbies once upon a time. She'd loved scrapbooking, working with different papers of various weights and printed with colorful patterns. But it'd be too obvious to get space-themed paper or stickers. Others would've done it. Boom was looking for something *different*.

Elisa's gaze fell on a nearby sales rack. "Have you ever done origami?"

Boom scrunched up her face. "Ori-what?"

"Origami." Elisa led her over to the rack and picked up a packet of square paper, colored in soft swirls of white and gold. It had a shimmery, pearlescent quality to it. "You fold fine paper in complex patterns to make different kinds of shapes. The Japanese do it. They make paper cranes and frogs and flowers, all kinds of things. I know there's a pattern to fold the paper into a sort of ball or balloon and we could attach it to your board in all the places where you're showing Pluto in orbit or in its place with the other planets of the solar system. Then we could take LED lights and put them inside the paper balls to make them light up with a battery. So it'll be different from just the lights and more unusual."

"Oh, I've seen the kids in some of the anime shows do the cranes and the stars." Boom beamed at her, the previous melancholy evaporated. "That sounds cool!"

Relief washed through her. It wouldn't cost Alex too much more, either. There were some fun sets of blinking LED earrings on sale over by the register that'd make installing them inside the origami planets easy. "Then we've got a plan."

They grabbed the rest of their supplies and headed for the register. In a few minutes, they were ready to head out and Elisa glanced out the glass doors of the store. She'd left her car parked in front of Revolution MMA a few storefronts down in the same shopping center. She wondered if she should check on it while she was here.

Abruptly she froze. Her heart jumped up and fear constricted her throat.

"What?" Boom stopped with her, small hand trapped in hers.

Her heart beat so loud the sound filled her ears as Elisa watched a man idly stroll by her car and look inside. Could be a random passerby. Maybe. But she didn't think so. Most people came to a shopping center with a purpose. They parked their cars and headed into a particular store. There was a purpose to what those people did.

"Boom, do you know if there's ever been car robberies in this area?" Elisa tried to keep the question light and mildly inquisitive.

Boom craned her neck to look for her father's car. "Not really. Sifu Gary and Sifu Greg say we should always pay attention to who is around us out in the parking lot and lock the car door as soon as we get in. They say we shouldn't ever sit in the car checking our phones or playing games. Because someone could just walk by and jump in the car with us or break the window to get at us and our stuff. But that's any parking lot and mostly at night."

"Those are good things to keep in mind." Elisa forced out the response in a whisper as the man she'd seen took a lap down the row of cars and came back to hers. Hers was the only car he peered into. And then he bent down to check out something near her tire.

Nope. She was not sticking around to watch more. If she and Boom headed to Revolution MMA, it'd be toward her car and the man messing with it, too. Better to go to Alex's car and put some distance between them. Now.

"Let's go." Elisa grasped Boom's hand more firmly and almost yanked the girl off her feet in the rush to leave the store and break for Alex's car.

Boom exclaimed in surprise but stretched her long legs to keep up.

Keeping her head down, Elisa hustled Boom into the car and then hurried to the other side. Every time she glanced back, the man was still on the ground between her car and another one, studying something under hers.

Boom's comment about never sitting in the car checking phones echoed in her spinning thoughts and Elisa decided not to call Alex, just get back to him. Locking the car doors, Elisa forced herself to pull out smoothly and drive away at normal speed. First of all, she wasn't sure if she knew how to peel out of a parking lot but it didn't seem like a good idea and would definitely attract the stranger's attention. Second, she needed to drive safely with Boom in the car.

Going for the calmest tone possible, she cleared her throat. "Boom, why don't you call your dad and tell him we're on our way back."

"Sure."

That way, if they were delayed, Alex would know something had gone wrong. Hopefully, it wouldn't.

Her heart raced the entire ride home and she could only give Boom lame excuses as to why she'd rushed them out of there. After a few abortive rounds of questioning, Boom settled back into the passenger seat.

When they pulled through the gate of the kennels and up the long drive, Boom reached over and patted Elisa's arm. "Don't worry, Elisa. We're home now and Dad's here."

*   *   *

Rojas had Souze on a lead, working through standard obedience training, when the girls returned. Boom rolled out of the passenger side with a smile and waved at him with her good arm. Elisa emerged from the driver's side more slowly.

Grinning, he returned the wave and headed toward

them. Souze walked at his side in a perfect heel position, attention on Rojas. The dog was good, very good, on most days. He had the energy, desire to work, and intelligence to easily complete his training every day. What seemed lacking on some days was his level of aggression and prey drive.

Oh, he'd go after the usual tennis ball Rojas and the other trainers used as a reward during training. And Souze had amazing scent skills. But when it came time for bite work and some of the more violent aspects of training key to ensuring dogs were ready for military or K9 work, Souze hesitated. The dog was wary, and when prodded to actually bite, he was formidable. More than capable of taking down a full-grown man. But a handler in a combat situation needed instantaneous precision from his dog, an eagerness Souze was lacking.

Rojas was convinced Souze had it in him. They just needed to work together to find the trigger. As Cruz's companion, Lyn, might've said, they needed to get inside Souze's head and understand his motivation. Until then, Souze wouldn't be a good fit as a military working dog or K9, no matter how otherwise capable he was.

"Dad!" Boom skipped toward him, completely unworried about the big dog at his side. "Elisa helped me come up with the best idea for my presentation!"

Rojas grinned and came to a stop, murmuring a command for Souze to sit. The GSD's big ears were up and forward, listening to Boom with detached interest. "Yeah? So the mission was a success."

Boom's face was flushed with excitement, but her eyes were somewhat glazed. She was running out of gas quickly, and it was just about time for her next dose of pain meds for the broken arm. "Getting the supplies was a success. There's still a lot to do."

"Yup, and to do it right, you're going to need proper rest." Rojas dropped to one knee and opened his arms to her, keeping an eye on Souze's reaction. The big dog sat obediently and otherwise could care less. In fact, Souze's gaze had settled on Elisa, who was approaching at a slower walk with bags of random craft supplies.

Boom came forward to throw her arms around his neck for a hug. She was a smart girl and only ever rushed him when he wasn't working with a dog. Sudden movement and approaching a handler too quickly could trigger a defensive response from the dog. He'd been careful to teach Boom to wait until he gave the signal the way he had—going on one knee and opening his arms to her in clear body language for both hers and the dog's benefit. Once he did give her the signal, though, his daughter didn't hold back on the affection, and he loved her for it.

After a moment, Boom straightened from the hug and gave Souze a thoughtful look. "I could go upstairs and take a nap now then work on my project later."

Which was a major indicator of how tired his daughter was feeling. Normally, Boom fought going to bed at all, tooth and nail.

Elisa smiled as she approached. "I can leave these on the porch."

Souze straightened almost imperceptibly as Elisa approached. Not eager and no welcoming signs. Just a sharpening of focus on the woman.

Rojas nodded. "Thanks. I'll put Souze away and come back to take the stuff inside on my way back."

"I'll go wash up." Boom jogged toward the house.

Before Elisa could follow, Rojas rose to his feet. "Anything you want to tell me?"

Souze's attention had given her away. Elisa was very good at pulling all of her fear and any telltale signs of anxiety and hiding them away somewhere. But a human couldn't hide that sort of state from a dog. Pheromones, modulation in tone of voice, minute twitches in body language communicated a human's mental state to an alert dog. And Rojas had long ago learned to read a dog's responses. It'd saved lives on missions overseas, including his. And soldiers who ignored the warnings died, plus got other people killed along with them.

Old memories reached up and hooked into him, trying to drag him into a continuous replay of missions long completed and in the past. Every one of them had been intense, none of them had been easy, and some of them had damaged him forever.

A whine cut into his train of thought and Souze's shoulder bumped his leg. Rojas looked down into the dog's eager gaze and gave his ears a scratch. Souze was becoming a lifeline.

Looking at Elisa, there wasn't any doubt that she stood ready to run. And in the short time he'd come to know her, he decided he didn't want her to.

"I have to go." The words came out as a whisper, controlled and measured. "I thought I could give this a try, and I owe you and your friends a lot already. I'll have to find some way to pay you someday. But I should leave as soon as possible."

Rojas blinked. He'd been willing to give the woman some space, but hearing her sound so defeated made him want to tell her, show her, she didn't have to be on her own. More importantly, Boom had been with her when whatever had happened to change her mind had hit. "Was my daughter in danger at any time?"

Elisa swallowed. She didn't shake her head or immediately blurt out a denial. She thought about it and met his gaze directly. "I don't think so. As soon as I realized there was an issue, we got in the car and I brought her back. Safe."

Well, it might've made more sense not to come straight back, but it all depended on how much danger there had been to make Elisa add that last qualifier on the end of her statement.

He let out a slow breath, reining in his anger. "Start from the beginning. Tell me exactly what happened."

She did.

For a nasty second, he wanted to rage at his own stupidity in entrusting his daughter to this woman and to shake Elisa for placing Boom in danger. But Elisa hadn't. Under normal circumstances, the trip should've been fine. Hell, he'd known Elisa had been running from something and they'd had friends nearby just in case. Elisa and Serena should've been safe and Elisa shouldn't be blamed for the persecution she was subject to. He needed to make sure the people he cared about remained protected. "I've respected your privacy up to now, but I do need to know if we should be expecting any unwanted company."

"I hope not."

He stared at her. "We'll plan for the worst-case scenario."

She bit her lip. "Which is also why I should leave.

The stranger I saw didn't seem to have noticed us. He was too busy looking over my car, under it. I got us back to your car while he was down there so I don't think he saw us."

"Take me through it one more time." He needed to see if the details were consistent, if she was remembering clearly. And he wanted her to get some distance from what'd happened by thinking it through.

He'd warn Cruz to keep an extra close eye on the security feeds tonight, just in case. Gary and Greg had security cameras with line of sight to the first couple of rows of cars in front of their school, so he could also check into the identity of this guy. Could be someone who'd dropped something between cars and made Elisa jumpy. But Elisa had demonstrated a presence of mind and practicality thus far, so he was guessing she'd really seen what she thought she'd seen. He wasn't going to doubt her until proof presented itself to say otherwise. And he had the means to verify what she'd told him.

His daughter was safely upstairs and about to take a nap, happy about the help and ideas Elisa had given her.

Elisa clasped her hands in front of her. "I'll call a cab, get back to my car and head out. Hopefully he didn't do anything to it and I can sell it in the next town I stop in."

Alex studied Souze. Souze continued to watch Elisa. The dog's ears were still swiveled to catch every nuance of what she said. His posture was tense, and his shoulders almost trembled with the tension he was sensing from the woman. As composed as she appeared, chances were she was frightened out of her mind.

His daughter was safe. He could help Elisa be safe, too. The men of Hope's Crossing Kennels had better means to protect the people they cared about than most. They didn't just keep their old military habits close; it was a part of who each of them was.

"You're not going back to your car." He pulled out his smartphone and sent a text to Forte and Cruz.

"I have to." She said it quietly. "I know he could still be there watching, but everything I own is in that car besides the overnight bag I left upstairs at Revolution."

He nodded. "Which is exactly why he'll stay out of sight and follow you until you feel safe. Then nab you. You're too attached to what's in that car."

"It's still afternoon. Broad daylight." Elisa unclasped her hands and held them in fists at her sides. "It was a busy parking lot with plenty of people walking back and forth. I can slip to my car and drive away. He wouldn't be able to grab me in front of all those people without me making a racket and drawing unwanted attention."

"True." And good for her for having thought of those things. "Do you know how to check your car for anything he might've attached to the bottom? You said he spent some time looking under there. What if he wasn't just looking?"

Her eyes widened, and her face paled. "Like what sort of things?"

What, indeed? Normal people didn't have access to things like tracking devices or worse, explosives. "It really depends on who you're running from and what sort of resources they have at their disposal."

She pressed her lips together in a thin line. Her eyes dropped, and her gaze settled on Souze. "He owned half a dozen dogs like him."

Rojas waited. Considering the pressure she was under, if he just let her uncork, it'd all come flowing out without her having a chance to filter it.

"My ex is a businessman. The CIO of his own company with all sorts of contracts and security clearances. He was very good at his job, and he was a control freak. He kept me under his influence until I finally gathered the courage to leave. To be honest, I should've left way earlier but it took a hard look at what he was really doing with his special projects to make me decide." She continued to study Souze, who in turn stretched his neck toward her, sniffing. The dog was inquisitive, which meant her fear was turning to something else. Rojas was hoping it wasn't her giving up. "There were dogs like Souze walking the property, loose. A lot of them were like him. They noticed everything. And I didn't know how to make friends with them. I thought about leaving a trail of hamburger patties across the lawn if I snuck away from the house at night, but dogs like Souze ignore food if they're trained well enough. I couldn't be sure one of them wouldn't pull me down as I was trying to get out."

True. Food was a powerful distraction, but all sorts of working dogs were trained to resist the temptation. A dog didn't have to be a military working dog, police dog, or other type of service animal to reach that level of training. Besides, guard dogs like those may have had training to ensure they weren't poisoned by potential intruders. Such training wasn't foolproof, but it reduced the chances of success.

"When I left, I only took what I could fit in my big shoulder bag. I pretended I was on my way to run some errands and took a detour. I just took a wrong turn and

kept driving. Didn't even plan it. It occurred to me that
the moment, the opportunity, might never come again,
and I just drove. I'd keep going until I couldn't stay
awake any longer and catch a few hours' sleep and drive
again. When I found a small town, someplace barely
on the map, I'd try to stop and see if I could get a
job and hide for a while. I even sold my car twice and
bought a used vehicle in its place. I'd stay for a week,
maybe two before there'd be a text on my new phone
or a strange man in town. Small towns always notice
strangers. And I'd leave. It's been six months and almost
as many towns." Elisa tipped her head to the side, still
staring at Souze. "You know, the only things I missed
about the house were the dogs. I thought I'd feel so
much more secure if one of them would be allowed
inside the house with me for accompany. German Shepherd Dogs are beautiful."

Rojas couldn't help a faint smile. She'd listened and
learned. She'd taken an opportunity. And she'd given
him a decent amount of information, most likely without
even realizing it.

She straightened her head and dragged her gaze away
from Souze. "At this point, I've driven across the entire
country. I can keep going. The stuff in the car I pulled
together along the way, things that were mine and a part
of the life I was building but I was never sure how long
I'd stay. I can leave it all behind again if I have to and
make do."

With nothing. Not even a car to live out of.

"How does he keep finding you?" Rojas watched her
blink, come out of her fugue of sadness. She had really
hoped to be happy at least for the morning.

"It's been a learning process for me. You already taught me about the phone." She lifted her fist and ticked off points on her fingers. "Cruz taught me about incognito windows not being enough. My ex is good with computers, has people who are good with them, too. Maybe they found the e-mail account I set up for myself and noticed when I logged in to check my e-mail in the first town or two. My mother means well, but she might've told them about it before I stopped checking in with her. I didn't realize I wasn't being careful enough. If I can learn to stay away from those mistakes, I should do better."

Maybe. Probably. But she didn't have the training, skills, survival instincts developed from mission after mission in hostile territories to draw from and he did. Forte and Cruz were soldiers, too. She wouldn't have the enhanced senses of canine companions like the ones here. She wouldn't have him.

"The next place you come to might not have the same type of people." In fact, the chances were extremely low. Somebody, well-meaning or ill, could give her right back to her ex in any number of ways.

"You and your friends are all very kind." Elisa looked toward the house. "Your daughter is amazing. I don't want to cause any more trouble for any of you."

He shrugged. "We've all seen our share of trouble. It's all sort of relative these days."

In fact, Souze had run down a gunman just a few months ago right there on kennel grounds. They'd had some truly unfriendly visitors when Lyn had first come to the kennels.

Elisa didn't argue further. She just took a step away. "I should go."

Should. But she didn't say she wanted to. Didn't say she had to. Didn't explicitly say she was going to. So he had no trouble lunging forward and catching her hand. "Don't."

She did yank her hand out of his. Souze surged to his feet and barked.

Rojas didn't reach for her again, but he stepped right into her space. She didn't back down. Her ex might've tried to repress her, but the core of who she was still had a whole lot of strength. He could push her, and she'd push back. Whether she consciously understood it or not, it was because she believed he wouldn't hurt her. And she was right.

CHAPTER ELEVEN

Letting her employer kiss her was definitely not the way to manage expectations. But Alex's lips were warm and firm against hers, and excitement zinged through her at the contact. Every bit of good sense she had flew right out of her head, and instead, she enjoyed.

The discussion had wrung every emotion out of her and then he'd gone and given her hope. He'd offered her protection, a support system, friends. And he was offering her this.

She almost believed in him.

But she was still going to leave, and the idea of leaving without knowing what it'd be like to kiss him would've haunted her forever. So she was going to savor this one kiss. Just one.

Alex's hand came up slowly to cradle the side of her face, encouraging her to tilt her head, and she did. He deepened the kiss then, his tongue running across her lips and coaxing them to open for him. She opened with a sigh, and his tongue swept into her mouth, gently tasting. She kissed him back in return, leaning into him until she had one hand braced against his hard chest.

A needy moan escaped her, and he responded in kind. When he lifted his mouth from hers, she almost tipped into him, her knees not holding her upright anymore and her head spinning. *Wow*.

She took not one, but several long breaths to clear her head, looking down at a black and tan face staring up at her with soulful, dark eyes. Souze wasn't shy about watching, apparently.

The thought brought her the rest of the way to her senses, because weird. Yeah. Weird.

She took a step back, and Alex let her. He'd done that since the beginning. Letting her go if she wanted. So why was it so hard to leave now even if she kept saying she should?

"Thank you," she told him, not looking up into his eyes.

"But?" Alex's voice came cool, deep, and so sexy it just wasn't fair.

"But I should go. Especially because this is obviously not a professional thing now."

"No. But none of your previous employers particularly cared if you left, did they?" He sounded reasonable. "Did they bother to try to check on you?"

"Not that I know of." She said it slowly. She'd had her phone with her, and she'd been checking her e-mail. Both big mistakes, she knew now. But she'd been paid under the table and they didn't really have a way to contact her after she disappeared.

"I think that's a little odd." Rojas lifted his hand, giving her plenty of time to avoid him, and brushed her hair back from her face. "Maybe this time, it wouldn't hurt to have someone care about whether you disappear."

Tempting. Oh, it was tempting. "Getting tangled up with my boss is exactly how I got into this mess in the first place."

"Ah." There was a pause. "I take it you started working at your ex's company, then got involved with him?"

Shame burned through her. She just nodded. This entire sharing exercise had gone way beyond her comfort zone. But Alex and his friends had already done so much for her, and this was some of what she could do to balance the ledger.

Personal information was a valuable currency, after all.

"Well, in the first place, your ex is an asshole, but only one representative of the human race," Alex said slowly. "And, secondly, you'll technically be working for Forte since he owns the place."

"Semantics!" Scandalized, she looked up into his eyes and saw humor and amusement.

"Details," Rojas countered. Then he cleared his throat. "Look. It's not just about how much I'd like to get to know you better. And believe me, I would. There's also something off about the way your ex has chased you. His texts to you to mess with your head. The unidentified creep messing around with your car, who I'm guessing is employed by your ex. A normal stalker is bad enough, but this is taking it up a notch in terms of money and resources invested in getting you back. I really do think your best chance of staying out on your own is to let us help."

He was right. Part of her wanted to scream at moving

backward, at admitting there was something she couldn't do for herself. The other part of her, the part with the survival instinct, admitted pride wasn't her best defense at the moment. Learning was. And Joseph Corbin Junior had found her a couple of times already. It was time to change the way she made her choices, break the pattern.

"You all can help me learn what I need to know to prevent him from finding me, right? Even if I decide to leave eventually." It was important to her, being the person to decide when to leave even if she'd been feeble, wobbling about whether to or not all this time.

Alex nodded, serious. He wasn't laughing or belittling this point, and she appreciated it. Everything about this conversation had become close to unreal in her head, and she was absolutely going to replay it in her mind over and over tonight, wherever she decided to go to sleep. Dissecting a conversation for every nuance and every possible way she could've chosen to handle it was sort of like counting sheep for her.

"I'm all about teaching a person to fish for themselves." Alex glanced at her to see if she caught the reference.

She raised an eyebrow at him. *Duh.*

The corner of his mouth lifted in a lopsided grin. "And I have a lot of respect for those who recognize they need some help to get to where they need to be going. People helped me along the way, and I consider it paying it forward."

Fair. She looked down at Souze. "You are a really patient dog."

"He is," Alex agreed. "And he's been paying more attention to this conversation than he has to his training sessions for weeks. It's interesting."

Huh. Elisa studied Souze more closely. The dog returned her regard with an enigmatic doggy silence. "He does seem to like to be part of conversations, or at least listen to them."

"Could be part of it," Alex agreed. "Why don't you stay here with him for a couple of minutes while I go inside and make sure Boom's settled? Then we can walk him back to the kennels and you can tell me what I'm getting into with Boom's project."

Sounded simple. "Okay."

Alex handed her the loop on the human end of the six-foot leather leash. She took it and slid it over her wrist, hoping Souze didn't suddenly try to charge off across the yard. The big dog simply sat again.

"Elisa." Alex reached out to touch her hand.

She looked back up at him. "Hmm?"

"I'm glad you decided to stay a little longer."

CHAPTER TWELVE

Gary and Greg had a date tonight, but we stop in a lot to check on the school or help out with the computers. They already said it was fine for us to review the security feed." Even though they were coming in through the back entrance, Rojas entered first with Souze, visually clearing the room once he'd turned on the lights and watching for signs from the big dog.

Souze first sniffed the floor, then lifted his head to catch the scents in the air. This was the dog's first visit to Revolution MMA, so he didn't expect Souze to signal a stranger's scent, but the big dog would alert him to the presence of a live person.

Once he and Souze had stepped inside, they continued on to check the few rooms on this floor including the office, bathroom, changing rooms, and supply closet.

Elisa entered after them with Cruz bringing up the rear. As much as Rojas enjoyed Elisa's company—and he intended to explore their chemistry more once she'd had time to catch her breath—it was easier to travel off kennel grounds with backup to help watch their six. Souze could come in handy both inside and out, plus he needed the exposure to areas off the kennel's property for his training, anyway. Cruz was the wiz with the computers.

Inside the MMA school, big blinds were drawn down over the front windows facing the parking lot, so they didn't have to worry about observers for the moment. Rojas made his way around the center matted class area to Gary and Greg's office. He could've cut straight across, but school rules were no street shoes on the mats, and he wouldn't disrespect those guidelines even after hours with no one to call him on it. Besides, dogs weren't allowed on the mats at all on the rare occasions they visited.

"This place seems a lot bigger with no one here." Elisa trailed along behind him and Souze.

The big dog didn't show any notice of her. Souze was in working mode and focused on the task of sniffing out any strangers present. Rojas was glad to see the big dog's attention to his work even with people he liked nearby. A good working dog didn't get distracted.

"The space fills up fast once you pile two dozen sweaty bodies in here actively moving around." Cruz passed her and proceeded into the office to sit at Gary's desk. He immediately brought the computer online and started tapping away at the keyboard, ignoring the mouse as much as possible.

It was a thing for Cruz. Rojas left him to it.

"The kids' classes get really crowded." He was proud of what Gary and Greg had established here. "It's a really good program. Boom loves it."

"She told me about it that first night." Elisa smiled at the memory, her eyes slightly unfocused as she thought back to it. "I couldn't imagine her wanting to get back to the thing that broke her arm so soon, but she seemed like she couldn't wait."

Rojas leaned against the doorway to the office, facing out toward the main class area. Souze sat to his left, relaxed and alert. "It was pure accident. The kids all wear proper padding when they spar. Greg was supervising. He always keeps a close eye on the kids to make sure it's as safe as possible."

"It's still direct contact." Elisa dropped her big shoulder bag and grabbed a broom from the closet.

"Yeah." Rojas wasn't going to argue, but he could provide some additional context. "The sparring isn't ever all-out for the kids, but it's important for them to apply the moves they've learned against a partner around their size and skill level. Otherwise, they might not be able to use what they know in real life if the need ever comes up."

Elisa slipped off her shoes and stepped onto the mats, starting in one corner and beginning to sweep in short, strong strokes. He noticed she never seemed to remain still for long, always looking for something to do.

"I guess I can see that, but it seems young to start learning to fight a real person."

He grunted. Hers was not an uncommon perspective. "Never too early for self-defense. Besides, learning the timing and how to move in response to someone else isn't a bad thing. I hear dancers and athletes learn similar skill sets when they train. In Boom's case, her arm wasn't even the result of a direct strike."

"No?" Elisa didn't look up from her sweeping, but she did sweep more slowly, more quietly, so she could hear better.

"Nah. Her protective gear would've prevented a break that way. In this case, somebody mentioned she'd learn fastest if she was continually pushing beyond her comfort zone to try new things." Rojas sighed. "Which is true."

"Hey, Forte felt real bad about what happened," Cruz called from inside the office.

"It wasn't his fault, anyway. Boom made me take a picture of her at the ER to send to him to reassure him." Rojas shook his head. "She tried a flying roundhouse kick. It's not even one of the core kicks Gary and Greg teach here as part of the Jun Fan Jeet Kun Do curriculum. She learned it from one of her friends at school who takes tae kwon do."

Elisa straightened and turned to face him. "How did she . . . ?"

He chuckled as she trailed off. "Break her arm doing a flying kick? She executed the kick beautifully. It was a sight to see. But she didn't stick her landing. She fell backward and put out her arm to catch herself. Too much momentum and she fell badly."

"Ouch." Elisa scrunched up her face.

"Needless to say, the proper ways to take a fall are being incorporated into the core curriculum this school year." Rojas crossed his arms, Souze's leash hanging loosely from his wrist. "Gary and Greg take their work very seriously, and it hit them hard that a kid was injured on their watch."

"Some parents would sue the school." Elisa's observation was made as she resumed her sweeping. There was actually a decent amount of dust on the mats. It was an ongoing struggle even with no street shoes allowed.

"Yeah." Alex raked a hand through his hair before crossing his arms again. "This was a true accident, and I'm not going to go after them. Besides, they offered to split any hospital fees insurance doesn't cover. I don't want to put them out, and neither does Boom. She loves it here."

"It was good of them to offer." Elisa made her way down the side of the mat and started back, keeping the dust she'd swept in a growing line to one side. Very systematic, the way she approached things.

He wondered if she ever noticed how much of her thought process came out in her actions.

"Well, they do have to be careful. Any owner of this kind of school has to be." Rojas visually checked the windows and doors, everything in sight for anything out of place again. Never knew when something could come up, but it was good to be vigilant, especially in places where something out of place wasn't expected. "Gary and Greg more so than others in some ways, but mostly the parents who bring their kids here are really positive people. The kids' program has received community awards for the confidence building and the anti-bullying program."

Elisa paused again. "How does a mixed martial arts school teach anti-bullying?"

Rojas watched her more closely. Her shoulders had hunched some and her tone had a slight note of strain.

"Not by teaching the kids how to fight." Rojas reached out to tap a poster on the wall. "The kids are taught to tell an adult and trust the adults in their lives to believe them. If not their teachers, their parents. Preferably both. The kids are also taught not to be caught alone. Use the buddy system, whether it's their friends at school or another kid from here. And the skills they learn in mixed martial arts give them a confidence they don't even realize they have. It's in the way they walk and everything they do. The confidence makes them unlikely targets for bullies. And if they are absolutely backed into a corner and have no other alternative, they have the skills to defend themselves."

Elisa stared at the poster. "It works?"

"For most kids, yeah. The confidence goes a long way toward making a kid a less likely target." Rojas studied her. "A lot of the same concepts apply to adult self-defense."

She gripped the broom handle more tightly. "Boom seemed to think I should take a seminar. And you gave me a card."

It'd be a benefit in a lot of ways. The added awareness aside, he would love to see her confidence bloom.

"It's a good seminar. There should be one in the next weekend or two." Alex moved to the counter Gary and Greg used as a reception desk, looking for a flyer. "They're usually on Saturdays, but I think Forte could be convinced to give you the day off to go. Sophie attends those even if she doesn't take regular classes."

"I'll think about it."

From the way her thin brows were pinched together in a pensive expression, she was already considering. It was important, and honestly, she might have real need of it in the near future. He, Cruz, and Forte were starting to put precautions in place, but the best defense started with Elisa herself.

It was a shit reality in the current world.

His vision started to blur in a red haze. Souze stirred next to him, leaning in until the dog's shoulder was pressed against the side of his leg. The movement and gentle pressure brought Rojas back to the present, and he decided it was a bad time to follow that line of thought.

Definitely not the time to ask her. Thus far, he'd tried to limit his questioning into her past to need-to-know items. Things that could impact the kennels or the school or Elisa's immediate safety. The rest could come out when she decided to share, if she did.

"Gary's computer is damned slow again. I'm going to need to come in some other time and give it some tender loving care." Cruz cut into his thoughts. "But I've pulled the feeds from this afternoon and started an upload of the video file to our servers. First look was interesting, though."

"Yeah?" Rojas got a good look at Cruz's glowering expression and turned to see Elisa sweeping the dust she'd gathered into a dust pan. "Elisa, did you want to go upstairs and change?"

Elisa met his gaze and raised an eyebrow. "You mean go upstairs and let you two exchange information while I'm out of earshot? I'd prefer not."

Cruz snorted. "Smooth, Rojas. Subtle."

Rojas threw up his hands. "Okay, I'm sorry. Could you please join us over here and not be insulted if we maybe don't phrase our exchange of information in the nicest way possible."

Because it was a real possibility. Hell, his ex-wife had

constantly picked fights with him over the tiniest details instead of focusing on the important concepts of a discussion. It got worse when she'd dragged her parents into any kind of decision-making. Cruz's own father had been far away in Peru and had never been part of the day-to-day yelling matches between Cruz and his ex-wife, so it never made sense to Cruz the way she'd call in her parents to back her. He'd wanted to get the information from Cruz without getting hung up with someone else interjecting.

Cruz just shook his head. "It's not encouraging news, but you should hear it eventually."

"Then it saves time if I'm right here." Elisa joined Rojas, leaning against the other side of the doorway and crossing her arms with a pointed look at him. "I'll try not to jump immediately into overreaction mode until we've heard everything."

Rojas winced.

Cruz brought up a video. "Well, you weren't overreacting earlier this afternoon. This guy is definitely shady."

The video clip showed a man walking past the car more than once and not actually entering any stores, just the way Elisa had described.

"And he is definitely messing with your car," Cruz finished as the guy first kneeled down as if he'd dropped something and then lay down flat on the pavement, reaching underneath the car as if to retrieve it. "I want to take a closer look at this video feed on my computer at home before any of us actually go to the car."

"Okay." Elisa's response was in a small voice, not frightened but definitely subdued. "What do you think he did?"

"Well, the tires didn't look flat when we came through the parking lot tonight." Alex rubbed his chin.

A smile tugged at Elisa's mouth, and he looked at her askance, but she waved it away. "No flat tires is good. But what's the worst-case scenario?"

Not everyone would want to know, but Rojas could respect her preference. He'd want to know the worst, too.

"Could be something as dangerous as an explosive if we're talking worst case." Cruz delivered that bit of information in a flat tone. "But not likely in such a public place, with your ex messing with you the way he has been. If your ex wants you back, he's not going to want you back in pieces."

Well, probably not. Some stalking scenarios did escalate to deadly situations. None of them was an expert, but it didn't look like it'd gotten there yet. Rojas had a call in to a friend at the police department, though. Just in case.

"More likely, he placed a tracking device on your car." Cruz finished his assessment. "Quick to install and easy to figure out where you are any time."

"So what do we do next?" Elisa asked.

"Well, I have a police friend I want you to talk to." Rojas watched her closely. "We'll give this video to them, too, and file a police report."

Her eyelids shuttered half closed, and her face went blank. After a moment, she spoke quietly. "I went to the police when I first left. They kept asking me over and over again if I was certain I wanted to file a report, apply for a restraining order. Instead of writing down what I told them, they kept offering me counseling."

Son of a bitch. Even if her ex didn't have influence at the police department she'd gone to, receiving that kind of resistance had to have been frightening. But if her ex did have contacts in the police department, it gave an added level of complexity to the sort of person they were dealing with. Rojas filed it away to consider later.

Cruz broke the silence. "Can you give us your ex's full name and address? I think it's about time we find out what there is to know about him."

Elisa nodded. "I can tell you about his company and his educational background. He doesn't really have much in the way of family. Parents retired out of country."

Cruz tapped the desk thoughtfully. "I'm not as curious about his bio. Can you think of why he's willing to put so much effort into tracking you? Hiring people—that takes money and effort to find the right, discrete kind of people. It's a risk when it comes to his reputation."

Elisa opened her mouth and closed it, a couple of times. She started to rub one hand up and down her opposite forearm. Her wrist brace was going to leave scratches in the skin of her opposite arm.

"Why don't you tell me while we get you settled upstairs for the night?" Alex offered. "Cruz is probably going to be here with Gary's computer for a few more minutes."

Cruz nodded. "Any information is good, but I'm going to do some searches, too, to dig into any background you might not know about. Tell Rojas what you can think of in the meantime."

"Okay." Elisa paused. "His name is Joseph Corbin

Junior. Chief Information Officer of Corbin Systems. The company is global, but the headquarters are in California."

As she gave them both home and company addresses, Cruz made notes on a pad of paper and nodded. "Good enough to start. Let me get Gary's computer back up to decent speed and double-check the network security."

Basic information wasn't what was eating at her. She hadn't relaxed after leaving Cruz with that much.

"C'mon, you must be tired." Rojas gestured toward the back stairs up to the studio above the school.

"It's been a lot for one day." She looked around, somewhat twitchy.

He watched her, considering. "Gary and Greg are going to be here soon and stay the night. If anything triggers the security, the police will be here in minutes. You won't be alone. I'd stay, but Boom—"

"Oh, no. Boom needs you. You've already spent too much time today on me, and she's still recovering." Guilt tinged her words, and she started to open the door leading to the stairs.

"Hold up. Let us go first." He wanted to address the guilt she was feeling over taking him away from Boom, but he applied his focus to clearing the stairs and the upstairs area first.

Stairs were always the toughest to clear, especially narrow ones like these.

Cruz called from the office. "Camera feed shows the upstairs as clear."

Rojas relaxed a fraction but didn't speed his ascent, letting Souze take the lead. Knowing the cameras didn't pick up anything helped, but nothing replaced the accuracy of eyes on the area. A skilled intruder could see security cameras and hide.

Reaching the top of the stairs, it took him a few extra moments to pie the corner in such a tight space. Then they were going down the short hallway to the room Elisa was staying in and clearing it, too.

Task completed, Rojas returned to the top of the stairs and called down to Elisa. "Clear. You can come on up."

The security system was good. He'd told her so himself. The likelihood of an intruder hiding upstairs had been minimal. But considering the latest issues she'd been experiencing, he thought indulging his tendency for overkill wouldn't hurt and might even help her feel safer coming up to the guest room.

Once she joined them upstairs, she headed into the guest room. Rojas lingered in the doorway.

The conversation they'd been having downstairs seemed weird to pick up now, and he opened his mouth and closed it a couple of times with false starts. Talking. Not exactly his forte.

Any of his interactions with women over the last couple of years had been infrequent and brief, limited to meeting in a club or bar, maybe heading back to her place. But he'd never stay the night and never tried to see the woman again. Standing here, wanting a different kind of connection, he didn't know how to approach it.

Elisa turned to face him from the middle of the small room. She looked lost, tiny, standing there alone.

Clearing his throat, he pushed back the clumsy self-consciousness swamping his brain. "Do you mind if I come in?"

CHAPTER THIRTEEN

He stood there for a long moment waiting for her answer.

She blinked. Startled. "You were just in here."

Of course. He sounded incredibly stupid. "Yeah, but that was to be sure it was empty. Now you're in it."

Brilliant. As explanations went, it wasn't the best he'd ever made.

But Elisa smiled. "Thank you for the consideration." She hesitated, dropping her eyes. "And, yes, you can both come in."

"I'm betting Souze appreciates you including him in the invitation." Actually, Rojas really liked her tendency to keep the dog in mind.

"So." She glanced around, opened her mouth, and then closed it again.

Glad to know he wasn't the only one grasping for what to say. "So."

"There's more." Her voice came out low, almost a whisper.

"It's okay. You can tell me." Alex stood waiting, tried not to press in on her or add pressure.

"Joseph designed programs to integrate with weapons systems and he was planning to sell the code instead of securing it for the US government. It wasn't right." Once she got started, she kept talking in a hushed stream of strained words. "He...he had it all on a laptop, locked up in his research facility. But he always took me with him. I was his key, he said. The security system required my fingerprints and my retina imprint to pass through."

Son of a bitch. Well, this explained the added effort to get a hold of her. This ex of hers was a special kind of obsessed.

Elisa stood there, shoulders hunched and head down. A tear fell and hit the carpet.

"Hey." He bent to one side and craned his neck, trying to get into her line of sight without crowding her. "Elisa, it's good you told me. It's going to be okay."

Her eyes met his and she hiccupped, straightening suddenly and wiping away her tears with her palms. He wanted to be the one to help her brush away her tears.

"Anyway, I hated being any part of that. But it is probably important to know."

Alex nodded. "It is. And you should know, you didn't do anything wrong based on what you told me. You know that, right?"

She swallowed hard. "At first, I was excited to see where he worked and have access to the restricted areas. He'd told me his work would have a far-reaching impact. And it could, but not in a positive way. I didn't learn about that until later. Going into that research center was all I did. I just opened the access points. I wasn't a participant. I was just a key."

Alex couldn't think of what to say, so he just held out his hand, palm up.

She hesitated, then placed her hand in his and let him curl his fingers around her palm. He gave her a brief squeeze. Her hand was so small in his and yet her return grip was strong.

A minute later, she'd reassembled her calm.

"What time do you need me at work tomorrow?" She pulled out her phone and started to set an alarm.

"There's a morning training session here tomorrow at oh-seven-hundred." Easy answer. "I'll come by to train and then take you back with me. Sophie's bringing a bunch of baked goods to try on us for breakfast. I hope you like sweet things."

Elisa visibly brightened. "I'll look forward to it and to meeting Sophie. She seems to be around a lot. Finances for the kennels. Getting you all new shirts."

Danger. Red flags popped up inside his head. This was the sort of moment where his late wife would have been poised to jump all over him for mentioning another woman.

"Yeah. She and Forte go back a long way. They grew up together. There's a thing between them, but they're pretending there isn't." It was nice when the truth got him so neatly out from under a metaphorical bus.

"Ah." A spark of mischief entered her gaze, and her voice held a touch of anticipation. "Then I'll really look forward to meeting her. I like her taste."

"I think she'll like you, too. She's been on us to get

someone to organize our front desk forever and she'll
love the rest of the stuff you're doing." Actually, Rojas
wondered if he'd sidestepped one minefield for another.
Once Sophie met Elisa, Sophie was sure to subject him
to a serious interrogation.

He really didn't want to think too hard about the sorts
of questions Sophie would ask about Elisa yet. Mostly
because he was still feeling things out. Thinking too
hard made things complicated.

It was simpler to act. Like he had earlier. And he'd
very much enjoyed the kiss that had come out of it.

"So, tomorrow at seven, then." Elisa hesitated, then
turned to put her phone on the bedside table.

"Elisa." He waited until she looked up at him. He
dropped Souze's leash and took a few steps to cover the
distance between them and stopped.

After a moment's hesitation, Elisa took the final step
to close the space, putting her within easy arm's reach.

Warmth rushed through him at the sign of trust, ac-
ceptance. It was getting hotter in the room. Or maybe
that was just him.

He looked deeply into her expectant gaze.

No. Not only him.

He leaned forward and kissed her. Her lips were soft,
brushing against his first before pressing in for real contact. Then she opened for him and he tasted her. She was
honey sweet and hungry. She only let him tease her with
a few flicks of his tongue before she nipped at the corner
of his mouth and claimed a deeper kiss all on her own.

Enjoying himself, and her, he raised his hands to cup
her face, and she gasped.

Freezing, he opened his eyes. "Is this okay?"

Her eyes fluttered open—dizzy, and with a slight hint of panic. "Yes."

It wasn't quite the truth. Maybe not a lie, either, but he eased back anyway.

"Don't." Elisa lifted her own hands and gripped the front of his tee. "You're not scaring me. I might be scaring myself, but it's not you."

"And that's all right." He dropped his hands to her shoulders without pushing her away. "There's a lot going on, fast. And this, this isn't anything we need to rush."

"I . . ." She didn't ease her hold on the front of his tee.

"I can stop if you want. You can absolutely tell me to stop." It was important for her to know that. He didn't want to apply pressure. "And I can also be a friend, if you need 'friend' more."

It'd require a shit-ton of self-control, but he could do that for her. He wanted to at least be someone she could lean on if she needed to.

"No."

His heart stopped in his chest. He started to release her shoulders. He should go if he wasn't wanted. And good thing if they settled it right away like this. Tomorrow morning he'd come back as an easygoing friend and do his best to let her settle into a comfortable rhythm with him again.

But Elisa released his tee to press his hands against her shoulders. "No, I don't want you to stop. I just . . . need to find my way through every step as we go. And this between us is new, and complicated, and I don't want it to get twisted up in the process."

He grinned. Better. Much better than he'd thought. "We can take it slow."

She looked up at him through long, dark eyelashes. "You don't mind?"

"Not at all." Because aside from the kisses, he hadn't really thought it through, either. This was going to be complicated from a couple of different angles, on both sides.

She smiled then, rising up on tiptoes to kiss him again. He was really starting to like her kisses. Especially when she placed her hands on the waistband of his jeans and tugged him closer, tipping her head back and angling it for an even deeper kiss.

He slid his hands over her shoulders and down her back. Time was starting to slip away, and he was more than happy to ignore its existence.

Then a dog whined.

Elisa jerked back like she'd been splashed with cold water. "Oh. I. Uh…"

He raked his hand through his hair. "Yeah. Uh."

He turned to regard Souze, still dutifully sitting in the doorway, staring right at them. The dog might be drunk on the pheromones in the room because his jaw hung open in a doggy grin.

"Not really into canine voyeurism." Elisa sounded breathless and hell, his ability to speak clearly wasn't in the best shape, either.

Mostly, his brain was scrambled. His pants also felt about three sizes too tight around the groin area.

"Rojas. You ready to go? Gary and Greg checked in; they'll be here any minute." Cruz's voice came floating up the stairs.

A beat of silence. "So did Souze whine because things were getting intense or because he heard Cruz coming to the stairs?" Elisa asked.

"Actually, I don't know." Rojas considered himself a good trainer, and he could read canine body language most of the time. But there just wasn't any way to know this time what exactly had nudged Souze to whine when he did.

"Well." Elisa let out a soft laugh. "Good timing either way, I guess."

Maybe. He was still arguing with the raging hard-on he had at the moment.

"I guess you guys are going to head back now. Boom's going to need to take her medicine before bedtime." Her voice had gone softer, but he heard the tremor anyway.

He turned back to her and brushed a stray lock of dark hair from her face. She'd be here by herself, and he really didn't want to leave her alone if at all possible. And he also appreciated that Boom was at the forefront of both their otherwise chemistry-distracted minds.

Inspiration struck. "Why don't I leave Souze here with you?"

Her eyes widened. "Really?"

"Sure." He jerked his head back to indicate the dog. "He's already demonstrated good behavior in your company, and it doesn't hurt to give him some exposure to a night outside his kennel. It's not like the two of you even have to leave this room. Cruz and I will lock up."

The relief was palpable in her expression, the tiny wrinkles between her brows clearing. "I mean, just the company would make a difference, I think."

He nodded. "If there's any issues at all, call us. If you hear anything outside or if he starts to fuss in here, it's no problem. Just hit my number on speed dial."

"Okay." She smiled.

"Rojas!" Cruz amped up his call a couple of decibels.

"Yeah!" Rojas called back over his shoulder. "On my way."

Elisa rose up on her tiptoes and kissed him, then gave him a decent shove. "Go on. And thank you."

* * *

Rojas murmured a quiet command and shut the door behind him.

"Doesn't hurt to lock it," he called back, muffled by the wood between them. "Gary and Greg have a room down in the basement so they won't disturb you."

Both Elisa and Souze stood staring at the closed door, listening to the sounds of Rojas and Cruz greeting Gary and Greg. Then her new friends were turning off the lights and locking up the school downstairs. When she couldn't hear any more, she watched Souze as the big dog continued to stare at the door, apparently still listening. After a few more minutes, Souze sat and looked at her.

"Don't ask me what we're supposed to do now. I've no idea." Elisa looked into those liquid, dark eyes and wondered what the big dog was thinking.

Souze seemed to be considering her, too. Or maybe she fancied he was.

After another minute, she crossed over to him. "Let me at least take off the leash so you don't drag it around behind you."

Souze watched her as she approached, and she decided it'd be prudent to move slowly as she reached for his collar and unclipped the leash. There was a tension. Not something she saw in his body language, but she felt it, and it eased once she backed away again. Casual petting was probably not going to be a thing.

"I should have listened more closely to the commands Alex used." Even if she wasn't using them, she decided to speak directly to Souze. It was what came naturally, and, at the very least, the dog would go along with natural. Right?

It was still better than being alone.

"Having you here is a hundred times better than the first night I was out on my own," she told Souze.

Or the nights after.

She grabbed up her big purse and set it at the foot of the bed. Then she unzipped her overnight bag and pulled out a few toiletries.

"I didn't unpack last night." Talking to Souze as she went about her business was actually a lot more relaxing than the silence she'd moved through the night before. At least then, though, she'd been tired enough to have fallen asleep listening to the late night class below. She hadn't heard Gary and Greg lock up for the night. Hadn't realized when she'd been left alone.

A cold, wet touch at her wrist made her jump. Souze backed away and sat again. She stood there, mouth open. "You can't pretend you didn't move. You're about five feet from where you were sitting before."

He sat there, ears up, looking about as innocent as a really big dog could. *So?*

"Did you want to sniff?" She held out her hand in a loose fist the way Alex had instructed her the first time.

Souze didn't move.

She stared at him.

Nope. Still not moving.

Then she realized she was trying to get into a staring match with a dog as if some sort of telepathic communication was going to occur. And Alex had told her not to make eye contact.

Following her line of thought, she continued to hold out her hand but awkwardly turned the rest of her body back toward her bag and resumed fishing around in there for her sleep shirt and sweat pants. She froze as a cool, wet touch brushed over her knuckles.

Souze sniffed her hand, her wrist, and a warm tongue briefly licked her fingertips before the air around her hands turned cold with his retreat.

"Did I pass inspection?" She used both her hands to gather her stuff and faced him again.

He was back to sitting, ears up, but now his head was cocked at an angle, giving him an inquisitive expression.

"I'm going to take a quick shower." She walked past him to the bathroom and stopped in the doorway. Just as she spun to face him, there he was again. Sitting. Facing her. Definitely closer to the bathroom than he had been before. Apparently, the wonderfully cushy carpet allowed the dog super stealth. "You do not need to accompany me into the shower."

She stepped backward into the bathroom and closed the door in his face.

Briefly, she leaned her forehead against the door and laughed. Quietly. This had been a day of ups and downs, and her heart might not survive the crazy flip-flop moments interspersed with bad scares. But this taste of the ridiculous was kind of fun.

Alex had done her a big favor leaving Souze with her. Beyond the security he provided, the company was invaluable. And she could not thank Alex enough for the amount of consideration he'd given her since the moment she'd met him. If she thought back, so many of his actions had been kind and generous, even when he hadn't any idea of who she was or if he'd ever see her again. There'd been no good reason for him to invest the effort.

Despite his intimidating exterior, he was a good man. Maybe that was why her gut told her she could accept Alex's help while her logical thought process repeatedly reminded her how much trouble it could get her into.

There was a lot of anger in him. She'd seen it a couple of times. And she absolutely could see it a mile away. That ability had developed over the last few years with her ex as a survival skill. But Alex kept it on a tight leash, controlled, and never directed it at his daughter as far as she could tell. Boom didn't show even the slightest fear of her father. If anything, Boom was the kind of bright and energetic child who might be allowed somewhat more license to go wild than she should be. So far, Alex hadn't directed his temper at Elisa, either. He'd stopped himself a couple of times, even. Visibly struggled. But hadn't exploded.

If anything, knowing it was there made him more trustable in her eyes. She'd rather see it there, below the surface, than completely hidden and likely to burst out without any warning.

Besides, his anger wasn't the only way Alex Rojas burned hot.

The memory of his kisses was enough to send her

into the shower. As the water ran over her, she remembered how much she'd enjoyed his mouth on hers, and it wasn't quite as embarrassing. No idea why, but there it was. The only issue was the way her imagination ran away with the remembered feel of his hands on her shoulders, her back, and took it further. She wanted him to hold her, slide his hands over her, and use his mouth all over.

Reaching out, she turned the taps to a cooler temperature. She could keep imagining things and maybe even give herself some relief. Nothing wrong with that. But then she'd be wobbly getting out of the shower and there was also a really big dog between her and the bed.

She was fairly certain he would absolutely know what she'd been up to. And the thought squicked her out.

When she did finally open the door to the bathroom dressed in her sleep clothes, Souze was still sitting there. His mouth was open and his tongue lolled out a little.

"Please tell me you're not laughing at me." She walked past him and repacked her overnight bag. No idea how long she'd be staying, but if her bag wasn't packed and ready, if an emergency came up, she'd have to leave things behind.

Luckily, she had what was left of her savings with her in her shoulder bag. But she needed to brainstorm a few ideas as to where she could keep emergency money in case she had to leave *everything* and make a break for it.

"It's only been forty-eight hours or so and Alex has already taught me way more than I realized I didn't know when I decided to leave." She started to turn down the bed, addressing Souze over her shoulder. "I mean, I got a few pamphlets, so I had an idea of what to plan to do before I left. Really left. But he's had a lot of good suggestions, too."

When she glanced back at Souze, he was still giving her his doggie grin. His tail swept the carpet back and forth once. *Tock-tock.*

Tail wagging was a good sign, as far as she knew.

Encouraged, she kept talking. "So I'll follow his example and keep trying to think of the worst-case scenario."

She climbed into the bed and turned out the small lamp on the nightstand. Through the darkness came the soft, reassuring sound of Souze panting.

"Then I'll have to come up with ways to anticipate those scenarios and plan actions to mitigate the circumstances." Yeah. It could be a promise to herself. A way she could act on her own fate.

"Good night, Souze."

CHAPTER FOURTEEN

Boom good for the night?"

Rojas nodded tiredly, joining Forte and Cruz in his living room. Forte handed him a beer. "She's gotten pretty far with her poster boards for her project. Apparently, the paint just has to dry and then she can work with Elisa tomorrow to fold paper into planets and light them up with earrings."

Cruz almost spit beer. "Come again?"

"Hey, it was Elisa's crafty plan." Rojas waved his beer bottle in the general direction of Revolution MMA. "She can come over tomorrow and show Boom how to do it."

"Elisa is good people." Cruz leaned forward and opened up his laptop.

Forte grunted agreement. "The dogs like her."

Rojas nodded. "I left Souze with her."

Forte raised his eyebrows. "Yeah?"

Rojas shrugged. "They're not leaving the one room, and he's not going to have to go out before morning.

He's housebroken and more than qualified for guard dog duty. She doesn't have any of the nervous tics that'd make him snap at her. Should be fine."

"He's not taking to the bite work readily." Forte leaned back and stared at the ceiling. "We've been giving him some time, but we're going to need to think of alternative careers for that dog."

Generally, alternatives meant they either found a home for the dog in question or sold him to a private buyer. With his training, Souze was valuable and could still live a long life as a guard dog. Preferably, a guard dog in far better circumstances than his initial environment. They took care to place any of their dogs in good homes.

"Maybe." Rojas didn't want to commit. He'd grown attached to the bruiser. Even if he didn't want to admit it. "It's not like he's all that sociable."

"Try not at all." Cruz snorted. "That dog had next to no socialization before he got here."

"But he got along with Elisa." Both Forte and Cruz looked up at him incredulously. He amended his statement. "In a standoffish sort of way."

Both men looked away again, Cruz to his laptop and Forte to the ceiling.

After a moment, Cruz spoke. "You're getting attached to him."

Tough part of training dogs for a living was risking the attachment. A trainer wanted to develop enough of a bond to train the dog well, prepare him for a tough job, and give him enough positive experience to bond well with a future handler. But some dogs got a little deeper.

Rojas didn't want to talk about Souze further. Not with more pressing points of interest to discuss. Instead he shared the information Elisa had given him about the additional reasons why Joseph Corbin Jr. was trying so hard to get a hold of her.

After an appropriate amount of cursing, Rojas looked at his partners. "What have you got from the camera feed?"

Cruz gave him a long, knowing look, then tapped his laptop. "We're lucky Gary and Greg are tech addicts even if they don't always keep their systems at optimal performance. They have good-quality cameras so their captured feed is in high resolution. I was able to capture a few stills from the video feed. Good enough to take to the police and see if they get any hits on him. Chances are he placed surveillance equipment intending to track her the next time she drove somewhere. She's too valuable to just blow the car up with her in it."

Rojas nodded.

"We'll also run the images around to a few personal friends still active in the information business." Cruz popped a few pictures up of the man so they could see his face in profile and head on. "He's good enough to seem casual but not skilled enough to spot the less obvious security cameras like the ones Gary and Greg like to use. Probably your average hired help. Maybe a civilian private investigator or similar."

Considering their last round of excitement had involved ex-Navy SEALs, Rojas was glad to hear the good news. The three of them could more than handle themselves. They'd been through hell and back multiple times each, deployed overseas. Serving together had made them brothers. But they didn't like to go head to head with anyone if it wasn't necessary.

"That said, private investigators cost money." Forte leaned forward, bracing his elbows on his knees. "What else do we know about our Elisa's ex besides what he was up to?"

Rojas shot Forte a look. Part of him, the thug evolved from caveman part, wanted to clarify that Elisa was his. But Forte remained relaxed and lifted his beer to Rojas.

Asshole. Forte was jerking his chain on purpose.

Cruz, probably aware of the interchange, chose to ignore them both. Easy for him. He had a steady sex life. Love life. Whatever. Cruz was happy, and he deserved to be.

"Our new friend, Joseph Corbin Junior, runs a tight ship over at Corbin Systems as the Chief Information Officer." Cruz pulled up a couple more windows on his laptop's screen.

Rojas didn't lean in to look. Unless there was a picture of the guy, Rojas would do better hearing the briefing as opposed to trying to read it on the limited real estate of the laptop screen.

"Looks like his business is definitely in information systems and content management," Cruz continued. "There's a wide range of publicly disclosed projects, but the company also holds a fair number of government and military contracts."

And obviously there were a few pet projects.

"Elisa did mention security clearances, didn't she?" Rojas briefly pondered, getting himself a notepad, then discarded the idea. He'd lose the notes anyway. Better for Cruz to keep it all organized and Rojas could review the information later on his own computer. His strengths were in active situations, and he'd had to review briefing data in the past. He could do it again.

Cruz only nodded before pulling up the next set of information. "Junior himself graduated Ivy League, high honors. Recommendations on his online professional profile all describe him as extremely detail-oriented and a strong leader."

Amazing what those professional networking sites could tell you about a person nowadays.

"His work history is all with Corbin Systems. Started at entry level and worked his way up in Daddy's company. Learned the business from the basement up to the corner office." Cruz straightened for a minute and rolled his shoulders before leaning in to the laptop again. "Good old Dad is still the CEO, but Junior runs the company in all but name, looks like."

"So we've got a man used to being the leader, no questions asked." Forte tapped the top of his beer bottle to his chin as he thought through the possible conclusions. "Probably a control freak, since most stalkers are, and Elisa wouldn't have bailed if it hadn't gotten bad."

Cruz tapped another couple of keys. "She did try to make a couple of police reports. Just like she said, they got buried. Counseling was recommended, but all of those counselors were affiliated with Corbin Systems' human resources division. Saves on insurance fees, apparently."

"He kept her fairly well corralled." Forte sounded impressed. "Family thinks he's the best thing since sliced bread and dismisses her as having anxiety issues. She herself has got some heavy-duty confidence problems now, too."

"I think she'll bounce back given the chance," Rojas tossed out.

"I don't doubt it." Forte nodded. "She's like a whirl-wind in the front reception area. All of our clients like her, and she's reduced our paperwork to a fraction of what it was. The only complaint she voiced to me was a need for matching pens. Good pens, with blue or black ink."

There was a beat of silence.

"So our Elisa is somewhat detail-oriented herself," Cruz ventured. "And apparently, she started at Corbin Systems at entry level, too. By that time, though, Junior was a VP. He had some heavy-duty influence already, aside from being the CEO's kid."

"Enough to get HR to look in the other direction." Forte was enjoying piecing the story together. A lot of it was conjecture, but all three of them were used to piecing together fragments of information to visualize an overall image.

Chances were, they were right.

"So Elisa finally decides to leave." Rojas took up the story at the key turning point.

"And she's successful," Forte added.

Impressive on its own.

"But Junior keeps finding her." Cruz brought up a few less publicly available files, from the color of the headers on the windows.

Rojas recognized the color system because Cruz tended to use the same categorization they used back when they'd all been active duty and reading their way through briefing reports.

"Some of it is his company resources." Cruz began scrolling in the file. "But some of this... I'm not seeing exactly how he found her jump out at me. Elisa is a quick learner, and she doesn't seem to make the same mistake twice."

"If she did, he'd have her back by now." It made Rojas angry to point it out.

"I can see him locating her by IP, even tracing her phone since he's got some influence with the police in his area." Cruz sat up and his eyebrows drew together in a scowl. "But he's found her several times, and he likes to play cat and mouse. He's gotten her number even when she hasn't checked her e-mails, based on what I can find in her back trail."

Cruz was an impressive IT specialist himself. Rojas didn't doubt Cruz had been able to backtrack through the Internet to see where Elisa had come from and thus also see how her pursuers were finding her.

But Elisa had family, and even if they hadn't believed her, supported her, she seemed too caring a person to leave them worried about her. "Can we pull her call records?"

"I can't with the databases I have access to. Hacking those could draw federal attention." Cruz shook his head. "But the police might be able to with a warrant if we can convince them to be somewhat more open about investigation than they normally are. We'd need to call in a few favors."

They'd supplied K9s to several of the police departments in the surrounding region and others across the country. Those officers would at least be starting points.

Forte finished his beer. "It'd be good to see who Elisa tends to call."

"I'll ask her tomorrow, too." Rojas preferred to get his intel direct from the source, and he didn't think Elisa would hide it from them. Or if she did, they'd have to reevaluate the situation.

"We'll look into it from this end, anyway." Cruz typed a few notes to himself on his laptop. "She might not realize she's following a pattern."

But humans were creatures of habit. Her ex was exploiting Elisa's patterns. The difference, the break in the pattern, was that Elisa had met Rojas.

"Tomorrow morning, I'll take Souze around the shopping center area and parking lot. I wanted to see what we got out of the video before doing a direct sweep and we won't stand out as much during the day if he's keeping an eye on the shopping strip. At the very least, we'll see if Souze can tell if the same scent by the car is anywhere else in the vicinity." Rojas paused. "Even better if we can find a piece of fabric or some other souvenir our snooper might've left under the car. We'll see if he actually left something for surveillance and remove it if he did. His scent should be all over it."

He'd take one of those fake rocks sold to hide house keys just in case he did find something and put the device in there. Then he'd leave it under the car so Elisa's stalker would think it was still on her car. If they needed to move her car in a hurry, they'd be able to without having to worry about a potential tracking device.

"I've redirected the video feed from the school to our network so we can keep real-time watch on the location, both outside and inside the school. Elisa's fine, by the way. Hasn't left the room." Cruz brought up a few video windows showing dark night and dimly lit areas.

"I copied some older video streams from last month into the cache directory. If her ex or his employees get nosey enough to hack into Revolution's system, all they'll see is normal footage. No sneak peeks of Elisa. I renamed the files so it'd look like the cached feeds from this week. I'll update them daily. Somebody might hack in, but they won't know the video feeds are from a prior month."

"Nice." Rojas lifted his beer to Cruz.

"So do we leave Elisa there?" Forte studied Rojas. "Our response time is going to be slow if she needs us."

Rojas frowned. He hadn't liked leaving her there tonight, even with Souze. Sure, he'd given her reassurances about police response time and the proximity of Gary and Greg, but it wasn't the same as direct intervention by him, Forte, and Cruz.

Rojas hesitated. But damn, Boom liked Elisa already and it was better than leaving her far away. He wanted her close and they could protect her best with her near. "She could come stay here."

Both Forte and Cruz stared at him.

True, he'd never welcomed a stranger into his home here at Hope's Crossing. He never brought a woman on the property, for damned sure. He hadn't ever wanted to put Boom through added stress after her mother died, especially if he wasn't ever serious about the occasional woman he did see. Hell, even Sophie rarely came into his house. Mostly Sophie ran riot through the main building and Forte's place. But what else could he do for Elisa?

"I'm good with that plan if you are," Forte said slowly. "I want to gather more intel on stalker-ex tonight."

"Let's ask her whether she feels safe here, too." Rojas took his first sip of his now warm beer. "I'm thinking she's had enough decisions made on her behalf. I think we can give her options but ultimately, she's got to decide on her own."

They all nodded in agreement.

"This is a lot of effort for a new administrative assistant." Forte set his beer on the table with a clink.

"Yeah, well, Cruz set the bar high when he brought in a supplemental training consultant," Rojas drawled. "Anyone good enough to work at Hope's Crossing is going to take some investment to make sure they stay."

Cruz held up his hands. "Hey, Lyn runs her own consulting business. She lends a hand nowadays, but I didn't request her in the first place."

Forte grinned. "I'm going to tell her you said so."

"Do and prepare for serious consequences," growled Cruz.

Lyn had a fairly formidable personality of her own. The best trainers always did, especially with the types of dogs they worked with. Considering the level of dominance and aggression working dogs had, a trainer had to have the kind of personality to not only dominate but win the dog's trust.

Thinking of Souze, Rojas amended his thought. Some dogs took longer than others. But he was making progress with Souze.

He could use the same patience with Elisa, and he had the gut feeling she was worth every bit as much effort. More.

* * *

"Welcome to Philadelphia, Mr. Corbin. I hope your flight was smooth."

Joseph Corbin Jr. settled into the back of the town car without bothering to glance at the young woman already seated inside. "Baggage handling is slow as ever."

"It is." The assistant made a sympathetic noise. "The driver will bring your bag as soon as it comes up on the carousel and we'll get you to your hotel. Your contractor will be ready to meet you first thing in the morning."

"No," Joseph snapped. "He'll meet with me tonight. I want an update and confirmation that my item of interest is ready for acquisition."

There was a moment of hesitation, then, "Of course. I'll arrange for a meeting at the hotel tonight."

It was already late at night, but his man wasn't far away from the city. Joseph stared out at the bustling Arrivals pick-up lanes. The East Coast was supposed to move at a faster pace than the California lifestyle but whenever he visited his offices either in Philadelphia or DC, all he saw was an insane amount of traffic. Not much different from LA. He preferred the steadier climate and temperatures back in California.

What had possessed Elisa to run here?

It didn't matter. Phase 1 of his highest priority project had completed this week, ahead of schedule. They were on the brink of finalizing the statement of work on Phase 2. It was time for Elisa to come home, where she belonged. He needed her.

"Arrange for a second contract, different vendor." He reached over and tapped the surface of the assistant's tablet. "I want a backup team on standby to ensure my item is acquired as soon as possible."

CHAPTER FIFTEEN

Elisa slept better than she had in months. That didn't mean she hadn't woken up in the middle of the night. More than once. But each time, the presence of Souze was a reassurance. He'd have given some sort of alert if something wasn't right.

The phone Alex had given her was another reassuring presence, cool and slim, just under her pillow.

One signal from Souze and she could call Alex for help.

As a result, every time she'd awakened, she'd been able to slip back into sleep. Free of fear and more quickly than those heart-pounding, agonizing late night hours she'd spent second-guessing herself and wondering if she should roll out of bed, get in her car, and keep driving.

So it took her a few seconds to come to her senses when she woke up slowly to the sound of snuffling, followed by a long sigh right next to her ear.

Groggy, she opened her eyes and turned her head, wondering what could be right...

A big, wet, black nose was inches from hers.

She sat straight up, and Souze backed away from the edge of the bed, sitting with his ears tipped back, scanning the room. Maybe he was looking around for whatever had startled her.

"You." She swallowed against a sleep-dry throat. "I didn't realize you were tall enough to have your head on the bed without even putting your paws up here."

Souze tilted his head then rose to his four feet, stepping forward and extending his head right over the edge of the bed to touch her hand with his nose. Damn, but he was a big dog.

"No need to prove it again." She grabbed the clothes she'd worn yesterday, because she didn't have anything else, and swung her legs over to set them on the floor. "I'm guessing you need to go out?"

Souze only sat again and stared at her expectantly.

Well, he wasn't going to start talking to her, but a bark or soft woof or something might have helped give her a clue.

Maybe not. She didn't exactly speak dog, and this wasn't a movie or television show. But Souze was a smart dog. And she, theoretically, was an intelligent human. If Alex Rojas, Brandon Forte, and David Cruz could figure out what their dogs were thinking, then she should at least be able to figure out one instance of Souze trying to communicate with her.

He had to be. Otherwise, he wouldn't have woken her up. All night, she'd heard nothing but the occasional rustle as he laid down or changed position on the rug next to her bed. Each of those times had been right after she'd tossed or turned in bed. Otherwise, he'd been extraordinarily quiet for something his size. All of her ex's guard dogs had been the type to bark. A lot.

Souze was both different and more than them, in her opinion. And since the moment she'd met him, he hadn't exactly been generous with the direct tactile contact.

It'd be worth an experiment to see if she could get a clearer response out of him. Standing, she headed to the door and placed her hand on the knob as she craned her neck to watch Souze. As soon as her fingertips touched the rounded surface of the doorknob, he came to his feet and wagged his tail once.

"That's pretty clear, then." She wondered if he could hold it a minute or two longer. "Just let me swap clothes and get a bra on, then we'll head downstairs. Hopefully, Gary and Greg are already down there and they can let us out the back door."

Alex had told her not to go outside until he'd returned in the morning, but she couldn't very well leave Souze in distress. She personally hated the feeling of needing a restroom and having to wait. Didn't seem fair not to care about Souze in a similar circumstance. Besides, she really didn't know how good the dog's discipline would be, and she didn't want him ruining the nice carpet up here. Somewhat gross, but could she get him to stand in the shower?

She'd prefer not to try the option. Instead, she hustled into the bathroom and splashed her face with cold water. Then she grabbed the hem of her sleep tee and started to pull it up over her head.

A quiet knock sounded at the door. "Elisa, are you awake? It's Alex."

She yanked the tee back down. Turning to Souze, she asked, "Did you know he was here?"

Souze only gave her a doggie grin.

Maybe that was why the dog had woken her. *Gah.* Either way, she needed to get a bra on.

Or maybe there were other priorities. Giving Souze a look, she rushed to the door, scooping up the leash. Undoing the deadlock and the lighter lock on the door-knob, she cracked open the door. Alex stood on the other side, dressed in a black Revolution MMA tee and gym shorts. It'd be interesting to ask him how many of those he had later. She shoved Souze's leash through the door. "Here."

Alex regarded the leash. "Um. There's supposed to be a dog attached to the other end."

True. And she had no idea whether Souze would let her put it back on again. "Give me five seconds to get into the bathroom, then you can come in and grab Souze. I'll meet you both downstairs."

There was a pause. "Five seconds it is. Should I count out loud?"

Oh, Alex was extremely entertained. She could hear the amusement in his voice even if he wasn't outright laughing. "Out loud can't hurt."

With that, she bolted past Souze for the bathroom, slipped inside, and shut the door.

Good for his word, Alex counted out loud. He even gave her a play-by-play account of what he was doing once he finished counting.

"I'm coming in now."

"I've got Souze."

"We're leaving now, and I'm closing the door behind us."

Great. Fantastic. She still waited until they both left
to actually go to the bathroom.

*   *   *

Rojas made it downstairs and caught sight of Cannon.
There were chances that'd passed Rojas by over the
years, and this was one of those moments he didn't want
to let pass him by just because he was too much of a gen-
tleman to give a woman an option she hadn't considered.

"Hey, Cannon." Rojas waved the man over. "You owe
me from yesterday."

"Huh?" Cannon walked over. Luckily, the man still
had his shoes on.

"Do me a favor and take Souze out to do his morning
business. When he's done, he can come back here and
hang out over in the corner while you guys train." Rojas
turned to head up the stairs. Cannon was a capable handler for a little while. Souze would be fine.

Cannon called a question after him, but he didn't answer. He didn't care what anyone thought, and possibly
he'd be right back down in about thirty seconds. But he
was hoping not.

He knocked on the door and heard a very muffled surprise squeak. After a few seconds, Elisa opened the door,
her hair in adorable disarray. Her eyes were narrowed.
"Did you forget something?"

He cleared his throat. Not exactly the reception he'd
been hoping for. "Did I do something wrong?"

Her cheeks colored, and she looked anywhere but at him. "No. You just have . . . interesting timing."

Oh, now there were some possibilities.

"Well, if I'm timely, maybe there's something I could help with." He smiled, nice and slow, enjoying the way her gaze zeroed in on his mouth when she finally looked at him.

"I do not need help getting my shirt off." The words tumbled out, and her eyes widened as she clapped a hand over her mouth.

It surprised a laugh out of him. "If you don't need help, can I watch instead?"

She narrowed her eyes again and uncovered her mouth, which was good because he liked looking at it and imagining naughty things. "Almost every time I'm about to take off my shirt, you've managed to knock on the door."

"I am sincerely sad I wasn't aware of this situation." He took a chance and stepped forward. She gave way, letting the door open and allowing him inside the room. "Is there any way I can make it up to you?"

Heat flashed in her eyes, and her lips parted. His groin tightened in response, and he decided it'd be good to lock the door after he closed it behind him. Uncertainty flickered across her expression then and he froze.

Reining in his raging hormones, he said slowly, "Any time you want things to stop, I will. I promise. I won't be angry. I will back off."

She swallowed, and a fraction of tension left her shoulders. "I don't want to lead you on."

"I want to be here." He smiled, gave her time to gain confidence again. He found her grumpy morning personality hot, challenging, fun. "We go as far as you're comfortable, and I will consider myself a lucky, lucky man."

The heat came back into her gaze, and she licked her lower lip. "I was going to take a shower."

His cock came to attention immediately. "That is a great idea."

And none of the knuckleheads downstairs would hear a thing. Not that he cared for himself, but for her sake, they didn't need to know what was going on or even that she was up here. Not this morning.

He waited, though, and thought he might strain a muscle holding still until she took a hesitant step, then another toward him. He held out his hands to her, and she placed hers in his, gently tugging him toward the close privacy of the bathroom.

Closed inside, he'd normally chafe at the tiny room, but right now he was completely focused on Elisa. She was facing him, searching his eyes with her cloudy blue gaze. Emotions swirled in a maelstrom through her, and he figured she could ask him to stop at any moment. Until she did, he wanted to give her as much pleasure as he could.

He reached out to touch the hem of her shirt, but she beat him to it and pulled the tee off in a smooth motion. His knees almost buckled on seeing her smooth shoulders, ivory skin, and very pretty breasts. He'd figured she hadn't had a bra on under her tee, but suddenly having her right there, exposed to him, was a sight to feast on.

Pulling a few brain cells together was almost painful, but he did and realized she was nervously waiting for him. So he figured fair was fair. Moving slow, he stripped off his T-shirt, too, taking his time so she could get an eyeful.

And she did. Her eyes widened as she caught sight of the workout holster he wore strapped around his torso, but she didn't back away. Instead she watched him closely as he removed it and set it carefully on the floor next to his discarded tee. Then he straightened, and her gaze followed him. She stared, taking in his chest and abs, before reaching out and running her hands over him. Her touch sent shocks of heat coursing through him and he closed his eyes to just enjoy it at first.

Her touch was featherlight, and he couldn't keep his hands to himself anymore. Opening his eyes again so he could see as well as touch, he started at her shoulders, caressing and learning the ultra-softness of her skin. The sight of his darker, tanned hands on her pale skin was only one contrast of many, and he wanted to explore them all with her. He moved his hands down her back until he settled his grip in the small of her back and gently pulled her close.

She closed her eyes as he did, splaying her hands across his chest and tipping her head back in invitation. He bent, brushing his lips over the temptation of hers and going lower to press his lips to the hollow of her throat. She uttered a tiny gasp and he smiled as he licked at her pulse point with the tip of his tongue. Encouraged by the sound, and planning to experiment to hear even more, he licked again. Just a flick against her skin. Fine tremors ran through her when he did and he experimented, kissing and licking his way up the side of her neck to her ear before he captured her earlobe and sucked gently.

He liked her little moans, guessed she didn't realize

just how responsive she was, and delighted in the way she responded to the barest of touches.

She was gasping when he finally settled his mouth on hers, teasing her gently with his tongue until her fingers dug into his chest. Desire flared as she did and he struggled to keep his grip on her firm but not painful. Then he deepened the kiss to match her hunger and sent them both drowning in the heat of it.

She tore free of his mouth, tilting her face up to look at him, her eyes stormy and wild. Her chest lifted as she tried to catch her breath, and he gave her the moment, easing his hold on her until she leaned back against the bathroom counter for support. Reaching into the shower, he flipped on the water.

She'd gathered herself during the brief respite, and he was very happy the hunger was still in her gaze. Biting her lip, holding his gaze, she hooked her thumbs in her oh-so-loose sweat pants and pushed them down off her hips, revealing very pretty blue lace panties.

He groaned. "Do you want to keep those?"

Her eyes widened. "I need to take them off to shower and...other things."

He leaned forward, bracing his hands on the counter at either side of her hips to keep them busy until he could clarify. Her breath puffed hot against his collarbone, and his scrambled brain registered how petite she was compared to him, how well she'd fit tucked against him. "If you want to keep them, tell me. Otherwise, they're going to end up in pieces."

Her lips shaped a very lovely *O* for a moment, and her answer came in a bare whisper. "I don't have many pairs right now, and I kind of like these."

"I like them, too." He knelt in front of her and very carefully slid them down. "Let's put these someplace safe. Okay?"

She lifted each foot for him as she gave him a breathless agreement.

Panties safely tucked into his pocket, because they could totally get lost in the bathroom, he returned his attention to her very lovely legs. She had slender ankles and muscle to her calves and thighs. Like she'd been in shape for a long time and only recently had gone sleek. He alternated between running his hands over her skin and gripping the muscles of her calves, the backs of her legs, until she was the one clutching the edge of the counter.

When he thought he might have some sort of control, he discovered a very hot secret. She kept herself immaculately groomed. Shaved. He pressed his mouth to the smooth lips between her legs. She sucked in air and held it.

He traced the edges of her labia with a gentle finger. "Breathe. We don't want you passing out."

"No?" she whispered.

"Uh uh. You are not going to want to miss this." He leaned forward and tasted her.

A whimper escaped her throat, and he smiled as he spread her for better access and took a long lick, then another. She trembled for him.

"You taste so good, Elisa. So, so good." He feasted then, licking and sucking as she gasped and tried to muffle her moans. The muscles in her thighs strained, and he gripped one thigh with his free hand to hold her open to his teasing.

He continued to torture her in the best of ways for as long as he could stand it, but he couldn't wait much longer. He slid a finger inside her and groaned as her wet heat clamped tight around him. He used his thumb to rub over her clitoris as he gently moved his finger inside her. He looked up the length of her body; she had her head thrown back, abandoning herself to the sensations he was giving her. Oh god, he shouldn't have looked up at her.

He wanted to be inside her.

Standing again, he admired the rosy nipples presented to him for a split second before he took one in his mouth, wrapping his free hand around her waist to steady her. Yelping, she brought her head up and clutched at his shoulder with one hand.

He continued to move his finger inside her, changing the rhythm of his thumb against her clitoris as she muffled her cries against his neck.

"Let go, Elisa," he murmured reverently. "Come for me, because I want to come for you."

Her fingers dug harder into his shoulder, and she stiffened. He kept his finger sliding in and out inside her, his thumb rubbing against her clitoris. Suddenly, she bucked against his hand, her inner muscles convulsing around his finger.

"Easy." He soothed her as he stroked her through the orgasm, lengthening it as best he could.

Her eyes were glazed when she finally lifted her head and looked at him. He smiled. "Enjoy."

Her smile was sweet, satisfied, as she nodded.

"Do you want to again?" He leaned forward until his forehead touched hers.

Her eyes widened. "But what about you?"

"Only if you want me." He ran his hands over the curves of her hips, enjoying the fine tremors still running through her. "I'm enjoying what I'm doing to you."

She ran her hands over his chest again, tracing her fingers over his abs and along the diagonal lines from the outside of his hips to his groin until she hit the obstacle of his shorts. The tip of his cock was peeking out above the waistband, and she teased him with her fingertips.

When she looked up at him, her lips were moist. "I want you."

"Yes, ma'am." He smiled, helping her undo the drawstring and letting his shorts fall to the floor. Reaching past her into the medicine cabinet, he retrieved a foil-wrapped condom. "Gary and Greg believe in stocking for any emergencies."

She gave him a wry smile in return.

He lifted his eyebrows in a dissembling expression. "Hey, it's against their rules for any of the guys to just bring any girl up here, but there can always be extenuating circumstances."

She ran her nails over his chest lightly and looked delighted when his cock jumped in response. "Like now?"

"Like now," he growled back.

Her gaze found his, clear and sure. "Come inside me, Alex. I want this."

He tore open the wrapper and rolled the condom on. Placing a hand on either side of her hips, he lifted her onto the counter and pressed forward between her legs. She reached down between them and helped him fit the tip of his cock into her entrance. Then she held on to his shoulders.

"Ready?" All he could manage was a strained whisper at this point.

She nodded. "More than ready. Please."

He slid into her, straining to go slow, but she was so tight around him he almost lost it right then and there. Somehow, he kept his control and he was buried to the hilt inside her listening to her moan. He took a breath to clear his head, and another, and then he began to grind his hips into her.

"Yes. Please, yes." She grabbed his shoulders again, her inner muscles tightening even further around him.

"Damn, Elisa." He drew out of her in a long stroke and drove back inside her. "I can't hold on."

"Don't. Don't let go of me," she pleaded against his neck.

Never. "I won't let you go."

He picked up his rhythm as his balls tightened, her cries driving him out of control, and moved deep inside her. Suddenly, her hold on him tightened and she shuddered in his arms, her inner muscles tightening impossibly harder around him. He came with her in a rush, buried to the hilt inside her.

CHAPTER SIXTEEN

Rojas walked down the steps to the martial arts school, workout holster strapped back around his torso and T-shirt in hand, trying to wipe the grin off his face. Heck of a way to start a morning. Elisa had been very happy, too. She'd also recovered her senses faster than he had and pointed out he'd left Souze downstairs.

So here he was, being sent down to check on Souze while she showered and finished her morning routine. Elisa had also brought up the practicality of them heading downstairs at different times. But she'd sent him off with a sweet kiss and a request for cuddles later.

Hell, he'd call it whatever she wanted, so long as he got to hold her in his arms again and enjoy the scent of her. Because he hadn't gotten nearly enough of her.

To be honest, he should try not to imagine what she was doing up there at the moment, but as he heard the water for the shower turn on, again, he couldn't help picturing water running over bare, cream-colored skin. And he very much liked the taste of her skin.

Maybe it was because he was already trying to banish thoughts from his mind. Or it could've been the blind foot of the stairway and the way it got darker right at the landing. But he suddenly became aware of the sounds of people moving quietly beyond the door leading out to the main portion of the school.

He froze on the steps, listening harder.

More than one person waited beyond the visual obstruction, closer to three or four people. None of them were verbalizing and all of them were moving with muffled steps. Attempting to conceal their approach, possibly.

He was walking into an ambush.

His heart started to pound hard as adrenaline coursed through him, heightening his senses and response time. He embraced the boost as he drew his handgun. He'd need both to get himself through the next moments alive.

Damn it, he'd give anything to know where his rifle had gotten to.

There'd be a fraction of a second, if he was lucky, when he broke through the door and threw himself clear. He might be able to take out one, possibly two of the people waiting for him before the others got their shots in. If they were seasoned soldiers, he was a dead man. But if they were civilians turned insurgents, he had a chance. They wouldn't have the same firing discipline, might not be ready to take a human life. And if they didn't shoot to kill, he would most definitely need to take them out. Because left to continue as they were, they would eventually kill someone else.

He opened his mouth, tasting the air. It was wrong somehow. The ever-present dust and dryness were absent. The sounds of vehicles driving by and the random noises of a town living in fear were off somehow.

Didn't matter. He needed to focus on the immediate vicinity and clearing downstairs before the person he was protecting walked down into this trap. No time to radio CC. Don't want to risk the threat hearing the click. Slow first step. Steady heel-to-toe pressure to keep the weapon steady in one hand while reaching to check belt clip for flashbangs out of habit. *Never have them when needed.*

Something cold nudged his hand hard, and he jumped, bringing his weapon to bear on the thing that'd snuck up on him. For several long seconds he stared at Souze down the sights of his handgun.

Souze.

The German Shepherd Dog stared back at him, dark eyes calm.

Oh God, what was he doing?

His hands trembled as he flipped the safety back on and holstered his firearm. He sucked in air as he leaned against the wall in the stairwell and sank down along it until his tailbone hit the step under his ass.

He'd had an episode. A thing. Whatever the fuck they called it. There'd been no warning. Suddenly, he'd been back overseas and treating everything the way he would've if he'd still been in a combat situation. He'd had nightmares before, been caught up in memories during the day even, but nothing as bad as this.

Those people he'd heard downstairs, beyond the door, were students of the school. Advanced martial artists come to train. Some of them were amateur fighters on the circuit. One or two were professional MMA competitors, competing in the organizations based out of Philly or Atlantic City.

None of them would've been able to react fast enough to him bursting through the door firing a gun to survive.

It would've been a bloodbath.

And maybe he would've come to his senses in the midst of the carnage. Or worse, he could've continued out the front of the school into the very public area, continuing to think he was in a combat zone.

Souze stepped forward and stuck his cold, wet nose right into Rojas's face.

"Ugh." Rojas pushed Souze's muzzle away, but the GSD returned and got in his face again. "I'm okay. I'm back. It's fine."

He pushed himself up to stand. The dog was responding to his agitation, and he was damned lucky Souze had responded at all. It wasn't in the scope of the dog's training.

Rojas stared down at the dog, then buried his hand in the thick fur along the back of the dog's shoulders. Souze's eyes closed in response to the good scratching Rojas gave him, leaning in as Rojas moved his hand up to massage around the base of the dog's ears.

"Thanks, buddy." Rojas could only imagine what would've happened if Souze hadn't been there. None of it was good. "I owe you. Big time."

He stood there with Souze for a few more minutes, listening to the sounds of the men downstairs training. He needed to be sure he was in the here and now, not trapped back in places he'd left far behind. As a Navy

SEAL, his missions had been in and out of hot spots, focused and comparatively short in length in terms of deployment. There wasn't any one mission haunting him. They all did, in one way or the other. It made figuring out his own triggers a struggle, made every day an unknown minefield to navigate.

When he was sure he was steady, he wiped the cold sweat from his brow and palms and pulled his tee on over his holster. Then he continued down the stairs, opening the door slowly.

Revolution MMA was exactly the way it should be. The blinds were up, letting in the morning light, and four men were training hard on the mats. One of them was Cannon. Cannon must've left Souze to hang out loose downstairs without a placement command. Good thing he had.

As Rojas stepped out, a couple of them gave him an upward chin jerk in greeting but didn't pause in their timing drills.

Rojas led Souze straight to the back door and let them both out into the open.

They should head back to Hope's Crossing Kennels, but he was steady now with Souze's timely help, and there was still a pressing need for action.

He had no doubts Elisa's car would still be under surveillance. Even though there weren't yet signs of someone tapping into the surveillance feeds at Revolution MMA, it was only a matter of time. Her stalker would likely hack into other stores with security coverage of the parking lot as well. Elisa hadn't been back in a day or more as far as her stalker could tell, and efforts would increase in intensity to gain some sort of control

over her again. If it'd been Rojas or any of his team monitoring a target, they'd have sent someone to keep direct
eyes on the car.

It was the most recently known connection to Elisa.

So he started them on a long walk around the
perimeter.

"Time to work." At his words, Souze's posture
changed from easygoing to alert.

It was a familiar phrase, one Rojas used at the beginning of every training session with Souze. It let the big
dog know they were getting to serious business.

He and Souze made their way around the front of the
building. At this time of the morning, there wasn't a lot
of foot traffic since most of the stores didn't open for a
couple more hours. But there were a few people walking
along the main road and a few joggers.

The two of them walked the length of the row of cars,
stopping at Elisa's and cutting between the driver's side
of her car and the one next to it. Rojas paused, mimick-
ing searching his pocket for keys as he let Souze sniff
around the cars. The big dog put his nose to the ground,
followed a scent trail practically under Elisa's car and up
the side of it.

Either the GSD had Elisa's scent or the man who'd
placed something on her car.

Rojas faked looking in the window of the car he was
facing, doing his best to look like a man who'd locked
his keys in his car, then led Souze away. They headed
straight out of the parking area up to Revolution MMA
and went inside as if they belonged. Because they did.
And it was much more natural-looking than their not-
friend snooping around the cars the previous day.

Stopping at the drink station, Rojas snagged a cup and let it fill with water. He wet his throat and then held the cup low for Souze. Summer heat was lingering even through the early fall and Souze's nose would be more sensitive if the dog was well-hydrated. Besides, Rojas wanted to give anyone who might be watching time to relax somewhat after he'd been near the car.

After a few minutes, he and Souze went back out the rear entrance and swung around the shopping strip from the opposite direction.

"*Such*." Rojas issued the command quietly, with a firm tone. The German word sounded like "tsuuk" where the *K* was almost silent. It was short, sharp, and Souze responded immediately.

The big dog moved ahead of Rojas, stretching the lead. Systematically, the dog moved in a zigzag across the sidewalk as he first scented the ground then lifted his nose to catch what he could on the air currents.

German Shepherd Dogs were extremely versatile and very good in a broad range of skill sets. Souze, in particular, had a good knack for scent work. Good enough for K9 or military if he didn't have other behavioral issues holding him back. As it was, Rojas was glad he hadn't completed Souze's rehabilitation yet because the big dog was proving himself a real asset now and a solid companion.

They'd progressed at a slow walk about halfway to Revolution MMA when Souze froze. Rojas studied the way Souze kept his nose to the ground, staring intently at the pavement. The person in question had to have walked across the pavement here.

"*So ist brav.*" Souze responded to Rojas's praise by

relaxing from his frozen stance and dropping his lower jaw to let his tongue loll out.

Rojas took in their location, right in front of the entrance to a Cluck U. If he was a betting man, and he didn't need to be to recognize a sure thing, he'd bet his target was conducting surveillance from a car of his very own and came into this place at least once to use the facilities and fuel up on grease-covered protein.

Not that he could blame the guy because the chicken strips were great and the wings could be amazing. Boom loved the potato wedges covered in melted cheese. And they had these fried dough things that could feed a hobbit for weeks.

Boom would've mentioned if she and Elisa had made a stop here, for sure, so he was certain he had the trail he was looking for now.

All right. They had a trail. Rojas didn't want to spook his man until he'd had a chance to circle around and locate him, so he gave Souze's lead a gentle tug and the two of them continued forward as if they were on a normal walk. Anyone watching them would probably assume Souze had paused at the smell of food like a normal dog.

As they walked, Rojas scanned the parking lot. More cars had arrived, mostly employees coming to open up the stores. There was one luxury sedan with tinted windows parked on the far side of a beat-up pick-up truck about midway down the aisle from the Cluck U. It was a straight path to the fast food place and back, minimum time away from his point of surveillance. Convenient.

First of all, no man owning such a nice car would

park next to a truck whose owner obviously didn't care about it when there were dozens of other parking spots to choose from. It was just asking to get dinged up, or its paint scratched, or worse.

Second, the tinted windows weren't a thing in this area. A car with them stood out almost as badly as an ominous black SUV could.

Rojas took Souze out to the end of the strip mall and around the far end of the parking lot as if they were taking a lap around the perimeter. A couple of joggers had done the same thing. He kept his pace easygoing and casually kept his gaze on what was in front of him as they closed in. Keeping an eye on the car of interest was easy, too easy. He looked beyond the car for what was less noticeable. Once he found what he was looking for, he had Souze turn and head back across the expansive blacktop.

When the two of them came around, Rojas kept the beat-up pick-up truck directly in the line of sight to cover his approach.

When they got within a few yards, Rojas gave the track command again, "*Such*."

Souze moved forward a step, maybe two, toward the luxury sedan and froze.

Positive confirmation.

CHAPTER SEVENTEEN

Well, it wouldn't hurt to introduce himself. Not to *this* guy.

Rojas lifted his arm, phone already in hand, and snapped a quick picture of the back of the vehicle with a clear shot of the license plate and the driver's incredulous face reflected in the side view mirror. Jersey plates. He could've approached from the front, but there were no parking blocks in this lot to keep the driver from pulling forward and running him over.

Approaching from the rear gave Rojas a little more time to get himself and Souze out of the way.

As it was, the driver didn't even start up the engine. The man actually got out of his car.

Rojas grinned.

"Just what do you think you're doing?" The man was dressed in a basic blue dress shirt and cheap khaki slacks. There were a few grease stains down the front of the shirt, and Rojas was willing to bet there was a discarded tie lying in the passenger seat.

"Making sure I can track you down if I have any questions after we're done here." Rojas made his statement simple in a flat tone.

The lack of intimidation on Rojas's part seemed to deflate the other man's bravado some but after a moment, the man recovered and jutted out his chin. No blustering boast or threat, though, so the man was at least somewhat intelligent.

Rojas decided to go with the direct question, the easy one. "What do you want with Elisa Hall?"

Elisa had her opinion on the reason for her ex coming after her, but there could be other possibilities.

The other man smirked. "I'm just here on an errand. No particular reason."

What a shitty liar. Or, more likely, the man wasn't bothering to dissemble. He was just going to try to mock Rojas into an altercation.

Rojas matched his smirk. "Errand? I could believe that. The real team is watching us speak. They've probably captured images of both of us with their telephoto lens and they're going to report back to your mutual employer that you were made. I'm guessing you'll be contacted soon to be told your services are no longer necessary."

The man's jaw dropped open. Rojas revised his opinion of the man's intelligence from somewhat to dubious.

"See. You were identified, caught on security feed." Rojas decided to add on to the pressure. "I'm guessing you placed a GPS tracker on a car and decided to wait for the owner to return. But none of the information you've gathered to date is anything your employer won't already have. Because he sent a second team to watch from a distance while you did the 'errand' run."

The other man's eyes darted left and right as he scanned the parking lot. Rojas watched as the man spotted the slightly dinged silver SUV with "baby on board" sun blockers in one too many windows parked down by the grocery store, much less noticeably. The man and the woman inside were dressed casually. They blended in. And there wasn't any reason to notice an SUV in front of a grocery store that opened significantly earlier than any of the other stores in the strip. One of them had even gotten out and made a run into the grocery store and come back out. But they'd been there way longer than they needed to be.

"What the fuck?" The man took a step forward, but Souze uttered a low growl.

The man blanched white and stepped back.

Rojas remained relaxed, unhurried. He planned to have a similar conversation with the others he'd spotted next. "Your job is over, regardless. It can't hurt to tell me what you're doing here."

There was a possibility the man would give up information they didn't already know, or a different spin on the situation to give them an angle toward resolving it more permanently.

"Maybe." The other man spit on the pavement between them. "For all you know, I could have backup."

"Really?" Rojas didn't bother to modulate the incredulity in his own tone. "Let's be real here."

The other man ground his teeth as he worked his way through admitting he'd already given away his ignorance. "Look. I was asked to locate and retrieve property for my client. It seems to have gone astray."

Rojas raised his eyebrows. What bullshit. "What's the property look like? Could be that I could help you recover it."

"Yeah?" The man cracked a grin and studied Rojas with a calculated look. "I might be convinced to split my fee if you lend a hand in retrieval. Your mutt there could be good at distracting people."

Rojas felt his face go blank as he shut down the reasoning side of his personality. No. There wasn't going to be an easy way forward with this situation. Not with this man's attitude. "Elisa Hall is not property."

"Not saying that's who I'm looking for but if it were, my client would think so." The other man shook his head ruefully. "And as you pointed out to me, there's other people here to ensure my client's property is returned in a timely manner. If you help me, then you can be sure she will be delivered in one piece. I won't harm a hair on her head. The others may not be so careful with her."

A red haze developed along the edges of Rojas's vision. "Leave."

"So that's a 'no' then." The man looked from Rojas to Souze and back again. "Look, it's best to stay way the hell away from this girl. Even if my contract ends here, they may have paid me very good money to locate her and possibly install a tracking device on her vehicle. My client's not going to stop just because of one scary boyfriend and his killer mutt."

Rojas took a step forward, letting Souze have some slack in his leash. The big dog took up the slack, his fur bristling until the GSD looked significantly larger than he had even a minute prior. "Tell me how you report in. What's the contact number?"

The man's eyes widened. He held up his hands, fingers spread wide. "No, man. No. I'm a private investigator. I guarantee my clients' anonymity. You'd ruin my business."

Rojas took another step forward. Then another. Souze was almost in snapping range, and Rojas wasn't particularly worried about this guy making a run for it. He wouldn't be caught running in front of his competition. No, he was going to try to keep up appearances.

"You can give me the number or I can hand over the security feed showing you tampering with Elisa Hall's car to the police." Rojas decided to keep his tone pleasant. It freaked people out more than rage. "After you spend a few hours explaining yourself to them, you can convince your *client* that you didn't breach his privacy."

The other man broke out into a sweat. Literally. Oh, he might be good at tailing spouses heading out for clandestine meetings with their illicit lovers. He might be good at tracking down the odd person trying to avoid a debt or fulfilling a contract. He was probably capable of putting on a good show, intimidating the run-of-the-mill person guilty enough to have something to hide. But he wasn't someone who made his life in the business of real violence.

As Souze uttered another low warning growl, Rojas made sure he had a good grip on the dog's lead. This man might piss himself in another five seconds, but if he did something stupid, Rojas didn't want to sully his dog on this slimy bastard's flesh. It was one thing to intimidate but another thing entirely to let Souze loose in an uncontrolled civilian environment.

Fortunately, the other man didn't know that.

"Okay. Okay. Here's the agency's card." With a shaking hand, the man fished a card out of his shirt pocket and tossed it to the ground at Rojas's feet.

Rojas didn't bend to pick it up. He kept his gaze steady on his target. "You can get in your car and drive away now."

* * *

Rojas pulled in to Hope's Crossing Kennels and put his car into park. "Why don't you take Souze for a walk around the perimeter?"

Elisa looked at him, surprised.

He'd disappeared once he'd come to get Souze and she'd ended up waiting a decent amount of time for him to come back. It'd been awkward, actually, but the men training at Revolution MMA had been very polite and charming as they invited her to wait on the benches where parents usually sat to watch the kids' classes.

Once he'd returned, Alex had hustled her into his car with little explanation. He'd also been silent on the drive over. The tension in the car upset her until she realized she was trying to make herself as small as possible as she sat in the passenger seat. Even then, she couldn't bring herself to ask him what he was thinking about or otherwise break the silence.

Conversation was not one of Alex Rojas's strong points.

"If you just took Souze for a walk, why does he need

to go again?" He might not be used to someone calling him out, but she wasn't going to just go do things without a reason. Employer or not.

Alex didn't seem irritated, though, only distracted. "I've got a couple of things to talk to Forte and Cruz about before we start the day. Souze is a little worked up, so the walk would do him good."

Elisa chewed on her lower lip and made a guess. "You went out to my car this morning. Did you find out anything?"

He hesitated for a long time. She got the sense he wasn't going to lie to her, but he wasn't ready to tell her what had transpired yet. "Some, but we've got a couple of facts to check first."

But he'd found out some things. Several things, if there were facts to check. She didn't want him to filter for her. "Will you talk about it with me there?"

His brows drew together but he maintained steady eye contact with her and didn't dismiss the question. "If you insist. But I think it'd be a lot clearer if you let us sift through what I've found out and make some sense of it first. Otherwise, it's going to be a whole lot of worrying."

"You all are way more involved than you should be. I hate dragging you into it." The sadness, guilt, twisted in her stomach. Suddenly she was glad she hadn't had one of the protein bars the guys had offered her this morning. It would've compacted into a rock in her belly by now.

"Hey." He turned in his seat to face her and reached out for her hand. After a moment, she placed hers in his. His fingers closed around hers, and she was struck by how much bigger his hand was. "This thing is more than one person should have to deal with. I'm very glad you and I met. I'm glad we can help you. Let us. I promise we're more than able to meet this head on and give you alternatives you wouldn't have on your own."

Maybe. But it'd taken everything she had to get out on her own in the first place. It shouldn't be only to hide under someone else's direction. "How is this different from letting him take over my life? You're going to leave me out here and make plans for me, at least for the near future."

The bitterness was back, but she didn't try to hide it from her tone. It was a fair question.

"Anything I do, anywhere I go, should be because I had all the information available to me and I made the decision. So far, what you're proposing to me isn't much different from what I left behind with Joseph."

Okay, with Joseph, he'd simply told her what to do. Alex seemed to be offering her multiple choices, but it was only marginally better. Frustration welled up and jockeyed for foremost position in her brain with the sheer anger she had at the idea of someone presuming to talk over her head.

Alex remained calm, listened. "I'm only asking you to wait a little while. Some of it is more about what decisions need to be made between me, Cruz, and Forte. I promise you we're standing with you as friends, trying to give you options. You still get to choose."

She considered his words, pressing her lips together. Intentions could make a big difference. And in a short amount of time, the amount of help and advice they'd been willing to give her had been without pressure. It was worth trust. Some. If she dared.

"You'll share everything with me once you've got all the facts you're looking for?" she asked, finally.

"Yes."

She sighed and opened the car door. As she stepped out, she called over her shoulder to Souze in the back seat. "C'mon, Souze. We're going for a walk."

Walking off the nervous energy was better than sitting at the front desk wondering what they were talking about in any case. She'd wait and hear what he had to say when he was ready, then she'd decide if he was telling her the whole truth.

And then...then she'd have to choose whether to believe in him and his intentions or leave.

CHAPTER EIGHTEEN

Rojas strode out of the main building in the direction he'd sent Elisa and Souze. Even if he felt he'd done the right thing in checking in with Forte and Cruz first, he still hated sending her away. He should let her know what had transpired so far and what steps they could take next.

So while Cruz was running the queries on the agency that'd hired the private investigator and Forte was putting together a big breakfast, Rojas was going to find Elisa and try to repair whatever damage he'd done by excluding her.

It didn't take long to find them. The grounds were fairly quiet on a Sunday morning with no classes going on, so he heard Elisa before he had them in his line of sight. She was talking to Souze and it occurred to him that maybe he shouldn't interrupt the conversation.

He slowed his pace, sticking to the wooded area along the walking trail until he got close enough to hear her more clearly.

"We all make stupid decisions." Elisa sat next to Souze on a grassy patch next to the trail. "So even when we start to try to make smart ones, we're not really sure they're the right decisions while we're making them."

Rojas paused. Elisa didn't seem to have a lot of people she felt comfortable talking to. She'd mentioned calling her mother occasionally but those calls seemed more obligatory than heart-to-hearts, especially since her mother hadn't supported her leaving her ex. A dog could be an incredibly helpful ear. And Rojas had a feeling she'd be talking about things he needed to hear if he was going to be able to protect her long enough for her to tell him these things on purpose.

Elisa sighed and drew her knees up to her chest. "I was too confident, too sure of myself when I started work at Corbin Systems. I'd spent a few years at entry level at a smaller company and landed the job at Corbin Systems with no trouble at all. I was going to be a project manager in their program management organization. I was going to have a high-powered corporate career leading project teams in the implementation of cutting-edge projects. I had every certification to back up the skills I had listed on my resumé, and I was absolutely sure my career would only skyrocket from there."

Impressive. Souze had his ears forward, the way he usually did with her, listening and looking appropriately interested. Rojas continued to listen, too, straining to hear every word and nuance. Every detail that could give him a better idea of how she came to be here and how she'd been found every time she'd stopped running before.

Aside from the immediate danger to her, a part of him

was hungry to learn more about her. Elisa. The person tugging at him in ways he hadn't thought possible anymore.

"So of course, when the CEO's son started paying attention to me, I was flattered." Hard not to be. But now her voice had turned bitter with a healthy dose of self-loathing. She wrapped her arms around her legs. "I held out for a few weeks, insisting I didn't date where I worked."

It would've only made her a more interesting target. Predators like the man chasing her down now enjoyed the chase. The stronger, the more bright the personality, the more fun it was to hunt them down and drive them crazy in the process. Rojas had seen it. Sure, it'd been overseas, but some things transcended culture, race, or religion. Some things were just about human nature.

Unfortunately, in this case it was the awful predatory side of what humans could do to each other.

"He was so good about being discreet around the office. And he was so extravagantly thoughtful about catching my interest. I couldn't help but enjoy the attention." She rested her chin on her knees and Souze lay down close to her in response, curling around her.

Did she realize she was slowly curling into fetal position? It was a natural reaction, a defense against what she was feeling. And it took everything in him to stay where he was and let Souze provide the comfort of his presence to her as she relived her nightmare from the pleasant beginning.

"Dating him seemed normal. I mean, he had his quirks. He demanded he pay for meals because he was insisting we go to restaurants outside of my budget, and since he was the one who'd been dying to try the place, it was only right for him to pay." Elisa tucked her chin and bumped her forehead against her knees several times. "I was stupid to let him build up the leverage from the beginning."

Souze lifted his head and nudged her wrist with his nose. She raised her head to look at the big dog and reached out to bury one hand in the thick fur around his shoulders.

Good boy. Distract her just enough to stop her from literally beating herself up over the memories.

"It was sneaky and gradual and cumulative. Every phase of our relationship became one where he provided for me, took care of me, and I felt so incredibly grateful to him for how much attention he showered on me." Despite her hand on Souze, her other hand curled around her leg and the fingers were pressed in a tight grip. "When he proposed, it never occurred to me that I could say anything but yes. It was the right thing in everyone's mind. His family, my family. And, of course, because we were engaged, I couldn't work at Corbin Systems anymore. It wasn't appropriate, a conflict of interest."

She shook her head, tears beginning to fall down her cheeks. Rojas wanted to hold her and kiss every drop of pain away. The way she tortured herself for those past choices was painful to watch.

"The job pool had dried up all of a sudden. There weren't any jobs within a reasonable commute. I gave up my career," she whispered. "The plan was to keep looking for a new job, but things kept getting in the way. There was the wedding to plan and he wanted me to focus on it full time. And then there was our home to redecorate to accommodate us both. Then the wedding was postponed due to company obligations and to better fit the timing to invite key investors as wedding guests. The wedding became more of a corporate event. And every day leading up to it, he nudged and prodded me into becoming the perfect executive's wife."

It wouldn't have taken long. She was intelligent and adaptive, responsive to feedback. All her ex would've had to do was present her with plausible reasoning for each change. There was a certain talent in making every argument sound like a reasonable idea.

"It happened a little at a time, and then suddenly I looked in the mirror and didn't recognize myself anymore." She huffed out a laugh devoid of anything close to happiness. "I was texting him for permission to spend money on anything over five dollars. I was taking pictures of anything I intended to buy for myself and showing it to him for his approval before I bought it. My clothing style had changed, even my reading choices. All because I wanted to please him, wanted him to like every aspect of what I was for him. I was doing the work of his administrative assistant because I could do it faster and better than she could. It didn't matter that I was overqualified and not paid at all. I was helping my fiancée. It didn't even occur to me to make it a matter of pride."

Of course not. She was a generous soul. It'd shone in the way she'd immediately jumped into helping Boom. There'd been no expectation there. Not from Elisa's side. "The first time I questioned him, he just went silent." There was a tremor in her voice. "He stared at me a long time, and just when I was about to apologize, he exploded right in my face. He screamed at me."

Souze shifted his position, getting closer to her, if that was possible, and curving his body around her. The dog was reacting to her distress and protecting her from the remembered onslaught.

"After that, anything could set him off. It was like his tolerance had gone to nothing and everything I did was an unthinkable insult to him. He wouldn't stop shouting, screaming, throwing things until the room around us was wrecked." Elisa started rocking slightly back and forth in an unconscious effort to comfort herself, too.

Explained her flinching at sudden movement and abrupt noises.

"It was escalating." All at once she stilled and looked down at Souze. Gently, she fondled the tips of the GSD's ears. Her voice had gone utterly calm. "He was going to hit me eventually. Almost did, once or twice. And I realized I needed to leave or I'd never get my life back."

Thank god she'd left before the man had actually laid hands on her. No one should have to live in a violent environment, but the emotional and mental damage could've gone from bad to exponentially worse. Souze sat up, snuffling his hair, and Elisa sat quietly petting him for a long minute or two. Rojas ached to hold her, comfort her.

"When I went to the police to report my concerns, they treated me like someone's prize show dog loose from the kennel. I wasn't a person. They wouldn't even look me in the eye." The bitterness was back in her voice, plus some heat.

Her anger was a relief to hear. Anything was better than the flat, monotone calm she'd spoken with before.

"It took forever to actually get any advice on how to

get away on my own." She adjusted her sitting position until her legs were crossed in front of her. Leaning forward, she touched her forehead with Souze's. "It's out there for women who need it, but the first thing it warns you about is the need to hide the fact you're looking for it from the person you're trying to leave. Joseph is really good at what he does. As a project manager, I figured I had decent tech savvy, but what he could do made me realize just how much I didn't know about computers and the Internet."

Rojas nodded even if she couldn't see him. There could've been keystroke trackers on the personal computers she was using before she left. Her ex could've been monitoring what websites she was visiting, her phone conversations, maybe even intercepting the streaming video from calls made on Internet-based calling software.

"I did my best. Only looked through pamphlets and written materials at the doctor's office. I memorized as much as I could and didn't take anything home." She left off petting Souze for a moment as she looked up at the sky. "I tried to be sure not to leave any clues on anything he might've touched. I just couldn't be sure how far he'd gone to keep track of me, but I didn't want to wait until he'd done something I couldn't undo."

Souze apparently decided she'd had enough of a break and gently tapped her leg with a paw a few times. She huffed out a laugh and started to pet him again. "So I waited until he had an important set of business meetings, a new project launching. The special project, the one even the government couldn't know about because he had other backers paying for it. Crunch time.

Couldn't be a business trip because he'd have just taken me with him. And I went on one of my normal approved outings to run some errands, then visit my mother."

Rojas made a mental note to check on her mother and her other friends. Their safety could be a concern as well and it'd kill Elisa to suddenly find out they'd paid for her disappearance. He wasn't sure what he could do, but at least he could look into it.

Elisa sighed. "You might think my mother helped me leave, but she didn't. She thought Joseph was wonderful. He could do no wrong. She didn't believe there was anything crazy about our relationship. She thought it was intense but must be a result of the pressure of his career. The couple of times I tried to talk to her about it, she thought I was being ridiculous. Then she reminded me how important it was to have someone to look after me, taking care of me so I wouldn't have to worry every day about how to make it to my next paycheck. She didn't want me to struggle the way she did, and I get that. But she'd have sent me right back to him with a hope that he'd help me through my momentary mental issue. So on my way I took a detour, deliberately, and never went to go meet her. I never said good-bye. She's been angry with me every time I've called to check in, too. She still tries to talk me into going back, so I haven't called in at least a month. Maybe it's been longer. I wanted to check in with her again when I felt safe, had some sort of life built for myself."

Her mother could be telling her ex enough for him to find her. Good intentions and whatnot. Rojas was certain Elisa had probably omitted any details of where she was to prevent exactly such an issue, but Elisa wasn't trained not to give anything away. And mothers had a knack for finding out all the things their children wanted to keep from them.

Only way to be sure was to go find out what her mother might be up to. He'd learned the hard way with his ex-wife and her mother. They'd worked together to hide his ex-wife's affair from him until the divorce papers were ready.

"I've decided not to call her while I'm here." The tired sadness in Elisa's voice tore at him. He wanted to do anything to ease it for her. Souze whined and stretched his neck forward until his muzzle rested on Elisa's shoulder. Elisa tilted her head to nuzzle the big dog. "It's better this way, until I can build a life for myself again, show her something she can be proud of. Show her I can be very happy away from Joseph."

Well, it was good she'd made the decision to adjust her pattern, too. Not calling her mother was a good step in changing up the way things had been working out so far. It also sucked. Hard.

Elisa was hurting, and he couldn't stand by and listen anymore. It was too much creeper and not enough real help for him, no matter how practical eavesdropping had seemed at the start of this.

He cleared his throat.

Souze pulled back and stood on all fours, looking straight in his direction. The big dog's ears were forward and his eyes locked on his location immediately. It was possible Souze had known he'd been there but the GSD hadn't alerted Elisa to his presence. Rojas wasn't absolutely sure what to make of the behavior there.

He stepped toward her and stopped about arm's length

away, crouching down so he didn't loom over her but not sitting until she invited him to join her. "Hungry?"

She considered him for a long moment. "Yes. Is there news you're willing to share with me?"

He winced. "Yes. We can talk about it over breakfast or after. Whichever you prefer. I'll show you everything we've gathered."

"Really?" There was quiet surprise and a healthy amount of doubt loaded into her question. "All of it?"

"Everything." Best way for him to gain her trust was to hide nothing. "We'll tell you what we make of it all, too, but it'll all be there for you to draw your own conclusions."

A faint smile played on her lips. "I'd appreciate it."

He tried smiling, too, and found he really wanted to be around her. "It's been a hectic couple of days. Come have breakfast and maybe you can experience what passes for a routine Sunday around here."

He straightened and held out a hand to help her up. She stared at it for a moment, then gave him her own and let him help her.

He chuckled. "And you can meet Sophie."

CHAPTER NINETEEN

Elisa was still caught up in her memories as Alex led her back to the main building. But he kept her hand in his as they walked, grounding her even as he left her to her thoughts. The contact was comforting, and yet every few steps he brushed his thumb over her knuckles or gently tightened his grip, kicking her heart into brief sprints and triggering a fluttery nervousness in her belly.

This thing growing between them was radically different from her relationship with her ex. That had been gradual, progressing in stages the way she'd expected it to. She'd embraced the predictability, anticipating the next step without meaning to.

But this chemistry with Alex was the opposite of predictable—from the first time they'd kissed to every intimate moment they'd shared since. She was off balance and constantly surprised, guessing and definitely excited. It was...fun.

For the first time in forever, she was having fun and wondering what was going to happen next.

The project manager in her was horrified.

"Dad! Elisa! Hurry, breakfast is just about ready!" Boom stood in the doorway waving her broken arm. Once she saw them wave back, she turned in the doorway and knocked her cast against the doorjamb.

Elisa winced. "Ouch."

Alex chuckled. "Actually, she needed fewer pain meds last night. She might've forgotten she was hurt until just then."

"It's amazing how fast kids bounce back from injuries." She shook her head.

"Speaking of which, how's your wrist?" Alex asked, looking down at her.

Elisa lifted her left wrist, opening and closing her hand. "Doing fine. I've been wearing the brace the last couple of nights. Helped a lot."

"Doc at the ER said it was a bad sprain?"

The night they'd met in the emergency room seemed a long time past, but it really had been just a few days. Amazing how caught up in Alex's world she was getting. Yet, now that she thought about it, there was a rightness to it she didn't want to overthink.

She nodded. "Ice, ibuprofen, and stabilize it to let it heal. I just hate wearing the brace when I'm typing and I figured since today is a work day I'd end up leaving it off."

"Doesn't hurt to bring it along just in case." Alex gave her hand a squeeze. Then he paused. "Feel free to grab a big freezer bag from the kitchen in the main house and ice from the freezer whenever. We use ice a lot around here."

"Okay." He'd brought her ice the first morning. Maybe she should figure out how to set a periodic alarm on the phone to remind her at regular intervals. The faster her wrist healed, the better. There was still plenty of organization she could do for the front office.

They arrived at the doorway, and he let her hand go, motioning for her to head inside. "I'll let Souze into his kennel so he can have water and some time to himself."

Boom rushed back to the doorway to meet her, grabbing her right hand. "C'mon, Elisa. I'll introduce you."

Elisa let herself be tugged inside and down the hallway into the kitchen area. David gave her a wave from his seat at the table and Brandon was manning the stove. Whatever he was frying smelled so good, her mouth immediately started watering.

Two women were arranging dishes on the breakfast counter. "Lyn! Sophie! This is Elisa!" They turned to her with smiles.

"Hi, there." The very pretty blonde turned to her first, offering a hand.

Elisa reached out and shook it, smiling at the firm return grip. When she'd been in an office environment, a solid handshake had been an absolute must to show confidence. Once she'd stopped working and had started meeting more of her ex's colleagues in social situations, the handshakes she'd received from other women had turned limp. Without substance.

It was nice to get a firm greeting again.

Boom continued her brand of introductions. "Lyn works with dogs all over the country, rehabilitating bad behavior. She travels a lot, so she wasn't here the day you started, and she's still getting over a bad cold, so don't let her breathe on you."

"Ah." Elisa fished for something to say and came up with nothing.

Lyn laughed. "No worries. I washed my hands just before you came in, and I'm on antibiotics now so I'm not likely to be contagious. I hope. Other people might've balked at taking antibiotics so *they* aren't allowed to breathe on Boom."

Lyn sent a warm glance in David Cruz's direction. He shrugged and winked. "I prefer not to encourage the breeding of uber viruses or bacteria."

"Uncle David!" Boom flapped her un-casted hand. "Still doing introductions here."

David held up a fork and waved it as if to say "continue."

"I'm Sophie." A dark-haired woman came around the breakfast bar to shake her hand, too. She had the sort of ever-young Asian features that made it hard to pin down her age, so she appeared to be anywhere between eighteen and thirtysomething. "I hear you're wrestling the chaos at the front desk into much-needed order."

Elisa blinked. "Well, I streamlined a few things and started up a client database so the forms could be just for newcomers."

Sophie nodded once, definitively. "Much needed. I've been telling them they needed to get someone with a good head on her shoulders to help out for months. If you let these guys go, they'll do nothing but work with the dogs and forget people even exist."

"I can believe that, actually." Elisa found herself smiling again. "It's nice to meet you both. Do you all live here?"

Lyn grinned and jerked her head toward David. "The two of us are in the guest cabin right now, but we'll be moving back into our cabin as soon as the expansion is done. I needed an office and a bigger bathroom."

"With a tub," Sophie sighed.

"A wonderful, deep soaking tub," Lyn affirmed.

"Ooh." Elisa sighed, too. How long had it been since she'd taken a real bath? The chance to soak and let all the stress go as the heat from the water seeped into her muscles would be so good.

Boom wrinkled her nose.

Elisa chuckled and looked at Sophie. "I actually have no idea where Brandon sleeps."

Brandon banged a pan on the stove. David barked out a laugh and almost choked. Lyn slapped a hand over her mouth, and Boom outright laughed.

Sophie turned a bright red.

"Sophie is a good friend," Alex said from behind Elisa.

As she turned to look up at him, he dropped a kiss on her temple in a seemingly absent-minded gesture and ruffled Boom's hair.

It was Elisa's turn to blush as Boom stared at her with a thoughtful expression.

"A friend who brings sweets and pastries to get us fat," Alex continued as he nabbed something from a dish.

Sophie slapped at his hand. "Elisa hasn't had a chance to get anything yet, and I use you guys as guinea pigs for my new recipes."

Alex stuffed his prize into his mouth unrepentantly.

A flustered Sophie handed a plate to Elisa. "Come

help yourself. There's scrapple and hash browns. Brandon's making eggs to order."

Elisa paused. "I'm sorry if I—"

Sophie shook her head. "Oh, no. It's no big deal. Honest mistake meeting us all in the kitchen like this. I'm just a friend from forever ago and come over all the time. Is scrapple okay or do you prefer bacon?"

Elisa studied the crisp fried slices of...something. "I've never had scrapple before. What is it?"

"Never ask what scrapple is." Boom leaned toward her and whispered loudly, "None of us talk about what's in scrapple."

"It's delicious," Alex said as he took up a plate of his own. "It's pork-based. And that probably *is* all you want to know about it."

Elisa smiled and took a slice. "I guess I can try something without knowing everything about it."

In short order, she was seated at the table with a plate of scrapple, eggs over easy, and hash browns, pondering whether she could eat her sweets first. There were sweet rolls baked a perfect light gold with some sort of gorgeous red berry filling and topped with rich vanilla icing. "Whatever these are, Sophie, they look amazing."

Sophie smiled. "Vanilla glazed strawberry rolls. Strawberries aren't in season locally right now. We're a couple of months late for that, but you can generally still find enough for this recipe at a decent price at most grocery stores. It's a Boom favorite, so I figured I'd bake a batch."

Elisa smiled.

"They're *so* good." Boom was happily gobbling up everything on her plate with the abandon of a young girl with a high metabolism and no worries about the need to do cardio later.

"They're sweet." Alex agreed. "And you like just about anything sweet."

"Mmm. I like other stuff." Boom sucked on the tips of each finger with exaggerated care. Then she looked directly at Elisa. "Pachamanca is super good for dinner when we go to Dad's favorite restaurant. I'm going to try it the way Dad had it as a kid when we go visit my *abuelo* in Peru someday. Papa rellena, too. They're these balls of mashed potatoes stuffed with super delicious meat filling. So good! And then I get dessert. Dad tries to make sure my sweet stuff is mostly fruit. He says sugar and candy should be treats and are even better when I don't have them all the time. He's kind of right, but some days I want sugar so much I'd take *baths* in sugar if I could."

Chuckles all around the table.

"Well, you could." Elisa ventured as she took a bite of her own strawberry roll. She lost her train of thought for a minute as the strawberry sweetness mingled with vanilla spread over her tongue and combined with the wonderfully soft texture of the roll. *So. Good.* When she came back to her senses Boom, Alex, David, and Brandon were staring at her. "Oh. Well, taking a bath with sugar. You could make homemade sugar scrubs. You don't eat them, but they can be really good for your skin."

"True," Sophie chimed in. "I never thought about it before, but Boom had dry skin so bad last winter she was itching a lot. A sugar scrub could help with that, and it's totally natural. It's also a great natural way to get the grime out of your hands instead of those nasty industrial soaps you guys use. They used to have a shop in New Hope that made all their scrubs and soaps themselves. They ended up moving to the West Coast and shutting down the store."

"That's too bad." Elisa pondered the details of a business making scrubs and soaps. Her brain automatically started going through the probable logistics, and she noted additional topics for research. It was a fun mental exercise. "I used to make my own scrubs back in college. And soaps in small batches. It's a calming hobby."

"Could you show me how?" Boom leaned forward over her plate eagerly, icing-covered fingers forgotten.

Elisa laughed. "It's been a long time, but I might remember some of the simpler recipes. If it's okay with your dad, maybe we can make it a weekend thing."

"Spa day at the kennels." Lyn tapped the table. "I'll join you ladies, if you don't mind."

"Sophie, you come, too!" Boom grinned at them. "It'll be a girls' day."

Not a one of the guys said a word.

Elisa hoped it was all right. It was one thing to work for them on a day-to-day basis, but getting more involved with Boom might not be what Alex wanted. But when she looked over at him, he gave her a slow, warm smile and...ate another strawberry vanilla roll.

How that was a turn on, she had no idea. But it so was.

"The supplies expensive?" asked Brandon.

Elisa shook her head. "Sugar, olive oil or almond oil or grape seed oil, a couple of essential oils like lemon or peppermint. That's about it. Could make bath salts the same way, with Epsom salt instead of sugar and a little bit of baking soda."

Brandon tipped his head sideways. "Could make the place a little classier. Make enough to have at the washup stations we've got by the kennel and class areas and put it on the kennel's accounts."

Both Sophie and Elisa voiced caution.

"Hold up, that has to be justified as a business expense…"

"They'd have to be properly labeled in case people have allergies…"

Brandon held up his hands in surrender. "Whoa, it was just a thought. I figured if you ladies liked them, clients would, too. Most of them are of the feminine persuasion."

"True." Elisa chewed on her lip. She'd only ever made them for herself and her roommates, but it wouldn't take much to research for use at the kennels. She'd really enjoyed making them before and hadn't been allowed to continue when she'd moved in with her ex. "It wouldn't take much to print proper labels, but you want labels so you're protected from liability. I'll look into it before we put those out."

Sophie nodded. "I'll check to be sure you can actually write those things off as expenses." She paused then turned to Elisa. "I do their accounting for them, but I am useless at organization and business administration. There's a lot more to it than most people realize. I'm so glad you're here."

Elisa smiled, a peculiar bubbly laughing feeling rising up from deep inside. "I'm glad I'm here, too."

CHAPTER TWENTY

"Why am I here again?" Elisa stood in the middle of the mats at Revolution MMA dressed in a Revolution tee and black yoga pants.

"Because I wouldn't leave any person alone with this many kids." Greg waved vaguely at the currently closed front doors to the school. "Alex is going to cover parents' night for us, and you're going to be his wingman. Person. Buddy."

Elisa had a sneaking suspicion she was being set up. But then she didn't mind, either. The week had gone by in a blur as she had started to fall into the rhythm of routine at Hope's Crossing Kennels. Each day started early, with breakfast and private training appointments. There were open mornings some days to work on the various projects she was developing for the business, and then afternoons of public classes. She got to see Alex every day, but they had very little alone time. With Boom back in school, Alex was busier helping his daughter with homework and spending quality time with her. Oh, Elisa had been invited a few nights to play board games or watch movies, and those had been wonderful.

But she didn't think any of that had prepared her for a night with Alex overseeing the well-being of other people's children. Gary and Greg obviously thought she was ready.

"A couple of things to keep in mind. The kids arrive in their Revolution uniforms to keep things nice and neutral. Different families have varying resources and the uniforms mean no kid has to miss out on parents' night because their clothes might be different from the other kids'," Greg said as he walked to the middle of the mat. "During class or parents' night, the kids' belts always come untied. Our instructors always have the child face them at an angle where their parents can see everything, and they retie the belt for them at arm's length with very clear motions. If a kid's *gi* has come loose, the instructor sends them back to their parents to get them straightened out. Those ties are too far inside the *gi*, and not every kid wears a shirt inside."

"The instructors? Not you and Gary?" She shut her mouth quickly and immediately wished she'd filtered those questions before letting them out.

A sad look passed through his gaze and the corners of his mouth turned down for a split second, then it passed. "Working with kids is always a sensitive situation. We're very careful not to make a move toward any child in any way that can be misconstrued. Gary and I generally have the instructors or the parents handle those things, just to be sure everyone is comfortable. On parents' night, the parents will only be around for the first half hour as they drop off the kids. They have to be back by nine thirty to pick their kids back up for the night."

A solid chunk of time when parents could go out and have a date night or quiet time. Meanwhile, the kids burned off energy in supervised play. Or chaos. Perspective could be everything.

"You're both really good teachers." She'd watched Greg work with the kids when she'd first arrived and Gary the next morning with the adult beginners' class. "More patient than I could imagine. I'm not sure I could be the same."

"You'll do great. Boom told us all about your game nights. And we love what we do." Greg perked up again. "Kids are starting to arrive, so why don't you grab a seat on the long benches over there? We'll introduce you in about twenty minutes or so."

Elisa took a seat as instructed and settled in to people watch.

The parents of Revolution MMA didn't even blink at a newcomer. They filed in with one or two or even three kids. The kids immediately ditched their shoes at the edges of the mats and ran out into the middle to start chatting. The adults weren't all couples, though. There were a good number of women gathering to sit on the benches. From their chatter and outfits, they were planning a ladies' night out.

Elisa wondered if Sophie and Lyn might be interested in one sometime soon. She hadn't really gone into Philly yet and it was so close by.

"Alex Rojas is watching the kids tonight." The feminine speaker was answered by a few gasps and a bunch of giggles.

Elisa kept her eyes on the kids but listened harder.

"He hasn't been coming in to work out as much on the weekdays." Another woman made the observation with a distinct sound of disappointment.

"His daughter has been out for the last week," the initial speaker informed them. "Broke her arm. It'll be weeks before she can come back to classes."

A round of sympathetic sentiments.

"Is there anything sexier than a single father as attentive as he is?" That question got a round of sighs.

Elisa sighed, too.

"Is there any guy here sexier than Alex Rojas?" One woman let out a wicked laugh. There were a couple of names mentioned, but for the most part, it seemed Alex was very popular.

Elisa squirmed in her seat, but couldn't tear herself away. She wanted to know what else they said.

Another woman sighed. "He has a knack for seeing everything going on in a room and yet not noticing any personal hints at all. I can't even tell you how many times I've tried to give him my phone number."

"Maybe you should give him your underwear." The suggestion was met by a gasp and several other laughs. "It worked for you at the club last month with the really hot bouncer."

"Look, every once in a while, a woman has got to get rid of some tension." Agreement there.

"I wonder how he is in bed."

Another woman snickered. "Forget a bed; how about up against a wall? All those muscles rippling and those biceps holding you up? Oh my god."

"In the shower..." More speculation.

"I bet his O-face is amazing." Squeals of laughter came in response to that one.

"Forget his; how many Os do you think he could get out of me?"

Gasps. Elisa's face started to heat up. They were going to notice her soon and wonder why she was eavesdropping. She should really get up and...

"Hey." Alex walked out of the changing room and headed straight for her.

The women on the benches let out a chorus of sweet greetings. Totally innocent, every one of them.

He gave them each a nod, a slightly awkward smile, then his gaze fastened on her. "Ready to go spend the night with me?"

Elisa let her mouth drop open, caught without a comeback. At least half a dozen stares sliced into her side as every woman turned to get a good look at her.

Alex's smile broadened into a wicked grin. "Parents' Night is started. You ladies have fun. My partner and I will watch over the kids."

* * *

Rojas stood with his arms crossed, struggling to maintain a properly mock-fierce visage as the kids battled.

Elisa had been "paralyzed" about a dozen times in Nerf scrimmage. She was currently lying slumped to her side on the mats feigning paralysis while two kids used her body as cover. One of those children was his daughter. Extremely practical child, his Boom.

The opposing team was on their last man. It looked like Boom's team was going to win. It'd bugged him, the first time he'd overseen parents' night. He'd thought this game was a bad idea. Emphasis on bad.

But Elisa had joined in the fun and the kids loved her. She'd laughed and gone down with all the drama of a Broadway actor. The kids ate it up. Plus Souze sat at his side, calmly watching over the chaos with him. It made the cacophony easier to handle somehow, having Souze with him, almost helping to keep an eye on things.

The kids took the competition and kept it friendly and fun. None of them claimed to be killing the other. The children's rules were to be tagged meant you were paralyzed, frozen until the end of the round.

He could live with those rules.

Movement in the lighted area outside the front doors of the school caught his eye, confirmed as more than simple passersby when Souze came to all four feet and issued a warning bark.

Hard not to notice every person walking past with the huge floor-to-ceiling windows facing out onto the parking lot. He'd drawn the blinds across most of the front of the school, leaving the door exposed so he could see the parents returning. Night had fallen, and it was a few minutes early, but, hey, some parents ran out of energy faster than the kids did. But these two people didn't move on after a quick glance in the doors. They remained waiting.

He didn't recognize the two men standing outside the door. Scowling, Rojas studied them as they peered through the glass. When one of them looked directly at him and pressed a badge to the glass, Rojas nodded and held up an index finger to indicate they wait.

"All right, recruits." He pitched his voice to carry over

the delighted shouts and squeals. Over a dozen pairs of eyes locked on him and the room fell silent. "We're doing a new thing tonight. We're going to send everyone into the big changing room and see who can stay silent the longest. Whoever the winner is gets first chance to choose their team next parents' night."

One of the young boys pumped his arm. "Nice. I'll win!"

A chorus of challenges came from the various children.

"None of you can win if you don't pile into the changing room and go quiet. I can hear everything from that room so you have to be absolutely silent." Rojas tapped his ear. "Consider this an exercise in discipline. Move out."

Elisa herded some of the less focused kids to the changing room in the back, her gaze going from Rojas to the men at the door.

He waited until their eyes met. "Text Gary and Greg. Our visitors flashed a badge, but I don't recognize them as any of our local police."

And he'd had reason to get to know some of them over the last several months. A few trained with Revolution MMA and at least one of their local police had his kid here tonight. But the staff at Hope's Crossing Kennels had interacted with the local police a few times when Lyn had first come to the kennels. It'd been interesting times and he'd gotten to know quite a few of the police in the area as a result.

Once Elisa had nodded and gone with the children safely out of view, Rojas headed to the door and snagged a *kali* stick out of the bin at the corner of the mats to bring along. Souze kept pace with him, leash dragging along the floor. Rojas wanted at least one hand free to act, and he trusted Souze to obey verbal commands.

Smiles and geniality weren't his thing, but he tried for as neutral an expression as possible as he unlocked one side of the double doors and cracked it enough to speak to the visitors. He kept his hand on the door bar, effectively blocking entrance across the opening. He carried the *kali* stick in his other hand, loose and re-laxed at his side, away from the opening. Souze stood at heel at his left side, an added obstacle in the partial entryway.

"Officers." He nodded at each. They were both av-erage height, not quite as fit as the police who trained at Revolution, and average build. Fairly non-descript. Their police uniforms had no name tags. "How can I help you this evening?"

There was a beat of hesitation as the other two men assessed the situation. They each returned his nod, glanced down at Souze for a long moment, then took a closer look at him. Hey, a handsome black and tan GSD standing ready to act had that sort of effect on a person. People had a range of reactions. Some were delighted. Others were intimidated and kept their distance.

People who planned to do shady things got fidgety and wary of the dog. These men both changed their weight from one foot to the other before steadying them-selves. They also each had their hands on their guns.

Rojas's attention focused and he kept his limbs loose, his joints relaxed to maximize his range of motion if he needed to counter an aggressive move on their part.

"Are you the owner of this school?" the one who'd

flashed the badge asked as he leaned in and placed his own hand on the edge of the door at about eye level. Not tugging it open, but definitely making sure to get a modicum of control on the door. He tapped his chest. "I'm Officer Wegner and this is Patterson. We're looking for an Elisa Hall. She's needed for questioning back at our division headquarters."

Rojas tightened his jaw a fraction. The guy's demeanor was meant to intimidate and it was scraping at Rojas's temper. The issue here wasn't whether or not the man made a move. Rojas was more concerned about the children in the other room and not giving these two creeps an excuse to remove Rojas from the premises.

Wegner leaned in a fraction more. "Do I need to repeat myself?"

Well. They were all in relatively defensive positions in the entryway. Hopefully things could be resolved with conversation, but they were all prepared to take action. This was a clear threat and Rojas settled into a cold analysis of the situation.

Souze was completely silent.

Which was a sign in and of itself. In relaxed situations, Souze gave the brief bark or warning growl. This was a serious encounter, and the dog had gone completely quiet. It was a personality quirk and a dangerous one. Souze was watching these men with potentially deadly intent.

"I'm actually not the owner." Rojas opted to answer the first question as pleasantly as possible. His dog was taking cues from his attitude, his voice, his body language. As long as he was in control, he was in control of Souze. Having the backup also reminded him to keep his

reaction in check. This wasn't overseas or a combat situation. Response with deadly force would not be called
for. Especially not with children nearby. He needed to
restrict himself to the minimum force required to maintain control of the situation and that was it. "But they
should be back in less than half an hour. We've got a
special children's event going on here at the school this
evening. We'd like to keep the kids feeling as positive as
possible. The presence of anyone they don't know can
be stressful."

There, he'd been completely reasonable. The next
couple of minutes were going to be telling. Could be
easily diffused or things could get ugly, fast.

Wegner bared his teeth in a smile, not a friendly one.
"No problem. Send Miss Hall out here and she can come
with us directly back to division headquarters."

Rojas allowed his features to twist into a grimace
of disappointment. "We'd like to cooperate, officer, but
there's reason to believe Elisa Hall is being pursued by
a stalker. I'd rather not have her out anywhere without
someone she knows. If you'd be willing to wait until after this event is over and all the parents have come to
take their children home, I'd be happy to accompany you
all back to your division headquarters. Where is that, by
the way?"

It was Wegner's turn to disregard a question. "We're
not waiting. You're not going. Just send out Elisa Hall or
we will come inside and take her into custody."

All of them were being so careful with their words.
Rojas hated word games. Souze's hip brushed his on his
left. The big dog was watching him, ready for the slightest cue.

Time for a direct question. "Is Elisa Hall under arrest?"

Wegner scowled and Patterson shifted uncomfortably a step or two back and to the side. Rojas resisted the urge to grin. No, Elisa wasn't. This was unofficial business, as far as Rojas could tell, maybe as shady as some off-duty extracurricular activity.

"Last chance," Wegner growled, dropping any semblance of pleasantry. "Send her out or we come in and take her."

Rojas raised his right hand up with the *kali* stick and brought it down smartly on the other man's fingers. Wegner withdrew his hand from the door immediately, cursing, and Rojas immediately yanked the door closed and locked it.

Wegner took a step back and drew his weapon, shouting through the closed doors, "Open the door or I will fire!"

Rojas dodged to the right of the doors for limited cover behind one of the counters. Was this guy crazy? Even with the kids in the back changing room, the walls were only sheetrock. There was no telling what could happen when he opened fire.

Souze was a reassuring presence at Rojas's hip. The situation still didn't require deadly force. Rojas struggled to consciously plan his next moves while he still had time to keep things at the appropriate level of response.

"Stop!" another, familiar voice called out. Even muffled through the glass doors, Rojas recognized the local policeman whose child was currently hiding in the back with the rest of the kids. "Hold your fire. Upper Makefield Township Police."

Silence.

Cautiously, Rojas rose up from behind the counter and took stock of the scene in front of him.

Officer Kymani Graves was approaching the two strange policemen, his own weapon drawn. There was a terse exchange of words. Rojas watched, tense, and decided to set the *kali* stick down on the counter in plain sight and easy reach. He'd let Graves handle things, but be ready to react again if things escalated. He didn't relax even once the men holstered their weapons. After a few minutes, they left looking murderous.

Rojas stooped to pick up Souze's leash and returned to the door, letting Officer Graves in.

"Excellent timing, Ky." Rojas shook the other man's hand. Rojas had some decent height at six foot, give or take. But Kymani Graves stood several inches taller.

The lean man smiled, brilliant white teeth showing in cheerful contrast to his dark skin. "I see you've battened down the hatches, Rojas. Tell me where you've hidden all of our children."

In answer, Rojas kept his eyes on the parking lot beyond Ky but called out over his shoulder. "Game's over, everyone line up on the mat! Miss Elisa gets to tell us who the winner is."

The kids poured out of the back changing room, babbling and full of questions. Gary and Greg arrived at a run, and Rojas gave Ky the quick version of what had happened.

Ky's eyebrows rose, then rose higher as Rojas added in some context with Elisa's situation.

"Good timing is right, then. If you'd had to resort to any additional action to keep them out, there could've been some major complications and possibly some charges for assaulting an officer." Ky sighed. "As it was, they were outside their jurisdiction."

Rojas jerked his chin up and down once. "They didn't actually say where they were from, just stated their names."

Ky pressed his lips together in a grim smile. "We'll have to look into exactly who they were and where their district headquarters are. But in the meantime, thank you for keeping my child safe."

Rojas shook his head. "I'm sorry we couldn't avoid it altogether."

Gary and Greg joined them. "Kids all seem okay. Some of them heard what was going on but Elisa kept them straight with the idea that you were having a discussion with strangers and because no one knew if they were police, they were not allowed in."

Ky's daughter Grace came running up. Because Souze had turned first to face the oncoming child, Rojas was warned that she was coming and he didn't jump.

Grace looked way up at her dad. "I didn't win the discipline contest, so I can't choose teams first next parents' night, but can Boom still sleep over tonight like we planned?"

Rojas winced then blanked his expression. This incident had probably left Ky with mixed feelings, and Rojas didn't want the other man to feel obligated to still look after his daughter for the evening.

Ky only smiled his generous smile, though, and placed his hand on his daughter's head. "Of course. Are you both ready to leave?"

Grace held up two fingers. "Two minutes! We'll say good-bye and get our shoes on."

Then she was running off.

Rojas caught Ky's gaze. "I understand if you'd prefer not to."

Ky's smile sobered a fraction. "I was sincere when I thanked you for my daughter's safety, Rojas. And I know something of what it cost you to keep things calm here. Not every man could do that. I'm honored that you'd trust me with your daughter after such an interesting evening."

Rojas didn't know what to say, so he put his hand out. Ky took it and shook it firmly. "When your Elisa feels comfortable, bring her in to see me at the station and we can see if there's enough evidence of stalking to have a restraining order put in place. We'll do our best to help her."

"She'd appreciate it." Rojas smiled then, genuine and sincere. "Thank you."

The other man nodded.

"Speaking of your Elisa"—Greg edged past Rojas—"I'm going to take her on upstairs. She looks like she's about to lose it."

Rojas quickly scanned the room for Elisa and saw her standing near Boom, holding Boom's backpack. Her smile was trembling, and her already pale skin had a faint gray tinge to it. "Yeah. I'll—"

"Finish up parents' night." Gary clapped Rojas on the shoulder. "We'll take her to unwind while you tie up loose ends here and straighten out the kids' stories so we know what kind of damage control we'll have when their parents ask about it."

Fantastic.

CHAPTER TWENTY-ONE

Sorry." Elisa sat on the edge of the small bed as Gary hovered near her. "Sorry."

"No worries. Don't you worry at all. This place needs a little excitement to keep us all on our toes, anyway." His voice was gentle, kind. There was no trace of anger.

A knock at the door to the room made her jump, despite knowing there was at least one trusted police officer and Alex between her and anyone planning to take her away. Not to mention any number of children and their returning parents still downstairs as witnesses if anything should happen at this point.

Greg entered the room carrying a small tray with three steaming mugs. "I brought up some tea."

Gary made an odd noise. Sort of a cross between a growl and a groan.

Greg rolled his eyes. "I brought coffee for *you*, ruffian."

"You like it rough, lover." Gary grinned and took a mug covered in cat images.

Greg rolled his eyes, but there was an affectionate smile playing around the corners of his mouth. Maybe they'd interrupted a good date night between Gary and Greg.

Another thing Elisa felt guilty about.

"I noticed you like the mint tea in the evenings when you've come back." Greg sat next to her and brought the tray close enough for her to see. "I brewed us a couple of mugs of this fantastic blend of mint and chamomile, with a hint of orange and rose blossoms. Doesn't it smell incredible? Most of the people we have training here don't have the palate to appreciate it."

Most of the people training at Revolution MMA drank water or sports drinks, as far as Elisa had seen. They always had their sports bottles with them and the only people drinking tea or coffee were parents waiting as kids were taking classes.

But then, it was one of those thoughtful touches. Elisa imagined other places might only have a water station. Gary and Greg went out of their way to have comforts and conveniences available for the people who came to their school. Even this room had been created for people who trained with them to have a quiet place to rest the night before a fight. It spoke volumes about the two men and the environment they'd created within their school.

Thinking about it, Brandon had wanted those sorts of touches for Hope's Crossing Kennels, too.

Here she was, bringing insanity down on all these wonderful people. "I'm not good for all of you. Every time I think I might be in a place to stand up for myself, my ex yanks the footing right out from under me. Worse, he threatens to hurt the people around me. I shouldn't stay anywhere near any of you."

"You should stay right where you want to be," Gary said quietly. He leaned against the far wall, sipping his coffee from his cat mug.

Greg lifted a mug with a German Shepherd Dog silhouette and a caption that said *I can make it to the fence in 2 seconds. Can you?*, holding it out to her until she took it from him. He took up his own mug, covered in cockatiels, and breathed in the rising steam from it. "You're a kind person, Elisa. And I can understand why you wouldn't want to cause trouble for the people around you. But you'd do more harm than good just up and leaving us all. For one thing, we'd miss you. And Boom would be heartbroken."

Elisa bit her lip, wrapping her hands around her mug until the heat almost burned her palms. "How is staying and letting my ex take potshots at you any way he can better? He's going to try to ruin your school or the kennels next. This was too public not to cause some trouble for you. He'll try to mess up the careers of anyone who gets between him and me."

"He'll try," Gary agreed. "But trust me. Greg and I have had plenty of people try to ruin us over the years. It'd be one more challenge. Not the end of the world."

Greg nodded. "And don't you worry about the boys at Hope's Crossing. Every one of them can handle himself."

She didn't reply, chewing on her lower lip.

"You're worth it." Gary came over to sit on her other side. "Don't doubt it for a minute. Alex is out there doing what he does because there's something about you that brings out the best in him."

"I don't know if it's the best." The words fell out of her mouth, and she grimaced at how bitter they sounded.

"He's got his issues to work through, and they're a little closer to the surface around you," Gary agreed. "But he'd have kept trying to bury them to be the perfect father for Boom if you hadn't come along. He doesn't need to be perfect around you. And he definitely doesn't need to be a father figure."

Greg snickered.

Finally, Elisa had to crack a smile. "You two are incorrigible with the innuendoes."

"Who, us?" Greg spread his free hand wide across his chest in mock affront. "If you catch what we're throwing around, your mind went there, too."

Elisa shook her head. With everything so serious, she'd been wound up so tightly she'd thought she'd snap. Being here with Gary and Greg, going on about completely inappropriate things, seemed silly.

And a huge relief.

She looked down at the mug. When was a person supposed to look at tea leaves for the answers, before or after drinking the tea? "Alex is trying to build a life for himself and Boom. He doesn't need all the complications I've got following me around."

"He needs you. And he's willing to fight for you." Gary raised his mug in the direction of the parking lot. "Without you, he wouldn't have faced his PTSD. He'd have tried to tough it out and pretend it wasn't getting worse. He'd have become a hermit and never gone out, eventually would've even stopped coming here."

"And that would've been a travesty," Greg interjected solemnly.

"I'm not helping him get better." Elisa wondered if he'd ever supervise a parent night again. Some of the parents might request he not do so. And even if there wasn't resistance from the parents, he might choose not to.

"You could, once you learned what he needs from you to help him relax." Gary glanced past her to Greg and gave his partner a warm smile. "Well, you've probably made progress in that direction, too, so let's say you can learn what you can do around other people. And you also made him open up. Once he did, he could admit he needed Souze. Which is a huge step in the right direction."

"He already had Souze." Elisa wasn't sure if Souze being at Hope's Crossing Kennels was the same as Alex directly claiming Souze as his dog, but she thought it was probably just a formality. "He's a great dog."

Gary nodded. "True. And all of the men at Hope's Crossing tend to train the best dogs and send them out in the world to partner the people who put their lives on the line every day. They don't keep those dogs for themselves. Without you here, Alex might not recognize how much Souze helps him. I noticed he brought Souze tonight, and Alex would never have done the right thing for himself in the past. He'd have come up with some sort of reasoning for why he could make do on his own."

"He's too selfless." She shook her head.

"And so are you." Greg reached out and tapped her on the nose.

She scrunched up her face. "Not really. I just stayed. I've been taking up all of your generosity."

She'd wanted more time to get to know Alex, explore what was between them. And then she'd become attached to Souze and to Boom and to all these people who were a part of the mini-world with Hope's Crossing Kennels at the epicenter. In a very short span of time, she'd come to love it here.

Gary grunted. "True. You stayed. And in my opinion, it was the best decision you could've made for you or for Alex."

"And we've definitely enjoyed you being here," Greg added, leaning in to bump his shoulder against hers.

It was impossible to remain hopeless around these two. They were such quiet wells of strength and encouragement. Well, maybe not quiet. "Thank you, both. I don't know what any of us would do without you two."

"I'm so glad you feel better, dear." Greg glanced at Gary. "So I have one thing I've been dying to know."

Elisa sipped her tea. "Hmm?"

"Alex. He's good, isn't he? We'll never know, but you could give us a hint."

Elisa's face suddenly burned with embarrassment. Sophie and Lyn could've asked her the very same question. Gary and Greg both seemed to know about her and Alex, though, and she wondered if it was obvious to everyone. "No kiss and tell."

Gary laughed. "Oh, the look on your face is enough. And there was definitely more than kissing. Good for you, girl. And *enjoy*."

*   *   *

About an hour later, Alex knocked on her door. She answered in her sleep tee and sweats, twisting the hem of the tee as she did.

His brows had been drawn together when the door opened, but his expression cleared when he looked at her tee. "So. How's my timing?"

She sighed. "Impeccable. I was just getting this on when you knocked."

He chuckled. The sound of it came from deep in his torso, rolling up and out and sending shivers through her. It wasn't necessarily filled with mirth, but it was a sound that lifted her up, excited her.

He stepped inside and closed the door behind him. "I have a question. You can absolutely say no. I won't be mad."

She looked up at him. He was different tonight, darker. An air of the earlier potential for violence still clung to him. Something fluttered low in her belly, but it wasn't fear. It was magnetic, exciting.

"Can I be with you tonight? All night?" There was raw need in his voice.

Instinctively she wanted to say yes, but he'd given her the choice, and she took the moment to think it through. "What about Boom?"

"She's sleeping over at a friend's tonight. She won't know I didn't go home."

And it might be better that way regardless, she realized. He was on edge. His temper was close to the surface, and she sensed he was struggling with it.

The question was whether she could handle being with him like this, tense with pent-up aggression.

Heat spread through her, and her nipples tightened. "Yes. Stay."

His clenched and unclenched his fists. "I want to be inside you."

It was a warning.

She crossed the distance between them, rested her hands against the flat planes of his chest, and rose up on her toes to kiss his jaw. "I want you inside me."

He set his hands on her hips and took a kiss from her, hungry and primal. He fed from her mouth, teased with his tongue, pressed hard until their teeth clashed ever so slightly before he backed off again, making her reach for him.

"I can't get enough of you, Elisa." He growled. "Be sure."

She wanted this, needed it after the stress of the evening. She'd crouched in the back room with the kids and listened to him stand up for her, protect her. And now here he was and they were alone and she could give herself up to him in every way.

She wanted it, and she trembled in anticipation. "I'm sure."

He walked her backward until the backs of her legs hit the bed. Stepping away from her, he yanked off his tee shirt and shucked the rest of his clothing, then reached for hers. In moments, she stood naked in front of him.

They left the lights on. His dark gaze took in every detail of her body, starting from her feet and rising. As his gaze lingered on her hips, then again on her breasts, her breath caught and her nipples tightened. He finally made eye contact and it burned into her. "You're beautiful."

He pulled her to him for another dizzying kiss, and when he tore his mouth from hers, she gasped for air. His hands gripped her shoulders, slid down her back, grasped her behind, and pulled her into his hips as he ground against her. The length of his erection was hard and ready between them, and she couldn't resist wrapping her fingers around the rigid length of him. He was huge, and she should've been afraid, but instead she was turned on.

He growled. "Too soon."

He took her hands off him and set his own on her hips, turning her to face the bed. With a palm between her shoulder blades and his other hand on her hip, he coaxed her into bending over, way over, until her hips were high and her face and shoulders were cushioned by the mattress. His hand moved from her hip to stroke her behind in soothing circles for long seconds until she steadied. Then he squeezed.

A low moan escaped her, and she turned her face into the blankets, trying to muffle the sound.

The hand on her behind slipped down, and his fingertips brushed over her, teasing her labia, then pressed at her inner thigh, encouraging her to widen her stance. She did, for him.

"I've been wanting to taste you," he rumbled from behind her. His breath scorched her skin as he kneeled low. And he did taste.

He teased her with long licks as he held her in place. His wicked tongue darted between her folds, almost reaching her but not quite. Then his free hand was pushing on the inside of her thigh again, and she widened her stance even further. His fingers held her folds open for him, and he blew a hot puff of air against her.

She groaned. His chuckle rolled over her again, and she shivered with it this time.

He tasted deeper this time, exploring her folds with

his tongue and darting farther into her entrance until she was whimpering into the blankets.

He was taking over her, seducing her body in ways she'd never thought possible, building a need inside of her stronger and more desperate than she'd ever experienced. She *wanted*, wanted him inside her.

"I'm rushing." His voice was tinged with guilt. "I need to be inside you."

Turning her head, she panted. "If you don't hurry, I am going to be so mad at you."

His hands gripped her behind, hard. She groaned and turned her face back into the blankets. His hands left her for a moment, but the heat of him was still close behind her. She heard the tearing sound of foil as he unwrapped a condom and rolled it on. Then the tip of him was nudging at her entrance. She couldn't wait. She pressed her hips back toward him as she arched, and he slid into her hard and fast.

"Alex!" His name burst from her as he filled her, stretching her.

He froze. "Does it hurt?"

She let out a groan. "You're so thick, *big*. I missed you."

An approving sound, full of male arrogance. "You like me inside you."

He rocked his hips against her, pressing his cock deeper inside her.

She whispered the word. "Yes."

"Good." He set his hands on her hips and withdrew almost all the way before he pressed deep inside her again, stretching her even further. He did it one more time before he picked up the pace.

He shifted his hands until one hand held her shoulder and the other pressed the base of her spine. The added pressure encouraged her to arch her back and bend into the bed while he drove into her over and over. She fisted the blankets under her as the pleasure built and she gave herself over to the sensation, to him. Every stroke inside her pressed a moan out of her until she was alternating between moans and hoarse whimpers as she asked him to go harder.

His hands tightened on her again, and he obliged. His hips pounded into hers as he drove inside her, hitting all the right spots on the way in and on the only slightly slower drawing out. Her stomach tightened as she approached the pinnacle of her pleasure, and she cried out as she fell over the edge and came.

His voice mingled with hers as he continued for a split second longer before shuddering into his own release.

CHAPTER TWENTY-TWO

Y ou know, sleepovers are definitely more fun than I remember from childhood." Elisa lay on her side with Alex pressed against the length of her back.

His chuckle rumbled up from his chest and over her back, sending delicious shivers through her entire body. "I hope so."

"I'm glad you stayed." She traced her finger down the inside of his arm, which she was currently using as a pillow.

"I'm glad you said yes to me." He shifted his hips against hers.

She let out a happy sigh. "Do you feel better now, too?"

He stilled against her back.

Hurriedly she tried to clarify. "We were both on edge last night. I don't mean…"

"It's okay." His other arm came across her in a brief hug before he set his free hand on her waist. "Last night definitely brought out some of the darker parts of me."

And she was as attracted to those parts of him as the kinder parts he'd displayed when they'd first met. At no time had she felt threatened or coerced by him, and she wanted him to know that. But he might not believe her if she just said it. Instead, she snuggled closer to him and went for a different response. "I can listen, too, if you'd like. I want to get to know you better."

"I've been a couple of different people over the years."

"You're still you," she responded. "But I'd like to understand how you got to who you are now, if you're willing to share."

He ran his hand over her hip, gently kneading as he progressed. For a moment, she wondered if he was trying to distract himself, because it was going to work if she didn't push the discussion. But he started talking. "It was rough overseas on active duty. Our SEAL unit tended to move out to forward positions to secure locations before there was a base established in the area. We were under constant strain. It wasn't a situation where a person could head out on a mission and return to a safe place at night to shower and get some sleep before going out again. We'd be out for days, even weeks at a time. And sleep was something you got while your teammates had the watch, but you were ready to jump into action at a moment's notice."

She snuggled in closer, unsure what to say but wanting to listen and take in what he was sharing.

"Thing is, we saw a lot of awful things." He fell silent for a moment, struggling for words. And then he dropped a kiss on her shoulder. "There isn't just one story; there's dozens. There isn't just one nightmare. And Forte, Cruz, and me...we all deal in our own ways.

For me, it was a state of hyperawareness, of being constantly on edge."

"Did it get better when you came back?" She hoped it had.

He huffed out a negative. "Uh-uh. I rushed home after each short deployment. I was married, and there was Serena to come home to. But at one point, I came home between missions to find divorce papers waiting for me. After that, I was looking forward to each new training, each new mission, because it was the easiest way to get through the time in between visitation with Serena. Then the call came. My ex-wife had been admitted to the hospital, literally as I was getting on a plane to come back to the States. She'd passed away before I even landed on home soil."

Elisa's heart broke for Alex and for Serena. "I'm so sorry."

He squeezed her hip. "Don't be. You weren't there and I try not to be. My ex-wife was a long-time drug user. Not street drugs or anything obvious. But she managed to get a hold of all the prescription meds she could ever want while she was cheating on me with some doctor. He made sure she had all the hydrocodone, oxycodone, diazepam, or alprazolam she could want, and she popped them like candy, depending on what new thing she didn't want to deal with on a particular day. She'd been hooked for years. When she came down with a cold, it advanced so fast into pneumonia no one knew what was happening until it was too late, and all the drugs she was self-dosing, thinking she'd make herself feel better, only made her condition worse. By the time her parents came to check on her and Boom...they called an ambulance right away, but the hospital couldn't save her."

"Oh no." Elisa didn't think there was anything she could say. But she felt for him, for the awful situation.

"After that, I didn't care about anything but Serena. My wife's parents wanted custody, made an argument about them being able to provide a more stable home environment, but I asked Serena what she wanted and she said she wanted to stay with me." His tone had turned fierce.

And she loved him for it, for how much he would fight the world for Serena.

"They threatened to take me to court, but their finances were already tied up in going after the doctor for providing my wife with all of those medications. I took advantage of their split attention and managed to keep custody of Serena." Alex relaxed against her again, brushing his lips over her shoulder. "Forte invited me here. Said he'd set this place up to start over on home soil. Close enough to a couple major cities to get work if we didn't want to get into training the dogs, but with enough privacy from the immediate community that we weren't constantly fighting our old selves to blend into civilian life. It's a steady income with health benefits for Serena and an actual house for her to grow up in."

"Hope's Crossing is a nice place." Simple statement, maybe. But exactly what she'd thought when she'd first come up the drive to return Boom's glove. "It's peaceful and active at the same time. There's plenty to do for all of you and it's not so quiet it drives you crazy."

"Exactly." He squeezed her hip again before running his hand up and over her hip in lazy circles. "When each of us arrived, we were all sort of raw. But we started getting better at our own pace. I just—I had to pull myself together right away to talk to schools and teachers for Boom. I kept telling myself I could handle things, but crowded public places got worse for me, too frenetic. It was harder and harder to keep my temper under control."

"Like at the ER." She turned in his arms and started to run her hand over his chest.

He made a deep sound of appreciation in his chest and pressed a kiss to her forehead. "Like at the ER. You coming in when you did actually helped me calm down. But my temper wasn't the most dangerous part. That's just hot air, and it doesn't make friends. I try to keep it under control to make social life easier for Serena. I don't particularly care if random strangers like me. The bigger issues come when I think I'm back overseas. The minute or two when I'm not sure where I am and I'm prepared to act as if I'm in a combat zone. I could come out of it amid a body count one of these days. And I can't do that. I can't."

"Do they have counselors to help you?" Elisa was absolutely sure his sharing would make a difference. With her, but with a professional, too, who could offer more advice.

"Yeah. Cruz has a contact for a decent one over in Jersey at McGuire Air Force Base." Alex sighed. "I didn't want to go because it'd give my late wife's parents leverage if they do decide to take me to court for custody of Serena. But I was avoiding public places more and more."

"And avoiding those situations wasn't helping you

handle them." She snuggled into the hollow of his shoulder. "What can I do?"

"Well, I realized the first weekend you were here that we have a mutual friend with unexpected talents." He chuckled. "Seriously, if Souze hadn't been there, things could've gone south fast."

"Really?" She struggled to figure out when he was talking about, but there'd been a lot going on that first weekend, and he'd been out and around Revolution MMA with Souze on her behalf multiple times.

"Yeah. I was caught up in one of my...moments. He poked and nudged me until I came out of it." He wrapped his arms around her and hugged her tight. "It could've been bad, but Souze brought me out of it. Natural instinct. His behavior could be positively reinforced. He could be trained to recognize the signs earlier and respond. There's a lot of other behaviors he could do to help me in public places. He could be trained to sit facing the opposite direction I'm facing when I stop so I don't have to worry about what's on my six. He'd be keeping watch over the rear approach for me. He could be trained to circle around me to make people in a high traffic area give me room and create a safe personal space. He's smart enough to learn several other behaviors to help deal with situations as they come up."

She lifted her head and nodded. "He's a big, intimidating dog. Some people would give him space just because he is the dog he is."

He smiled. "Exactly. I'll need to work it out with Forte and probably coordinate with the psych over at McGuire, but Souze could become a PTSD service dog.

And if he can help me function, I can be there for Boom whenever and wherever she needs me."

Elisa couldn't stop smiling. "I'm so glad for you all."

"All?"

She stretched her neck and kissed his jaw. "Yes, all. Serena gets you. You get Serena and Souze. Souze gets to stay here with people he likes, doing interesting things that have nothing to do with chasing down awful people. I think it suits him."

And she was attached to the black and tan fur monster, too.

Alex was silent for a moment. "Will you come out with Souze and me for our first outing to test this?"

"You and Souze have been going out in public." Confused, she tipped her head to the side.

Laughter danced in Alex's eyes. "Yes, but this time it'll be with this purpose in mind and I can't think of something I want to do more than take you out to dinner."

"Oh." She bit her lip and blinked back emotion. "I'd like that a lot."

More than that. To be included, be a part of it. She'd love to.

"Good. After work, I'll get Cruz or Forte to give you a ride with a two-hour head start over to Revolution to get freshened up. Then Souze and I'll come pick you up for an early dinner. Sound good?"

She smiled. "Absolutely."

He kissed her then, and his hands roamed over her.

Laughing, she came up for air. "We do have work today."

He growled against her throat. "And it'll still be there for us."

"I refuse to be late!" She squirmed and gasped when he slid a finger inside her.

"We'll be quick."

She clutched at his shoulders and answered, breathless, "Okay. Quick. Quick is good."

He was ready. It was hot. And oh wow, his idea of quick blew her mind.

* * *

"I'm home!" A ten-year-old whirlwind blew into the front reception area.

Elisa smiled. Or maybe she was still smiling from when Alex and she had made it back to Hope's Crossing just a couple of hours earlier. "Welcome back. Your dad's wrapping up the first morning agility class and then he'll meet you up at the house for second breakfast. Mind if I join you two?"

She loved the idea of second breakfast on the weekends. Actually, the men of Hope's Crossing did it all through the week because they ate like training athletes. Five to six small meals a day. But on weekends, they did it so Boom could snack with them and get in quality time with her father.

"Duh. Food is always better when you join us. Dad actually talks." Boom stampeded past the front desk. "Heading up to the house now."

Elisa actually glanced up from entering the data for the latest new client and did a double-take. "Whoa. Hold it."

Boom froze, ducking her head and lifting her shoulders as if cringing would hide what Elisa had already seen.

"Let's see." Elisa stood up to see over the high counter of the reception desk better.

Slender shoulders slumped, and Boom turned to face her.

No laughing. Laughing would be bad. "I take it you ladies had a sort of makeup experiment last night?"

Boom heaved an exaggerated sigh. "This morning before breakfast."

Oh, dear. So the raccoon-style eyeliner and mascara had been on purpose and not the result of a night sleeping with it on. "I see. And all of you have similar... looks?"

"Maybe?" Boom scrunched up her face. "Marlene brought her mom's makeup kit, and we each did our own. Grace and Marlene have more practice."

"Ah." Elisa struggled for a light tone. "Even with someone teaching me, it takes me a couple of tries to get it the way I want it to look."

A dam burst inside Boom. "I don't get it. I don't. You and Lyn and Sophie always look like yourselves. I don't want to look like somebody else. What's wrong with me?"

"You're incredible," Elisa said simply. "Nothing's wrong with you."

Boom stared at her for a moment. "Makeup is stupid."

Elisa chewed her lip for a minute. Boom was young, really young, and more interested in sports and mixed martial arts, to boot. Most of her friends were boys. That's why last night's sleepover had been unusual, according to Gary and Greg. But Boom was still a girl and going to school with other girls.

"Here's the thing. I don't think liking any particular

thing is stupid. I like what I like, and I try to respect what other people like." Not the easiest perspective to maintain sometimes. "So if a person likes makeup, it's their thing and that's okay."

Boom grabbed a pen from the container and flipped it over and over between her fingers, clearly still agitated. Elisa watched her and wondered if Alex did the same thing.

"Liking makeup doesn't make you any less able because you can still go toe to toe with any of the boys at Revolution MMA." Elisa tapped the counter in front of Boom, bringing the young girl's gaze up to meet her own. "But being able to do anything the boys can do does make it kind of uncomfortable with some girls, doesn't it?"

"They shouldn't matter." The stubborn tone was something Boom had inherited from her father.

Elisa smiled as she recognized it and admitted silently that she loved it in both of them. "They shouldn't. But leaving yourself open to their kind of criticism isn't fun, either. Besides, there's a good reason to learn how to do your nails and experiment with makeup."

Boom's eyes widened. "There is?"

Elisa nodded. "Skills are always good to have and learning to do your own makeup is a skill. It lets you look the way you want, when you want, at will. You can go natural any day of the week with no cosmetics at all. And if you have the skill, on the one night in a million, you also can give yourself a Cinderella moment. All on your own. Minimum stress."

"I never thought about it that way." Boom tipped her head to the side.

Elisa shrugged. "You don't need it. Honestly. You've got a great face with healthy, lovely skin and a natural blush to your cheeks. But if you ever want to learn, just so you know how to accentuate what you've got at the right time, we can sit down together."

Any person looked a million times better when they could step out with confidence in themselves. For Boom, ten was way too early for the works, in Elisa's opinion. But a little dab of gloss here and maybe a touch of powder could do wonders for her confidence level in simply knowing she could do it if she wanted to.

Then Boom could go back to being herself without the doubt.

Boom nodded. "Let's do it. I want to learn to do it right so I don't ruin my face."

Elisa blinked. "Who said anything about ruining your face?"

Though that was another consideration. It could totally happen with bad habits.

Boom lifted a shoulder in a half shrug. "It's one of the things those girls talk about when they make fun of girls who try makeup when they don't know how. Mess up your face forever or end up with ugly, yellow fungus nails."

Ugh. No wonder Boom had been twisted up about this. Elisa would've been, too, even as an adult.

"Good call. I like your face, so I've got a vested interest in helping you keep it the way it is." Elisa winked. "A lot of beauty regimens are mostly about properly washing and moisturizing your face, anyway. The better you take care of what you have, the less you ever need to tweak the way you look."

"Washing? Like taking those sugar baths you talked about?" Boom perked up at the idea.

Elisa laughed. "There's different kinds of stuff. Sugar scrubs could be for your lips once in a while but mostly you use the scrubs for the parts of your body that take a lot of abuse, like your hands and feet or elbows and knees."

"Break out the big guns for the extra rough spots." Boom nodded sagely.

"Something like that." Elisa shook her head.

Boom gave her that brilliant smile. "Thanks. I kinda like my face, too. It's why I keep my guard up 'cause a punch to the face can ruin it, too."

Elisa raised her eyebrows. Apparently Boom had taken a lot of talk into consideration. "Good point."

Boom was going to grow up into one heck of a woman. Alex might not survive it.

"You know, Dad spends a lot of time looking at your face." Boom's voice took on a sly tone.

"Oh?" Nope. Elisa was not going to take the bait from a pre-teen.

"He seems to like you whether you have makeup on or not." Boom chewed her lip.

Wait. Elisa deliberately stopped chewing her own.

"I bet if you did your makeup all special, his jaw would hit the floor." Boom tipped her head back as she continued to consider. "But most mornings he has a silly kind of smile on his face when he sees you before you've had your coffee, and you don't wear makeup most days. So I guess that's a different kind of like, too."

"Maybe." Faint response, but it was the best she could manage.

Alex watched her that much? And she hadn't noticed. Well, maybe it wasn't a big surprise since it seemed to be before she'd had her morning caffeine, but still, she'd never thought he paid much attention.

"Yup. Maybe." Boom bolted then, heading back to the kitchen and out the back door closest to her house.

Outmaneuvered. By a ten-year-old.

This round went to the Boom.

CHAPTER TWENTY-THREE

The outdoor patio was a good idea." Rojas watched Elisa take in the décor of the cafe with a soft smile on her face.

This place was busy even on weeknights, a popular spot for couples of every age. Sitting inside would've been a nightmare for Rojas but out here, they could enjoy the autumn colors on the surrounding trees. The owners had set tall heat lamps out at intervals between the tables to keep patrons warm.

Rojas had taken mental note of the various couples, mostly younger and middle-aged sets braving the evening. All of the wait staff were teenagers and in fact, the entire restaurant was run by young people. It was trendy and hip, with a sophisticated menu. Exactly the kind of place he'd wanted to treat Elisa to.

Her dark brown hair was done in soft curls falling around her shoulders, and she'd worn makeup this evening, making her blue eyes brighter and somehow more striking. Her lips were even more tempting than usual, and he was sure he wasn't going to get through the whole meal without wanting to steal a kiss. She was beautiful every day, and tonight, she'd highlighted a few of her charms specifically for him. He liked it.

"This restaurant has some interesting backstory, according to Sophie." He took a sip of his water. "And Cruz has brought Lyn here a couple of times for dinner."

"I like that it's pet friendly." Elisa leaned to one side to scratch the side of Souze's face.

Rojas liked the way Elisa thought about Souze's comfort, too. The big dog lay next to his feet, relaxed and wearing a service-dog-in-training vest. Lyn had sent it along from her supplies since the vests they had at Hope's Crossing were mostly military working or K9 dog vests.

The staff at this café had welcomed them both and Souze, too, bringing out water for all three of them. Souze had his very own bowl under the table. As long as Rojas could remember not to kick the bowl, both Elisa and Souze would be happy with him. He hoped. It'd been a damned long time since he'd taken a woman out to dinner.

Drinks, one-night stands, even 0200 breakfasts at a diner after a booty call. Yeah, he'd done those. But this was *dinner*. He wanted Elisa to enjoy it, and he wanted this to be the first of many.

No pressure or anything.

"But you haven't been here yet?" Elisa tipped her head sideways, and he wondered how he'd ever manage not to nibble at her neck in public.

It was a good thing the tables at this café had them

sitting opposite each other. If they'd been in a booth, there'd have been some serious necking. "I figured we'd both have fun if it was a restaurant we're both checking out for the first time."

He was rewarded with one of her bright smiles. She'd started smiling for real after they'd included her in Sunday brunch. The small, polite smiles the day or two before had been nice but didn't chase away the sadness in her eyes. Now when she smiled at him it took his breath away.

"New Hope is less crowded than I thought it'd be, the way Boom was talking about it." Elisa sipped at her water.

"Yeah, well, Boom runs up and down the streets trying not to knock anybody over." Rojas considered the menu. It was prix fixe so he could make his choices up front and not worry about it through the rest of the meal. "A ten-year-old takes up a lot of space."

Elisa nodded in concession. "True. She was saying we should walk down to the end of the street and get cupcakes."

Rojas grinned and leaned forward over the table. "Two reasons we're not going to do that. First, I'm told there's really good desserts here. I think you'll want to try these. And second, the cupcake store Boom likes is around the corner and way down the end of the main strip of stores here in New Hope and it'll be closed by the time we walk there. If she was hoping we'd bring her some cupcakes, she can hope for dessert on a different day. Sophie's probably baking something full of sugar and bad for us for tomorrow's brunch anyway."

Elisa narrowed her eyes. "Ooh. Good points on all

counts. Though I wouldn't mind a walk through New Hope after dinner if you two are up for it."

He glanced down at Souze, who looked back up at him with eyes half-lidded, and shrugged. "Could be. Let's enjoy dinner first and play it by ear. Any idea of what you want?"

"I'm super hungry," Elisa admitted. "The pickled beets and goat cheese look interesting, and the braised pork shank sounds amazing."

"It does." He put his menu down. "I'm thinking I want to try the fried risotto balls and don't tell Gary or Greg."

She raised an eyebrow. "Because of the innuendo they'd make?"

"Nah." He shook his head. "Because there's mushrooms in the risotto and they'd get on my case about eating fungus."

"They don't like mushrooms?" Her brows drew together in her puzzlement. She was extremely cute.

"It's a long story involving Boom and this phase she went through where we had to justify to her why she needed to eat anything. We had protein and vegetables covered but fungus was a harder sell."

Elisa laughed.

Dinner went faster than Rojas thought possible. Service was good. Souze was well behaved. Every table at the café was filled and it was a small space, but the outdoor seating had enough room for him to relax. He wouldn't have chosen to sit outdoors if it hadn't been for Sophie's suggestion and the fact that Souze sat with him. Despite the GSD's chill demeanor, his ears twitched back and forth with every sound. Watchful. Meaning

Rojas could ease his watch a little. Enough to enjoy the evening.

Elisa had just tried one of a trio of mousses, and her eyes almost rolled into the back of her head, when a woman in a dress suit approached their table.

"Elisa! There you are!" The woman's voice had been pitched to carry and everyone in the restaurant turned to look as she took the last few steps to their table.

Startled, Elisa blinked up at the woman. "Julie. What are you doing here?"

"Looking for you, obviously." As the woman waved her hand, a strong mix of cheap perfume and hairspray wafted over to Rojas. "Your mother is incredibly worried, so when Joseph contacted us to let us know he'd found you, I offered to fly over on the first available flight."

He held his breath until he thought the evening breeze must have dissipated the pungent smell. "Did you fly in alone?"

Julie looked at him as if she'd only just noticed him. "I don't see how that's any of your business, whoever you are, but yes."

Julie crossed her arms, forcing her low-cut shirt lower and showing off some very impressive cleavage. There was a calculating look in her eye for a split second and then it was gone. She was checking to see if he'd checked her out.

Rojas didn't lean back or away from her, instead reaching forward to brush Elisa's hand on the table with his fingertips. Hopefully, she'd take it as a comfort. Whoever this Julie was, she'd caught Elisa by surprise and the tension was becoming palpable.

"I'm sorry I've been out of touch with my mother." Elisa didn't take her hand away from his, but she didn't look at him, either. "But I did share my reservations about checking in with her."

Julie rolled her eyes. Hard. "Which is why we are all incredibly worried about you. Disappearing without *any* warning. Leaving your *fiancé*. Hopping *all over* the country over the last few months. You were under a lot of stress planning your wedding, and I really think taking all those pills was getting out of hand."

Rojas went cold. "Pills?"

No. Absolutely not. If there was one hard line he had, it was abuse of those damned medications.

"Oh? Don't worry, they're all prescribed medications." Julie fluffed her hair. "Taking a couple a day is no big deal. I took a diazepam before I hopped on the flight over here. Couldn't fly without it. But, really, it got to a point where every time we saw Elisa, her eyes were vacant and glazed. She was always bumping into something."

"I was depressed, not drugged. And I don't bump into things more often than anyone else does. When I've gotten distracted, I've bumped into the front desk back at work even. You *know* this." Elisa tried to turn her hand to catch his, but he withdrew it. "Joseph got the medications for me, but I wouldn't take them."

He didn't want to hear it. The words "prescribed" and "medication" echoed inside his head, and all he could think of was his late wife's slurred voice yelling at him over the phone, telling him it was his fault she needed her pills. After all, he was never home, always out of communication when on missions. They'd never known exactly when he was leaving or when he'd be coming back.

"Please." Julie's tone turned sarcastic. "You expect us to believe the way you changed, the way you were walking around like nothing around you was touching you, was because you were depressed? I don't think so. Your mother was already talking to Joseph about maybe limiting those prescriptions. He said you insisted you needed them to cope."

Rojas stared at Elisa, hard. He'd told her about his late wife. She knew how he felt about those damned pills. "You should have told me."

Elisa's eyes widened, hurt flashing, but he clamped down on the part of him that cared whether he hurt her or not.

She set her jaw. "There's nothing to tell. This is completely out of context."

Of course there wasn't anything to tell. He didn't want to listen to any lies. "No one with a drug problem thinks there's actually a problem."

His wife hadn't, right up until her problem killed her.

Elisa's breath left her in a *whoosh*, like he'd punched her in a gut. "You don't believe me."

"I think the way a person reacts when they're caught by surprise says a lot." He snapped.

He stood up abruptly, and Souze scrambled to his feet to join him. The woman, Julie, stood her ground just long enough to brush against him accidentally before taking a few steps back. "Oh, are you leaving?"

He glared at the woman. "I think the two of you have some catching up to do."

She smiled, fluttering long fake eyelashes at him. "We

do. But after she's checked back in with her mother and her fiancé, maybe Elisa could introduce us properly and we could get to know each other."

Disgust filled him. Scavenger. "Pass."

Elisa came to her feet. "Alex. Please don't leave."

He took a couple of steps away. Hell, he couldn't even look at her. "I need to clear my head. Text me when you're ready to head back."

"Oh, don't worry, I have a rental car. I plan to take her to wherever she's staying and help her pack up." Julie brushed a hand down his back, and he stiffened. Souze growled. Her touch disappeared. "Elisa should really go back to where she belongs."

Red haze crept across his vision. Suddenly, the café was too crowded. Conversations, whispers going on around him left him vulnerable, exposed. There was no room to get clear and no place to take cover. He'd just get enough distance to cool down and she still had her phone. Rojas left before he exploded.

*   *   *

Elisa watched Alex leave, incredulous. He didn't believe her.

Julie, who was supposed to be her friend, let out a disgusted sigh and sat in Alex's seat. "He's got a crappy attitude. Where did you even find him?"

Elisa closed her eyes. "Why are you here, Julie?"

It didn't make sense. Julie had been a friend since her last year in college. Elisa had shared everything with her about getting her first job, dating, even meeting Joseph. Julie had been excited for her through it all, supportive.

But when Elisa began to see the reality of belonging to Joseph, Julie had been more inclined to make the same arguments as Elisa's mother so the two of them had grown distant.

Once Elisa had left, she sent Julie one e-mail to let her friend know she was okay, but she hadn't been in contact since. Her being here made no sense. Her being in communication with Joseph was crazy.

"I told you, your mother and your fiancé are worried about you." Julie's voice dripped with sweetness.

It probably wasn't worth noting that Julie hadn't claimed to be concerned about Elisa's well-being. Wouldn't want to be struck down by lightning or anything.

"My mother, I'd believe. Joseph wouldn't be worried about me so much as concerned about what people would think when they found out I left him." Elisa pulled out her purse. Hopefully she had enough cash to cover dinner so she could go after Alex. They needed to clear the air, at least, even if he was done with her. And he shouldn't go walking through New Hope angry the way he was. She'd promised to help him tonight and she would, even if he was beyond angry with her.

"See, I don't understand why the fuck you would leave Joseph." Julie leaned forward and took a spoonful of Elisa's dessert. "He's got money, influence, looks. He's the full package. He had the most incredible house set up for you."

"A house surrounded by guard dogs as likely to keep me from leaving as keep anyone from coming in." Elisa tasted bile as she thought about it.

"Obviously, you don't mind dogs." Julie waved a

spoon in the general direction of where Alex and Souze had gone.

Everyone had their own definition of what they were looking for. Elisa had been happy exploring the connection she shared with Alex, but it wasn't until he'd walked away, believing awful things about her, that she realized how much his opinion mattered to her. The absence of his trust left her aching, hollow. Worse, she was angry. Betrayed. He could've at least listened to her. But like everyone else, including the former friend sitting across the table from her, he hadn't.

"You have no concept of the difference." Elisa glared at Julie. "You didn't understand when I tried to explain why Joseph wasn't the right partner for me in the first place, and I don't expect you to now. But I'm assuming he told you how to find me. Didn't you stop to wonder how he knew? Or how incredibly insane his behavior has been, chasing me from state to state across the entire country?"

Julie sighed. "You don't appreciate the attention people give you. You never did. I don't see how you even deserve it."

Elisa waved at the waiter and mouthed a request for the bill. She couldn't just leave without paying for dinner, and she was starting to be afraid Alex wouldn't come back. If he didn't, she wasn't sure what she'd do but she definitely wanted the chance to talk this through with him.

The mix of anger and fear churned her stomach. Part of her wanted to stand up for herself and the other wanted to beg him to realize he'd been misled. And, honestly, she had a right to both emotions at the moment. She embraced that at least and figured she'd untangle the whole mess once she talked to him. It could fix things or they might be broken past mending, but at the very least, with Alex she wanted understanding.

"I don't think you're done with dessert yet." Julie took another spoonful. "Or at least I'm not. Is this any way to treat a friend who's flown across the country to find you?"

Elisa glared at her. "I don't even understand you. But let's get this clear. We are not friends."

"No need to find the waiter, dear." A voice come from over her shoulder, and her heart stopped. "I've already taken care of the bill. You can have another bite of dessert, but then we have to be going."

Elisa turned in her chair but the newcomer was standing so close, she couldn't rise without stepping right into him. "Joseph."

CHAPTER TWENTY-FOUR

Rojas wasn't even sure how many turns he'd taken down the side streets leading away from New Hope's main street. He'd barely had the presence of mind when he'd gotten clear of the crowded café to turn left and head away from River Road. That was where most of the evening's foot traffic was and that was exactly where he didn't want to be.

God, he was so angry. It'd taken several blocks before he could think at all.

Elisa should really go back to where she belongs.

Maybe Julie, whoever she was, was right. He'd known Elisa for all of a week. Okay, a week and a day. They'd never run a background check on her, only taken her at her word. She'd played them all for suckers. Played him. The others only followed his lead.

As he walked, Souze kept pace. The big dog had liked Elisa, though, and Boom would be heartbroken when Rojas returned to tell her she couldn't spend time with Elisa anymore. It'd rip him up to hurt Boom, but he absolutely would not expose her to another adult abusing drugs or indulging in any destructive addiction. Boom had lost her mother. She didn't need to start caring about another woman who'd progressively destroy herself.

Elisa's face rose up in his memory, the look of hurt in her eyes when she realized he didn't believe her.

He drew a hard line with addiction. He wouldn't, couldn't get sucked into another life and expose Boom to it all again. He'd have to talk to Forte. Find a new administrative assistant and maybe help Elisa get a new job, assuming she didn't leave town. Her friend had come to help her pack, after all.

Something about his line of thought bugged him, though. He was pissed, too angry to run through it again for another couple of minutes. And then he came to a stop and cursed.

Forte would hate having to get a new admin assistant. And whoever it was would need to figure out Elisa's organizational system and the spreadsheets she'd set up. They'd need the computer skills to keep up the newsletters and update the websites. In the space of a week, Elisa had overhauled the way Hope's Crossing Kennels did business, for the better. The clients loved the new check-in process and were relieved not to have to fill out the same forms by hand every time they came to a class. It was seriously possible they were getting more return clients because Elisa had made checking in so much easier. She'd changed the kennels.

And if she had proven herself and those skills, didn't that indicate a certain level of honesty? Integrity?

His phone buzzed in his pocket and he answered without looking to see who the caller was. "Elisa?"

"No, man." Cruz's voice came through the phone. "Isn't she with you?"

Rojas swallowed another curse. "Long story. What did you need?"

"I got information back on the agency behind the private investigator you spooked last week and those two out-of-town cops." Cruz was tense, worried. "The agency specializes in discreet services. High-level executives contract with the agency and the agency hires the actual resources to go and carry out the dirty work. If anything backfires, there's a degree of separation so the executives can keep their hands clean. Plausible deniability or some shit."

"Sounds in line with what Elisa told us about her ex." Rojas considered his own words. Elisa hadn't done or said anything yet to deserve having her word questioned.

"Yeah well, you didn't exactly make great friends with those two officers. I'd be more worried about them than the PI. For the PI it wasn't anything personal. He took his contract money and went on his way. He was local staffing and has plenty of business chasing adulterous spouses." Cruz sounded disgusted. "The officers, though, we've got positive ID on them based on the security feed from Revolution MMA. They're out of Richmond, Virginia, and were off-duty on vacation when they happened to stop by."

"Long way out of their way for a visit." Rojas didn't like the sound of it.

"Yeah, Ky didn't like it, either. He's going to take it internal." Cruz didn't sound sad about it.

"As long as they don't come back, I'm okay with that." Rojas had plenty to worry about as it was. "What else is on your mind?"

Because Cruz hated talking on the phone as much as he did and his friend was lingering.

"This is a shit-ton of effort and resources to track down one woman." Cruz let the air out of his lungs in a *whoosh*. "This is beyond early stalker behavior. He doesn't just want to keep tabs on her. It's escalating in an insanely short period of time and all signs point to him wanting to have her back in his hands ASAP."

A cold knot started to gather in Rojas's stomach. "Is there more information?"

"I did some digging and called in a favor or two. This guy is a textbook narcissist. I'd bet megalomania isn't far off the mark, either. He doesn't care about anyone but himself and it shows in his business." Cruz's voice turned grim. "Corbin Systems contracts services to several private military organizations. Everything on the record is too clean to believe."

Meaning there had to be shady shit going on behind the scenes, just as Elisa had told them. Rojas didn't like where this was going.

Cruz continued, "The CIO himself has been on a couple of discreet news releases as heading up a massive two-year project on some new weapons system design and integration. So there's Elisa's story confirmed. But here's the catch. Phase one of the project just completed, and he is on the brink of closing a huge deal for phase two. It's enough to take up the time of five heavy-hitting project managers. Why is this guy splitting his focus between the project and Elisa?"

A good question. "She's an obsession."

He could sort of relate to that. He'd thought of little besides Elisa since the night he'd met her, Boom being the number one exception.

"True. But why not be satisfied with knowing exactly where she is and what she's doing? Why not be satisfied with occasionally messing up her head with the texts? Why escalate right now when focus is needed on this huge business deal?" Cruz's questions all hit hard.

"He needs her. In person."

"Didn't Elisa say he took her everywhere with him? And she's his biometric key, right?"

"Yes." Rojas barely choked out the affirmative.

"This guy has high security at almost all of his facilities. The research and development plants all require fingerprint and retinal scan." Cruz picked up momentum. "If you wanted to breach any of those security systems, who is the first person you'd grab?"

"Him." Easy choice. The man probably had access to everything.

"Uh-uh." Cruz was starting to sound very worried. "He hasn't taken a tour of the facilities in six months or more. It's mentioned in the a few speculative articles regarding the upcoming deal."

Six months. Because Joseph Corbin Junior couldn't access his own facilities. Elisa wasn't with him. It was her fingerprint and retinal scan that were required.

"No." Rojas shook his head, searching for holes in the theory. "They're his companies. He could have the systems re-keyed. There's always a password reset, even for biometrics."

"For access to the facilities, yes." Cruz shot back, ready

for the challenge. "But he's been able to keep tabs on her all this time. He knew where to find his key when he really needed it. But what if his pride and his obsession push him to go get his property, especially with phase two of his particular pet project about to be finalized?"

"Shit." Cold spread through Rojas's chest and out toward his limbs. "And this time it's different. He's losing control of her. He doesn't know where she is all the time."

"He's on a time crunch now," Cruz finished.

Her friend had walked in and pushed a button for him. And he'd completely gone ballistic. But it was too damned convenient for the woman to have found them away from Hope's Crossing Kennels, in a restaurant in a completely different town.

He turned on his heel and started back, cursing himself as he went. Souze kept with him watchful in response to the sudden urgency. "Get a hold of Ky. I think there's a problem. Tell him to head to New Hope."

"You need me and Forte?"

"Stand by," Rojas responded. "I'd appreciate it if you could keep an eye on Boom for me."

"Always."

Rojas ended the call and started running back to the café.

*　*　*

Joseph leaned in, grabbed Elisa's arm just above the elbow, and whispered in her ear. "Continue to make a scene and I will be forced to create a distraction. A horrible accident, perhaps. It would be terrible for business if a random driver were to lose control of their car and drive directly into the dining room. People could be hurt. The business would have difficulty recovering. You would be responsible."

His lips brushed the shell of her ear as he spoke, and she trembled. He'd do it. She wouldn't doubt him there. And he probably had a driver waiting outside because in all the time she'd been with him, he'd always had a driver and a backup mode of transportation ready in case something happened to the primary. Flat tires, bad traffic—Joseph had always been prepared to do what it took to get where he was going.

Julie watched, unconcerned and even gleefully interested, as she continued to gobble up Elisa's mousse trio. "This is really good, by the way. You sure you aren't going to take your last bite?"

Elisa spread her free hand over the phone on the table, the one Alex had given her. She dragged it off the surface, trying to hide it with as much of her palm as possible and trying to make it look like she was just her putting her hand into her lap. Julie might've seen her phone on the table earlier but her "friend" had been very focused on pissing off Alex. Hopefully, Elisa would have a chance to get a message out.

"What do you get out of this, Julie?" Probably not anything Elisa needed to know, but she wanted to.

Joseph's fingers dug into her arm. "I said not to continue making a scene."

Elisa closed her mouth and carefully smoothed the expression from her face. She'd only set the phone to a swipe to get past the screen lock in case she needed quick access. Under-the-table texting wasn't something she'd ever been good at and she only hoped the message would go through.

The pressure on her arm ceased. "Excellent. You look lovely this evening in a simple sort of way. Wear a darker lipstick in the future and put more effort into your hairstyle. I prefer up-dos at dinner, even at...casual establishments like these. I've missed you."

A scream was crawling its way up her throat, so she took a sip of water. Joseph watched her patiently, or with what passed for patience with him. It was the anticipation of a snake, waiting until a moment of inattention. Then he'd strike out at her and she'd have no time to avoid him. She wasn't sure why he hadn't moved to leave yet, then she remembered. He'd given her permission to take one more bite of dessert.

Hand shaking, she lifted her spoon and scooped up a small bit of chocolate mousse Julie hadn't devoured. She brought the spoon to her lips and ate, trying not to gag.

The corners of Joseph's mouth turned upward. "Good girl. Let's go now."

He didn't let go of her arm as she rose, and to anyone else's eye, he was helping to steady her. Having him touch her again made her skin crawl. He was always one step ahead of her and she'd learned already that making a scene would only result in awful things later. Unless she was absolutely sure she could get away, she had to do things as he told her. Had to.

Her thoughts started to scramble and she struggled to catch someone's eye, anyone. As they turned to head through the café's main dining room to the entrance, he held her back for a moment and took her phone from her hand.

"It would be unfortunate if the authorities were to attempt to track this phone via the GPS locator." He glanced at the screen, pulling up the call log, and Elisa's heart froze. There were no recent calls, none made in the last half hour or more. With a satisfied huff, he tossed it back toward the table and it hit a chair before tumbling to the floor. "I'll give you a new one."

She didn't dare glance after the phone he'd taken away. It was another one of his tests. It would be a mistake to focus on anything but what he was providing for her. He'd find a way to hurt her for anything less than the perfect response. So, instead, she met his gaze steadily. "Thank you."

He smiled his faint, reptilian smile again.

It was the perfect billionaire boyfriend smile. Where less was more: only the upturned corners of the mouth and perhaps a hint of teeth if a woman was lucky. She'd found herself eager to do something to make him smile in the past. Trying so very hard for such a small amount of good humor. She hadn't known it was all he had in him.

He ushered her out of the café and down to the sidewalk. She tried to look up and down the street without turning her head too much. Make it too obvious and he'd tighten his control on her somehow, and she wanted him to think he had her. He hadn't checked the text history, hadn't seen her call for help. She might have a chance.

Please, Alex, please be right on the street somewhere.

She'd been hoping Alex and Souze weren't far. He'd said to text him when she was ready to go back, so he hadn't intended to leave her behind completely, regardless of how angry he was. But there was no sign of him.

Despair crashed down on her, and her vision blurred as tears threatened.

"No need to be frustrated, dear." Joseph leaned in to murmur in her ear again. "Our driver had to go some blocks away to park. He'll join us shortly. You won't be waiting long."

"I parked around the corner." Julie flipped her curls over her shoulder. "I'll meet you at the airport."

Joseph nodded. "Your flight information will be sent to your phone."

Julie batted her lashes. "I thought I was riding in the private jet with you."

"Speed is not a concern in your return home." Joseph's tone was dismissive. Of course. He was done with her. "You can take a commercial flight."

"That's fucking ridiculous." Julie's face twisted in anger. "I did everything you asked me to and you're going to ditch me on the way back to DC?"

As Julie proceeded to give Joseph a piece of her mind, Elisa pulled her thoughts together. Okay, so Alex wasn't nearby and wasn't going to save her. She had very little time to save herself because once she was in Joseph's car, she'd be enfolded in the layers of security he maintained. There'd be a driver for now and maybe a bodyguard. Once they arrived at the airport, there'd be another bodyguard or two. They'd be in private lounges until their flight was ready and then the private jet would transport them to wherever he had in mind, whether it was back to the DC area or someplace else. When she'd been running from Joseph, distance hadn't been important because he could chase her anywhere. It'd been the randomness of the location she'd depended on to hide from him.

And random was what would help her now. She needed to behave as he expected and create a chance for herself.

What would Boom do?

Julie stormed off with an ear-splitting screech. Joseph muttered a curse and tugged Elisa across the street.

"Where—"

"That entitled bitch Julie thinks she's going to cause a fuss, going off to catch the attention of the authorities." His lips pressed into a thin line, and the muscles in his jaw jumped as he ground his teeth. "Her temper tantrums are an excellent asset on occasion, but the timing is currently less than perfect. I'll have to consider her punishment later. Perhaps a few choice photographs will leak out to the modeling agencies she was hoping to sign with. She has rather delusional aspirations, unfortunately. Attractive charms, yes, but she is not striking. She really is unwise about sending images via phone."

Elisa could only imagine. "Julie often criticized me for being too conservative and not sexy at all when texting with you. I felt it was unwise to have images out there when so many celebrities have their privacy invaded. You don't like scandals."

One corner of his mouth lifted. "You were always considerate, dear. Until you decided to leave. But everyone has second thoughts and I didn't mind letting you go off to experience a modicum of freedom within limits. I'm relieved you did nothing to embarrass me during your adventures."

They reached the other side of the street and he hustled her toward a set of stone stairs by the quaint old bridge. Its stone and wood construction made it perfect for pictures in the daylight but with the fading light, it cast shadows across the adjacent stairs. In the gloom, there were too many ways to be overlooked.

The stairs led downward, toward a water-filled canal and a dirt running trail. Away from people and the regular foot traffic on the main shopping strip. New Hope was a small historic town; high traffic here did not mean the same thing as it would in the city, even on a Saturday night. The trail was almost deserted.

Oh, she had to do something. Quick. Her chances of finding help, of catching anyone's attention, had gone from decent to close to zero.

You're not trying to win a fight. You want to hit once and run. Give yourself enough time to get away.

She tried to take in her surroundings. Think. She could do this. She didn't have to wait for someone else to do it for her.

They reached the bottom of the stone steps and, sure enough, there wasn't anyone on the dirt trail or even in sight up and down the river. The banks on either side of the canal were steep. Too steep for her to hope to climb. Other than the occasional steps near bridges like the one they'd come down, there wasn't any quick way back up to the houses and streets that she could see. And it wasn't likely for someone in one of the houses to see down into the canal at the moment. Sounds from the street were muffled on the trail running next to the canal. She wondered if shouts from down here would be similarly muffled to people up in the houses or the street beyond.

Calling for help wasn't going to do her much good if Joseph still had his hands on her.

"Come along." Joseph tugged at her until she stumbled into a faster walking pace. "There's a parking lot at the end of this godforsaken little hiking trail. I'm going to need to change my shoes after this."

It was a good thing she was wearing low heels. Otherwise, she'd have had a lot more trouble catching up. As it was, these were comfortable and broken in. If she had to, she could run in them. Looking at the odd stones in the well-worn trail, it might be better for her feet if she kept her shoes on. Plus the other parking lot she'd seen, where Alex had parked, had been gravel. She wouldn't be able to run far on gravel in bare feet if they reached a similar parking lot. So the shoes stayed.

A phone rang, and Joseph pulled it out of his pocket. "Yes? We've left the restaurant. We're heading toward the parking lot you are in. Have Quinlan come down the trail along the canal and meet us en route."

The phone conversation continued, but Elisa only partially listened. Instead, her awareness centered on the way Joseph's grip was loosening on her arm as he split his attention. There might not be another chance.

She yanked her elbow back at a downward angle, ripping free of his hold. Then she kicked out, aiming for his shins. The inside of her foot caught him just below the knee, and he stumbled away from her with a surprised yell. Inspiration took her and she risked shoving him.

He fell into the canal.

She sprinted for the bridge ahead of her. It was closest, the nearest set of steps back up to the street and other people. Because when Joseph came out of the canal he'd be angry. And he was a much faster runner than she was.

CHAPTER TWENTY-FIVE

I'm sorry, sir, but she left." The waiter looked genuinely distressed.

Rojas drew in a slow breath, struggling to remain and project calm. "Do you mind if I take a look around the table where we were sitting?"

"S-sure." The young man indicated for Rojas to proceed ahead of him. "They're clearing the table now."

So Elisa and her friend hadn't left too long ago. "Did the woman who was with me leave on her own?"

"I don't know, actually. I was with another table when she stepped away."

Rojas nodded to acknowledge the waiter's answer and started scanning the area on and around the table where they'd been sitting. There, under the table, almost under the railing. He bent, grabbed Elisa's napkin from the table, and used it to gingerly pick up his find. It was the phone he'd given Elisa, screen cracked from a sudden unceremonious dumping on the floor. Not good.

"Please work." Rojas figured talking to electronics might yield more help than he'd gotten talking to random people.

The phone lit up despite the spiderweb fracture pattern across the screen. It'd been dropped mid-entry and the text was addressed to his number.

Its hium. Hes here. H

Garbled—it must have been done in a hurry. She'd been interrupted sending him the text. The last word could've been a lot of things, but he swallowed hard. His girl had been trying to ask him for help and he'd been out of reach. He never should've left her. Stupid to think she was safe with him a text away.

She'd said her friends and family hadn't believed her when she'd gone to them for help, had even supported her ex. He should've remembered, kept that in mind.

He straightened and headed out of the café. Once he was out the front door, he turned to Souze. "Time to work."

The big dog almost vibrated with eagerness to be given a job.

Good, because Elisa needed them, STAT. He bent to show Souze the phone. The big dog sniffed it over a couple of times, ending with a single long and low whuffling intake. Once he was sure Souze had Elisa's scent, he gave the command. "*Such. Such* Elisa."

Adding her name wasn't standard, but Souze knew Elisa. If there was any chance Rojas could strengthen the command, it was using her name to emphasize who they wanted to find. Souze dropped his nose to the ground and got to work.

An onlooker might not notice, but Souze was system-

atic about the way he searched for scents. He went to
work in the area Rojas had set him in, moving back and
forth in a grid-like pattern. Checking the ground, any
plants or walls a person might have brushed past, and
even lifting his nose to the air to catch airborne hints.
In less than two minutes, Souze froze to indicate he'd
found her scent.

"*So ist brav,*" he praised Souze. Then he gave him the
next command with terse urgency. "*Revier.*"

Souze ranged out ahead as far as the six-foot lead
would allow him. Rojas desperately wanted to give
Souze his head. Let him off the lead so he could get up
to his full speed of thirty miles per hour. Too risky, no
way to know who or what was ahead, and Rojas didn't
want to lose sight of the dog.

Souze had the trail for sure and led them unerringly
across the street and to a set of steps headed down to the
canal trail. They vaulted down them three, four, five at a
time.

As they hit bottom, Rojas speed dialed Ky. Souze was
getting into it now, taking in huge, loud snorts of air as
he worked in a quick grid to re-establish the scent trail.

"Officer Graves."

Souze froze for a heartbeat, flipped an ear, and without a word needed between them, the two moved fluidly
back into a dead sprint north up the canal.

"Ky. Rojas here. Elisa's stalker made a grab for her."
Rojas hated the pace he needed to keep to remain un-
derstandable. He needed to make this quick. "Get to the
Delaware Canal Towpath between West Mechanic and
Ferry if you don't want anything permanent to happen to
this bastard before he sees justice." That duty done, he

ended the call and began to focus on setting a personal record for speed.

You don't believe me. Elisa had been hurt. By him. And he'd walked away from her.

Don't let me be too late; please don't let those be our last words.

Souze pulled on the leash, snapping Rojas's full attention past the slight bend in the canal and the outgrowth of bushes obscuring the rest of the trail ahead. He had visual.

Elisa, his Elisa, was running hard down the trail away from him. She was headed toward the next bridge and another set of stairs out of the canal farther east.

He slowed ever so slightly. The resultant clearer vision and hearing allowed him to take in every angle of the situation as he approached.

Between him and Elisa, a soaking wet man was climbing out of the water in the middle of the canal, yelling. Farther down the canal, beyond Elisa, a figure was quickly picking out footing as he came down from an awkward lookout-style perch on the far side of the bridge. The far man was clearly moving to intercept Elisa.

Rojas wasn't sure what she'd had in mind, but if she was trying to get to the bridge and the next set of stairs, the other man was going to catch her on them. Rojas wasn't going to be able to reach her in time, not even at top speed.

Without slowing his pace, he pitched his voice to carry and bellowed, "Elisa! Freeze!"

Elisa stumbled to a skidding stop, falling to the side against the steep bank. Thank god for practical, intelligent partners who could *think* and think fast.

With his previous target stationary and to one side of direct line of sight, Souze wouldn't misunderstand Rojas's next command. Rojas dropped Souze's leash and pointed. "*Fass! Fass!*"   •

The German Shepherd Dog streaked forward. He'd been desperate for the command.

The oncoming man's forward progress faltered, and he even turned to run as an oddly high-pitched little whimpering noise seemed forced out of him—so he did have a brain cell or two. The sight of eighty-five pounds of incoming black-and-tan German Shepherd Dog intent on doing you harm was enough to challenge any person's courage.

Souze picked up even more speed at the sight. Sure of his target, the dog drove forward, following his instinctual drive to run down prey. In moments, the big dog caught up with the man and launched himself. Strong jaws clamped on the man's right arm, and Souze's forward momentum swung him around his anchor point, the man's shoulder. The resultant forward jerk took the man completely by surprise, and they fell forward to the ground, landing heavily. Souze regained his footing first, jaws remaining clamped on the downed man's arm.

Rojas turned his attention to the man just stumbling out of the canal.

"Bitch!" the man screamed. "I don't need you. I could take your hand and your eye and leave the rest of you to rot. How dare you!"

"Stop." Rojas had to warn the man. Had to give the man the chance to leave off. Minimum force necessary. He reminded himself over and over against the rising tide of rage he was feeling. "It's over. Leave her alone."

"Fuck you." The man squared off with his fists up. "The bitch is my property. She belongs to me."

"No." Rojas didn't bother with more words. He slipped under the sloppy punch the man threw and with a small twist of his knees, foot, torso, and legs buried his own right into the man's gut with a precise uppercut. He followed up with a left body hook to the man's kidney as he had so obligingly bent down and forward. When the man arched backward and straightened in pain, Rojas finished his striking combination with a right hook to the jaw.

Joseph Corbin Junior fell backward, back into the canal...and didn't come up for air.

"Ah, shit." Rojas waded in and felt around in the water until he had the man's suit jacket. Yanking the other man up to the surface, he dragged Junior onto the bank where he wouldn't drown and patted him down for weapons. Clear. He put Junior's suit jacket back on him. As makeshift cuffs.

Satisfied, Rojas ran down the trail. As he reached Elisa, he asked, "Are you okay? Can you hang on another few seconds?"

Elisa's gaze met his in one lightning second and relief washed through him. She was alive and all right. And she was going to be safe.

Breathing hard, she waved him on. "I'm okay. Souze. Don't let him hurt Souze."

All this insanity and she was still more concerned about his dog. God, he wanted to wrap her in his arms and hold her, but he did as she asked and ran on down the trail.

Souze still had hold of the other man's arm. The man screamed and beat at Souze's head and shoulders with his free fist, but the GSD shook him and didn't let go. The entire struggle was silent on the part of the big dog. No growling. There was only the relentless determination to hold on. Blood was running freely from the man's shredded forearm, and every time he tried to yank free, Souze shifted his grip for a better hold. The man's flailing only damaged him more as it forced Souze's teeth deeper.

"Freeze!" Rojas shouted at the man. "Police are on their way, and you are not going anywhere. Freeze and the dog will let go."

The man glared at him but stopped struggling.

Rojas issued the quiet, firm command. *"Aus."*

Souze let go, stepping around the man to stand with Rojas, never dropping the other man's gaze.

"Pass auf." Souze sat and watched his target, comfortably between Rojas and the potential threat. Meanwhile, Rojas warned the man. "Move and he will be on you. Stay where you are and he'll let you alone."

Sirens were approaching. It'd only be another few minutes and Elisa would be safe. Rojas turned and jogged back to her, gathering her in his arms. "Are you hurt?"

She shook her head, burrowing into his shoulder as she held on to him.

"Are you sure?" The fear sliced through him now. He'd been ignoring it as long as there'd been a purpose, action he'd needed to take, but now he was shaking because he'd almost lost her. "Not anywhere?"

Elisa raised her head. "I'm okay. I just…"

She trailed off and drew in a slow breath, then another.

"Yeah?" Concerned, he searched her face for any signs of pain.

She closed her eyes slowly then opened them to meet his worried gaze. "I need better cardio."

CHAPTER TWENTY-SIX

Elisa woke up from a doze. It took her a few seconds to recognize the private room in the ER.

"Hey. Have a good nap?" Alex's voice was gentle, gruff and low.

There was a stirring beyond the edge of the bed, and Souze's face popped up as he rose to an upright sitting position from where he must've been lying on the floor.

She smiled at them both. "Maybe. How long was I out?"

Alex shook his head. "Not long, maybe twenty minutes tops. The doctor hasn't come back yet."

They'd been brought by the police to the same emergency room where Elisa had first met Alex and Boom. There'd been a storm of questions until her voice had started to crack from the strain and Alex's police friend, Officer Graves, had exchanged a few words with the investigating officers. Then, only one officer at a time had sat down to talk with her, with Souze in the room to help reassure her. Alex had remained outside the room but within earshot if she needed to call him.

A doctor had come in to examine her and mentioned an IV bag of fluids to treat dehydration but otherwise gave her a clean bill of health. The ER had received an influx of patients, though, and out-processing was going to take a while, so Alex had told her to get some rest while she was still getting fluids via IV.

It seemed crazy to fall asleep in such a public place, despite the private room. She'd been exposed and frightened and worried that the man who'd been helping her ex would be brought to the same ER. Officer Graves assured her he wouldn't be.

"How much longer on this bag of saline?" She craned her neck trying to get a look at the bag hanging behind the hospital bed.

Alex glanced up then back down at her. "Not long. It's almost empty."

"I feel like I've been run over." Every muscle in her body ached, and if it was this bad now, it'd be far worse in the morning.

He didn't stop staring at her, his gaze boring into her as if he could see every fear, every insecurity. She bit her lip. Maybe he was going to tell her she was fired. He'd helped her, but that was because he was a good man. It didn't change things. He needed to think of Boom first, and Elisa was definitely not good for either of them.

"Elisa." He stopped and then started again. "Elisa, I'm so sorry I left back there."

She held her breath for a moment as his words sank in. So totally not what she'd been bracing herself to hear. "You came back."

It was all she could think of.

He shook his head. "You were right. I didn't believe you, and you never gave me any reason to doubt you. It was worse than betraying you."

Tears welled up before she could stop them. "Do you believe me now?"

It was important for him to trust her. Because it mattered more than she had words to explain. He needed to believe her, always, or she might as well leave as soon as she could get released from this emergency room.

Alex placed his hand on her bedside, palm up. She stared at the invitation for a long moment and placed her hand in his, hoping he'd be very careful with the heart she was placing in his care, too.

"I wasn't being fair to us," he said quietly. "I was trying to compartmentalize too many things in life. Asking you to separate the work we were doing for Hope's Crossing from the conflict I was causing for you by pursuing you. Asking you to ignore the way your relationship started with your ex to risk exploring what was between you and me. Ignoring my own issues while I was trying to do everything for Boom and for you. But when it came down to even the hint that you might have an issue I couldn't accept, I ditched out and walked away. Like it was black and white, no discussion required. I was making decisions as if I was the only person whose opinion mattered, and I couldn't have been more wrong."

Elisa wanted to stop him, but at the same time she wanted to hear him out because every statement he made settled a piece of unrest inside her—a worry, a fear that he'd be just like Joseph.

Fundamentally, Alex Rojas and Joseph Corbin Junior couldn't be more different.

Alex squeezed her hand, held on to it as if it was a lifeline. "I thought I'd lost you. And even though I've found you again, I want you to realize you got away on your own. You're free of him now. You can choose to stay here or leave if you want to. And if you stay, you can decide if you want us to stay together or I will respectfully step back. It's completely up to you. But I was hoping you'd let me ask you a question before you make those decisions. I was going to ask tonight, but dinner went all to hell."

A big question. Her brain kicked into overdrive. It'd been a little over a week. There weren't many questions he could ask, and she'd drive herself crazy wondering what if she didn't let him ask.

As Boom would've said, *Duh*. "Ask me."

"Would you like to give living with us a try? Full time? You could have your own room or you could move into mine with me. We could go in phases at whatever pace is comfortable for you. But I've realized I enjoy seeing you every morning and I'm hoping you'll accept."

Her heart thumped hard in her chest. It wasn't too big a question, or too scary. It had a lot of flexibility to make it the right fit. "Are you sure Boom would be comfortable?"

He grinned and fished his phone out of his back pocket. "Serena thought you might ask that, so she had me take this pic for you."

There in the picture was Boom, his Serena, giving a thumbs-up and holding up a sign: COME LIVE WITH US!!!

And sitting next to her was Souze, with a sign around his neck: PLEASE.

Elisa laughed, taking the phone into her hands.

"This." Alex caressed her hands as she held the phone. "This is why I love you, Elisa Hall. Because your first thought is for my daughter and me and my dog. Because you're selfless and brave, and I don't think I deserve you, but I'm going to do my damned hardest to make you happy."

Before she could answer him, there was a knock at the door. A very disgruntled doctor stood in the doorway. He pressed wire-rimmed glasses up his nose and cleared his throat. "Miss Hall. There are several very insistent visitors requesting to see you. While I don't usually make exceptions to hospital policies, they make compelling arguments."

Alex got to his feet and so did Souze.

The doctor's gaze went from Elisa to Alex to Souze and paused for a long moment before returning to Elisa. "If you do not wish to see these visitors, I will not let them in. But I have been convinced that you should at least be given the opportunity to know who felt it was too urgent to wait, until you are properly discharged, to see you."

Alex brushed his hand over hers and then withdrew, staying within arm's reach.

Elisa considered for a moment. There shouldn't be anything to fear anymore. Joseph was in custody. Anyone else, she could handle. Even facing him, she could if she had to. "Who is it?"

The doctor consulted notes he'd made on a tablet he was carrying. "Mr. David Cruz, Miss Evelyn Jones, and a Captain Jones. Mr. Brandon Forte, Miss Serena 'Boom' Rojas, and Miss Sophie Kim."

Relief swept through her. These people were wonderful. Hearing they'd come to find her filled her with an unexpected warmth, and she wondered how it all could've snuck up on her so quickly. "Yes. Yes, I'd like to see them."

"Normally, we limit visitation in these situations to the emergency contact and direct family members." The doctor's tone was distinctly disapproving.

Elisa gave him a peaceful smile. "Doctor, they *are* family."

The doctor harrumphed, but then his expression cleared, and he gave her a smile. "I'll have them escorted in."

* * *

Brandon and Sophie were the first to enter. Sophie looked back out the door to see if the nurses or doctor were in sight, then pulled an insulated lunch bag out of her canvas shoulder bag. "It has to have been hours since you last ate and hospital food is awful. I figured you could use a snack."

"Oh, I love you." Elisa exchanged a heartfelt hug for the lunch bag. She'd have been as enthusiastic to see Sophie either way, but good food was a fantastic bonus.

Alex leaned forward and whispered, "If food is all it takes, I'll cook for you at the house sometime when Boom is away on a sleepover. Clothing optional."

Elisa blinked and tried not to blush. Based on the way

David grinned when he and Lyn came in, she'd failed utterly.

"Who said something naughty in your ear?"

Lyn whacked him across the shoulder.

David rubbed his arm in mock hurt. "What? Look at her face. We know that look."

Lyn briefly dropped her forehead into her palm before recovering as a man in Navy uniform entered and closed the door behind him. If it was at all possible, Alex straightened next to her.

Brandon and David stood equally as tense.

Elisa decided this was going to be a new experience and she was going to meet it head on. "Hello. I'm Elisa Hall. You wanted to see me?"

The man in uniform stepped forward and offered his hand. "Miss Hall, I'm Captain Francis Jones, United States Navy."

She nodded. "What brings you here, Captain?"

Honestly, she wasn't sure how to address him but figured she couldn't go wrong with his rank.

"I need to request your help."

Elisa raised her eyebrows. "I'm not sure how I can be of help."

But she had a sinking feeling her time with Joseph wasn't completely behind her. Corbin Systems was a major military contractor.

"I'm in the midst of a deep undercover investigation. It brought me here a few months ago and into contact with David Cruz and Evelyn Jones." The captain glanced at Lyn and then away.

Elisa studied the two of them for a minute and decided the surname wasn't a coincidence.

"What is discussed between us does not leave this room. I'm currently tracking the progress of a forming private contract organization made up of ex-military resources, a mercenary group, if you will. It seems they are looking to gain footholds in several aspects of the private sector, including integration with weapons systems that should not be in the hands of mercenaries. You are currently the most expedient way for us to conduct investigation into the activities of Mr. Joseph Corbin Junior." Captain Jones didn't scowl, but his look was definitely stern. "We have reason to believe he used you as his biometric security key."

Elisa swallowed hard but refused to wilt under the captain's regard. She hadn't done anything wrong.

"When we were together, he preferred I accompany him on all business trips. When he toured his manufacturing sites, I was there. I thought it was a compliment, his way of showing his affection, that he set access on my thumb print and retinal scan. I thought it was a demonstration of his trust in me." She hesitated. "I assumed he'd reset all of those systems when I left."

Captain Jones shook his head. "The suspect in question had extreme confidence he could get you back. What he has in custody could be evidence to resolve several ongoing cases under my purview."

She shook her head. "I never saw anything unusual."

"You may not have known what you were looking at," Captain Jones pointed out, not unkindly. "We have reason to believe the suspect has an air-gapped laptop stored in his facilities containing sensitive weapons designs and integration code intended for sale to various foreign interests. What weapons and who they were intended to be sold to are best not shared in current company."

David nodded to Alex. "Phase 2, behind the scenes."

Captain Jones scowled at David.

"So you need me to go with you?" She hadn't even given Alex his answer yet and she might have to leave. "For how long?"

"Actually, no." Captain Jones looked at Alex, Brandon, and David in turn. "We can digitally assimilate your biometric information and create replicas. I have the equipment to copy both your fingerprints and your retina imprint. That is information that should not leave this room. What we'd need to do while the investigation is underway is assure your location at all times, to verify you are not being used by someone else to access the same systems. We need to know where you are and what you are doing, who you might be communicating or interacting with, and any possible ways you might become compromised."

Alex stirred next to her. "And how are you going to do that?"

Captain Jones cleared his throat, obviously ruffled about someone other than the person he was speaking to directly asking questions. "Normally you would be taken into protective custody. You'd be moved to a secure location and kept under watch."

No! Elisa leaned forward and clutched the blankets covering her. She'd only just gotten free. She didn't want to be kept hidden away, separated from friends she'd just made. The idea of having to leave Serena and Souze, of leaving Alex, ripped a hole in her chest.

But Captain Jones wasn't finished. "However, it has been pointed out to me that you are already employed by an organization with unique specialization in multiple applications, including security work. While it is unorthodox to leave a key asset with non-active duty personnel, each of the men currently at Hope's Crossing Kennels has an exemplary service record. There may not be a safer arrangement than the one you are currently in, without significantly limiting your freedom or quality of life. If you agree to stay at Hope's Crossing Kennels with certain additional safety precautions, we may not need to take you into protective custody."

The older man glanced at Lyn and his face colored a fraction.

Elisa considered. "This is a lot of information you're sharing, if you don't mind my saying so. I can't imagine civilians usually get to hear this."

It didn't surprise her to hear Joseph had been involved in illegal dealings. Not at all. He'd been a driven man and ethics were for less powerful people. She was glad to be away from him. But there were more connections in the room than she was understanding, and for once in her life, she wanted the full deal.

"I'm making exceptions," Captain Jones said.

"That seems to be going around," Elisa responded.

The older man pressed his lips together. "Every time I deal with any of you people, you have a knack for disrupting well-laid plans."

Every time?

Elisa caught Lyn's eye and her new friend mouthed a single word, *Later.*

That was going to be a story to follow up on and get all the details.

"But you also flush out evidence I might not other-

wise have been able to acquire," Captain Jones continued. "So I am making exceptions. I hope the idea of
cooperating with me and my people is somewhat more
palatable as a result."

Lyn made an odd noise.

Captain Jones glanced at Lyn, and his expression soft-
ened. "And you are involved with people I trust."

Lyn's eyes widened, then started to glisten suspi-
ciously. "There's a lot of family in the room."

Well, Elisa hadn't been sure. Jones was a fairly common surname but, maybe there was a lot she had to learn
about her friends. In a good way.

Captain Jones cleared his throat. "In any case, I became aware of the inquiries your people were making
into Joseph Corbin Junior and decided to trade information for aid. You cooperate as much as you are able and
I will see to it that you have the option to stay at Hope's
Crossing Kennels. I have every confidence you'll be in
safe hands while we conduct our investigation."

David caught her eye. "This kind of thing doesn't
have a clear time limit. Consider that. You'd be staying
with us until who knows when."

"You don't have to choose this." Anger made Alex's
voice rough. "We can find alternatives if you want."

She looked askance at him. "Does that mean you're
taking back your invitation?"

His eyes widened. "No. I just don't want you to feel
trapped."

And she knew he'd fight to make sure she could go
out on her own if she wanted.

She smiled, suddenly calm. "I don't." But she might
be enjoying Alex's discomfiture a little too much.

She returned her attention to Captain Jones. "I would be happy to help, sir."

It took a few more minutes to work out the next steps, but eventually they had a plan and a timeline, starting first thing in the morning. Apparently, more organizations than Hope's Crossing Kennels worked seven days a week.

With a nod, Captain Jones let himself out of the room.

Boom entered before Elisa had a chance to ask Lyn anything additional, and the tiny whirlwind chased any serious thoughts to the back of Elisa's mind. "You're okay!"

She gave Elisa a hug as best she could from the side of the hospital bed, careful not to jostle the arm with the IV still installed.

It didn't stop her from poking it, though. "Aren't these cool? They've got a bendy tube inside the vein so you can flex your elbow if you have to."

"It's definitely cool," Elisa agreed.

Boom looked from Elisa to her dad and back to Elisa. "Did he ask you?"

Elisa smiled. "Yes, he asked me."

"And he showed you the picture?"

"He showed me the picture." Wow, this girl had made her way into Elisa's heart and lit it up from the inside out.

Boom gave her dad a shrewd look. Before meeting Boom, Elisa wouldn't have known nine-year-olds could manage those looks.

"You didn't answer him yet, did you?" Boom looked around the room. "We all need to leave so Elisa can answer my dad's question. Somebody find an oxygen tank in case he passes out from holding his breath so long."

There were grins all around but Alex looked like he'd swallowed something large and maybe sour. Everyone shuffled out. Brandon called over his shoulder even as Boom planted her hands on his behind and shoved him out the door. "We'll be in the waiting room. Whenever you're ready to go home."

It took a minute to get used to the suddenly not-crowded space. Souze popped up at the side of the hospital bed, and she wondered if he'd hidden underneath it the entire time everyone else had been in the room. Very likely, actually. It'd been the only floor space available.

Alex resumed his seat, looking worn out. "So."

"So." It was her turn to hold out her hand for his.

He gave it to her with no hesitation.

"Either of us is completely capable of going on all on our own. We could do everything we need to and manage just fine." She sighed. "But it'd be lonely. And there wouldn't be any energy left to actually enjoy life. There'd be no one to share the pleasure or pride of what we've accomplished at the end of each day."

She intertwined her fingers with his. "I want to build a life for myself, but I don't want to build one alone. And I don't want to be with just anybody. I love you."

He let out the air in his lungs in a *whoosh* and squeezed her hand. Rising out of the chair, he leaned over her. She happily let her eyes fall closed as he kissed her, long and slow, until her pulse quickened, and she nipped at the corner of his mouth, hungry for him.

Then he grinned at her. "So that's a yes."

She laughed. "That's a yes. Now get me out of here and let's go home."

Years ago, Sophie gave up any hope that her crush on Brandon Forte would turn into the real thing. But now he's back from active duty, and the girl-next-door he left behind has grown into his every waking dream...

Please see the next page
for a preview of

ABSOLUTE TRUST

CHAPTER ONE

It was a quiet Tuesday afternoon in New Hope. Few people were out and about on the main street, which was perfect for Brandon Forte. The jet black German Shepherd Dog (GSD) walking just ahead of him needed space for this excursion, a couple of things to look at, but not too much to excite him. A few people to see was good for both of them, too, as long as they weren't going to be overwhelmed with requests to pet or take pictures.

Besides, the bake shop all the way down at this end of town tended to have day-old baked goods at a discount and the shop owner occasionally gave Forte a cupcake or cookie on the house along with the special home-baked dog treats he bought for whichever dog was with him. It gave the dogs, and him, something to look forward to on the walk.

Today it was Haydn. Haydn was a seasoned veteran and one of the dogs Forte had trained on active duty for the Air Force. Haydn had come to Hope's Crossing Kennels now for a new kind of training. The black GSD had a lot of physical therapy ahead of him. He'd been fitted with a prosthetic to replace his front left leg prior to arriving, but it was up to Forte to help Haydn figure out how to use it. The big dog had walked the kennel grounds fine, but was obviously getting bored. It happened with intelligent animals, same way it could with people. The two of them were more than ready for a change of scenery and terrain.

Thus the outing and the very slow walking.

Besides, it took skill to stuff a chocolate cupcake with cookie dough frosting, dusted with sugar, in one bite. A man needed to practice once in a while to make sure he could still manage it.

And it was a necessary skill as far as Forte was concerned. His friend Sophie tended to bring her own baked treats to Hope's Crossing Kennels every weekend. If she caught him partaking of other sweets, she'd never let him hear the end of it. Thus the entire bite-and-inhale technique. Because she had a knack for popping up out of nowhere.

Now, if it was about dating, she'd never had a word to say about any of the women he saw or one night stands he indulged in now and then. He'd bumped into her once in a while in Philly on the weekends. They both dated and it couldn't matter less to her who he chose to spend his time with, but take a taste of someone else's baking and he was in for a world of hurt. Which made it more fun when he took the risk and did it anyway.

Of course, he had a long history of crossing paths with Murphy's Law, and apparently this was his day for it because who should be walking down the street but the very person he was just thinking about?

Sophie Kim was five feet two inches of nonstop energy, and she was heading out of a small art gallery with a large paper shopping bag. The woman had expansive peripheral vision and excellent spatial awareness. Which meant she'd spotted him and changed course immediately toward his direction.

Forte swallowed hard.

She must've come directly from work because under her very sleek trench coat, she was wearing a sharp matching pencil skirt. Three-inch red heels popped in contrast to the severe black of the rest of her outfit. Which did all sorts of things to him. Naughty things.

The kind of things that were so good they were really bad. Especially when a woman was off-limits.

"Hey! Is that the new guy?" Sophie slowed her approach, keeping her gaze locked on Forte's face.

She'd been around tiny dogs all her life. But she'd spent enough time at Hope's Crossing Kennels over the past couple of years, while he'd been establishing it, to have learned how to meet the much bigger dogs in his care. Training working dogs were his thing. Or, in Haydn's case, retraining.

Always a work in progress. And she'd been there when he'd come back after being too battle-weary to continue deploying. Trouble was, he still wasn't sure if he belonged. What mattered more was there'd been no question about where he'd end up. He always came right back here.

His mind was wandering on a sugar high; and there was Sophie, her bright smile fading as she waited for him to answer.

"Yeah." Forte brought them to a halt and murmured the command for Haydn to sit.

Instant obedience. Despite his injury, surgery, and current need for recovery, the dog was as sharp as he'd been on active duty. The mind was eager, ready to work. The body, not so much.

Sophie's smile renewed, the brilliant expression stopping his heart, the way it had every time he'd seen her since they'd first met way back in school. She came to a stop in front of them, barely within arm's reach. "He must be doing well if you've got him out here for some fieldwork."

Haydn remained at ease as Forte and Sophie stood there, unconcerned with her proximity. Curious, even, if Brandon was any judge of body language. And he was. For dogs, at least.

Forte shrugged. "Easy going with Haydn. He needs a lot of light walking, over different kinds of surfaces, to get a feel for his prosthetic. We're not out for too long. I don't want to tire him out or put too much strain on his legs."

Sophie nodded in understanding. "Glad to meet him though. I thought I was going to have to wait until I stopped by this weekend."

While they spoke, Haydn watched them both. Then he stretched his neck and sniffed the back of Sophie's hand, which she'd been holding conveniently within reach.

Introductions were simple with dogs. Stay relaxed, let the dog know the approaching person wasn't a threat via body language, and give the dog time to investigate on his own. Her body language was naturally open and non-threatening. Sophie had learned from Forte not to look his dogs in the eyes. The dogs he trained tended to be dominant, aggressive, and they required a more careful approach than the average pet on the street.

Usually, Forte preferred if a person asked to be introduced, but this was Sophie. If he'd been anyone else, she'd have requested permission to say hi to the dog. Instead, she spoke to him and took it on faith that he'd tell her if she needed to keep her distance. But then again, he also wouldn't bring a dog out into public that wasn't ready to be socialized.

It was all in how well she'd come to know the way he worked in the last few years.

"What's your plan for him?" Sophie glanced down at the dog, now that he'd sniffed her hand. "Haydn, right?"

Forte gave her a slight nod and she ruffled the fur around his ears. The big dog's eyes rolled up and he leaned his head into her hand for more enthusiastic scratches.

Definitely no problems socializing. Then again, in Sophie's hands, most males turned to Silly Putty.

Or...he needed to stop thinking about what could happen to him in Sophie's hands.

"Yeah." Forte cleared his throat. "He's got a couple of weeks of physical therapy first. Then we need to coordinate with the Air Force on his adoption."

"Ah." A world of understanding in the one syllable. Part of why Sophie was one of the few people Forte felt easy around was because she got it. Only needed to explain once. And she *listened* the first time. Sometimes no explanation was required at all. She had the kind of caring heart to fill in the gaps when something went unsaid. "His handler didn't make it?"

Forte shook his head. "Same IED that injured Haydn took out his handler. The deceased's family has been contacted and they'll have first choice to adopt. We haven't heard back yet on their decision, but those kinds of things can take some time coming through the communication channels."

Sophie nodded and looked down at Haydn. "We'll give you time to figure things out while all the paperwork goes through, huh? It's nice to meet you, Haydn."

The black GSD leaned into her, his tongue lolling out in response to the attention and the use of his name. Dog knew when someone was talking to him and apparently, he liked Sophie's voice.

"Where's your car?" Forte was not going to stand around long enough to be jealous of a dog. Not at all. "We'll walk you."

"Right across the street." Sophie jerked her head in the direction of the small parking lot.

They headed over, Sophie falling into step next to Forte. She didn't try to take his hand or tuck her own around his arm. They weren't like that. Besides, she knew he didn't like to be all wound up with a person when walking out in the open. And she demonstrated it all the time. It was a regular reassurance. A comfort.

Better than free cupcakes.

"Has Haydn met Atlas?" Sophie asked casually.

The first rehabilitation case at Hope's Crossing Kennels had been Atlas, a dog suffering from PTSD after his handler had died. One of Forte's trainers and close friends, David Cruz, had worked with Atlas and still did now that the dog had become a permanent part of the kennels. But Atlas's challenges had been psychological. With the help of Lyn Jones's approach to working with dogs, Cruz had successfully brought Atlas back up to speed.

"Briefly." He glanced at Sophie and caught her making a face. "The dogs don't need group therapy sessions."

The psychology aspect of the rehabilitation was something Forte was only willing to entertain so far. Lyn got results with her work, yes, but he was not going to go all the way into the deep end with the dog whisperer approach.

To Sophie, he made a stupid face right back. "You do not need to come over and sit Atlas and Haydn down to compare notes on what they've been through."

Sophie was silent a moment, a sure sign his guess at her thought process was on target. "Well, they do need to play with each other sometimes, right?"

"Dogs are social creatures and, yeah, some playtime is good if they can socialize with other dogs that way." He'd give her that. Forte made sure the dogs trained at Hope's Crossing Kennels could socialize well with both human handlers and other working dogs. "Haydn's the second military working dog to come to us for help after active duty but his challenges are mostly physical. We have to watch him carefully with the prosthetic on until we all know what he can do with it, including him. But, yeah, he's gone out with Atlas on a couple of group walks without the prosthetic."

Honestly, Haydn was pretty spry even without the prosthetic. Dog just had better mobility with it.

"Okay." Sophie let it go. "I just think you and your working dogs could use a little more playtime in your lives. Like a doggie field day or something."

He snorted.

Sophie's car was a sensible sedan, the sort to blend into a lot of other normal, everyday cars. What made it easy to spot was the pile of cute stuffed animals across the back. Not just any stuffed animals. A gathering of cute Japanese and Korean plush characters from her favorite Asian cartoons.

As they approached, Sophie juggled her shopping bag to pull her keys out of her purse and triggered the trunk.

"Need help?" Forte came up alongside the car, scanning the area around the parking lot out of habit.

"No worries." Sophie lifted the trunk door and carefully placed her shopping bag inside the deep space, leaning in to move things around to where she wanted. "I need to make sure this is arranged so stuff doesn't shift. It's delicate!"

He was not going to admit to anyone, ever, how much he was willing to stretch his neck to catch sight of her backside while she was leaning over.

Haydn was sniffing the side of the car. Forte tore his attention from Sophie. Actually, the black dog was very interested in the car.

Then Haydn deliberately sat and looked up at Forte. It was a clear, passive signal. One Haydn had been specifically trained to give as a military explosives detection dog.

Shit.

"Sophie. Step away from your car."

She popped up from the trunk. "Huh?"

"Do it."

Sophie always listened to him, Rojas, or Cruz when they were urgent. She complied, thank god. He gave Haydn a terse command, then circled around to grab Sophie and get more distance, reaching for his smartphone.

They got a couple of yards away and Sophie craned her neck to look back at her car, even as she kept moving with him. She always did as he asked immediately, but she had a brain and she insisted on explanations after she complied. "What—"

Behind them, the trunk hatch came down with a solid thunk.

Forte let out a curse and grabbed her, pulling them down to the ground and rolling for cover of other cars as an explosion lifted the entire driver's side of her car.

Sophie screamed. Maybe. She was pretty sure she did, but wrapped in Brandon's arms and smooshed up against his chest, she wasn't sure if she'd gotten it out or if it'd only been in her head.

The explosion was crazy loud. The concussive force of it slammed into both her and Brandon despite the shelter of the cars he'd pulled them behind.

He covered most of her, one of his hands tucking her head protectively into her chest. His other arm was around her waist. They were horizontal.

Not the way she'd daydreamed this would happen.

After a long moment, all she could hear was the ringing in her ears. Her heart thundered in her chest. And she thought, maybe, Brandon's lips were pressed against her temple.

Or was it her imagination.

His voice started to penetrate the roaring sound filling her head. The words slowly started to make sense. "Are you hurt?"

His weight lifted off her and his hands started to roam over her, gentle and with purpose. Looking for injuries.

"Haydn?" She sounded funny in her own mind, but Brandon met her gaze for a moment and jerked his chin to one side.

"Don't turn to look until I check to see if you hurt your neck or head." His admonishment came through sharp. It was the way he talked when he was worried. People thought it was meanness, but it wasn't. He was frightened. For her. "Haydn's right here. He's fine."

As Brandon continued, a cold nose touched her cheek. Big ears came into view and warm, not so sweet, breath huffed across her face.

"I'm glad you're okay," she whispered. It was for both Brandon and the dog.

A brief whine answered her. Then a large, furry body lay down next to her, just barely touching her shoulder and side.

"He's going to stay here with you." Brandon rose. "Can you lay here until the ambulance comes, Sophie? Please?"

Then she realized things hurt. Her shoulder, her hip. Shooting pain was coming from her ankle. Maybe the only thing that didn't hurt was her head.

"Is it bad?" She stared up at Brandon as he lifted his smartphone to his ear. Sirens were already approaching.

Brandon held out his hand. "Give us space please. Stay off the black top!"

People must be gathering. He was stepping out to take command of the situation. He was walking away from her. Again.

"Don't leave me," she whispered it. She always said it quietly. Because she didn't want him to actually hear her.

A soft woof answered her instead. Careful not to turn her head, because Brandon asked her not to, she looked as far to her side as she could. There was Haydn lying next to her. His eyes were dark, almost as black as his fur. And his gaze was steady on hers. Calming. He wasn't going to leave her.

"Okay, Haydn," she whispered to her new friend. "We'll wait right here for him."

It's what she'd always done. And this time, she had company.

ACKNOWLEDGMENTS

This book was written with the support of so many, from the initial draft to the final edit round.

Thank you to Courtney Miller-Callihan for helping me figure out the best path forward from the initial concept of the True Heroes series to the challenges faced in seeing this story completed.

And thank you to Caroline Acebo for your patience, helping me really take Alex and Elisa's story to the next level. I am grateful to be working with you both.

Thank you to Christopher Baity, executive director of Semper K9 Assistance Dogs, for the opportunity to meet some of your dogs and for answering my questions about the training of service dogs for psychiatric alert.

Writing can be an isolating profession in many ways, but once in a while you meet people who inspire you to do nifty things. Huge thanks to Katee Robert and Christi Barth for your advice, feedback, and help in brainstorming. If I am still sane, it's only because your encouragement and reality checks helped me stay that way.

Home isn't always about a building or a room. Sometimes it's about the people in your life who are home to you. Thank you to Matthew Beckerleg for reminding me to take care of myself, and for taking care of me when I'd forgotten to. And thank you to Alex Delgado for being the best roomie I can ever imagine.

I've saved the best for last. Massive thanks to my readers for joining me on this journey. There wouldn't be a True Heroes series without you, and I hope you'll continue with me for more to come.

ABOUT THE AUTHOR

Piper began her writing career as "PJ Schnyder," writing sci-fi and paranormal romance and steampunk, for which she won the FF&P PRISM award as well as the NJRW Golden Leaf award and Parsec award.

Play Find the Piper around the Internet for insight into her frequent travels and inspiration for her stories.

PiperJDrake.com
Facebook.com/AuthorPiperJDrake
Twitter @PiperJDrake
Instagram.com/PiperJDrake
YouTube.com/PiperJDrake

Fall in Love with Forever Romance

NACHO FIGUERAS PRESENTS: RIDE FREE

World-renowned polo player and global face of Ralph Lauren, Nacho Figueras dives into the world of scandal and seduction with this third book in The Polo Season. Antonia Black has always known her place in the Del Campo family—a bastard daughter. And it will take a lot more than her skill with horses to truly belong within the wealthy polo dynasty. She's been shuttled around so much in her life, she doesn't even know what "home" means. Until one man shows her exactly how it feels to be safe, to be free, to be loved.

Fall in Love with Forever Romance

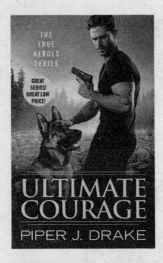

ULTIMATE COURAGE
By Piper J. Drake

Retired Navy SEAL Alex Rojas is putting his life back together, one piece at a time. Being a single dad to his young daughter and working at Hope's Crossing Kennels to help rehab a former guard dog, he struggles every day to control his PTSD. But when Elisa Hall shows up, on the run and way too cautious, she unleashes his every protective instinct.

WAKING UP
WITH A BILLIONAIRE
By Katie Lane

Famed artist Grayson is the most elusive of the billionaire Beaumont brothers. He has a reputation of being able to seduce any woman with only a look, word, or sensual stroke of his brush. But now Grayson has lost all his desire to paint...unless he can find a muse to unlock his creative—and erotic—imagination...Fans of Jennifer Probst will love the newest novel from *USA Today* bestselling author Katie Lane.

Fall in Love with Forever Romance

LOVE BLOOMS ON MAIN STREET
by Olivia Miles

Brett Hastings has one plan for Briar Creek—to get out as quickly as possible. But when he's asked to oversee the hospital fundraiser with Ivy Birch, a beautiful woman from his past, will he find a reason to stay? Fans of Jill Shalvis, Susan Mallery, and RaeAnne Thayne will love the next in Olivia Miles's Briar Creek series!

A DUKE TO REMEMBER
By Kelly Bowen

Elise deVries is not what she seems. By night, the actress captivates London theatergoers with her chameleon-like ability to slip inside her characters. By day, she uses her mastery of disguise to work undercover for Chegarre & Associates, an elite agency known for its discreet handling of indelicate scandals. But when Elise is tasked to find the missing Duke of Ashbury, she finds herself center stage in a real-life romance as tumultuous as any drama.

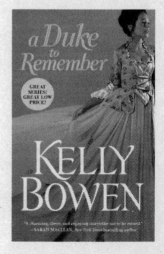